She couldn't be what he thou **impossible . . .**

He heard the sound of the key in the lock and made himself a shadow, unbreathing, almost unthinking, melding with the darkness. It was the long, dead time of early morning, right about half past two, the dark thick and absolute before false dawn began to creep up through the cracks of night. The knife was steady in his hand, and the beginnings of combat-sorcery tingled on his other fingers. Blood dripped into his eyes, warm salt stinging; his shoulders both hurt and his wrists were bracelets of agony. His knee was destroyed too. He'd taken a bad shot, and the shirt she'd given him was going to be a rag, useless, slashed, and bloody. He felt bad about that.

Another lock unlocked, the faint sound loud to his Drakul senses. He heard only one heartbeat, as familiar to him as his own by now.

The door opened, a slice of golden light from the hall outside appearing. "Hi, honey, I'm home," she whispered, and stepped inside, closing the door and locking it. Two deadbolts, thudding home, then the lock on the knob. The smell of stonekin hung on her, stonekin and Inkani; she still smelled of the demons that had attacked the Shelaugh, the demons he'd thought had taken her.

Rage brought him to his feet, the knife thudded into the wall in the kitchen as he went through the arch into the hall. His fist slammed into the wall over her shoulder, the combat sorcery spending itself uselessly, his body pinning hers. He dropped his head, inhaled deeply, taking in her scent. Yes, there was the taint of the Inkani, but she hadn't been touched. The smell of stonekin was much stronger. Under it, the smell of her shampoo and the taint of demon, his own smell, very strong; another Drakul would recognize it on her. The smell of Inkani was just a faint fading tang under the smell of the night outside. She was safe, they hadn't gotten close to her.

And under it, the fresh golden smell starting to wear through her human camouflage. He should have noticed it first off, but he'd been confused. It was true.

Holy God, it was true.

For librarians everywhere

Other Books by Lilith Saintcrow

Dark Watcher
Storm Watcher
Fire Watcher
Cloud Watcher
Mindhealer

The Society
Hunter, Healer

The Demon's Librarian

***

Lilith Saintcrow

ImaJinn
Books

The Demon's Librarian
Published by ImaJinn Books

10 Digit ISBN: 1-933417-44-7
13 Digit ISBN: 978-1-933417-44-8

10 9 8 7 6 5 4 3 2 1

PUBLISHER'S NOTE:
This book is a work of fiction. Names, characters, places and incidents are products of the author's imagination or are used fictitiously. Any resemblance to actual events or locales or persons, living or dead, is entirely coincidental.

Books are available at quantity discounts when used to promote products or services. For information please write to: Marketing Division, ImaJinn Books, P.O. Box 545, Canon City, CO 81212, or call toll free 1-877-625-3592.

Cover design by Patricia Lazarus

ImaJinn Books
P.O. Box 545, Canon City, CO 81212
Toll Free: 1-877-625-3592
http://www.imajinnbooks.com

One

She ended up knee-deep in slick rotting garbage with one hell of a shiner and a stitch gripping her side, holding a glowing-blue knife while something with tentacles thrashed toward her in the foul stinking water.

How the bloody blue hell do I get into these situations? Oh, yeah. Bond issues and politics. Sure.

While the good citizens of Jericho City would pay thousands yearly for plastic surgery and to pad the pockets of the mayor's friends, they simply would not vote a couple of measly bucks onto their property taxes to take care of her library. *Lovely. Remind me to spit in a city councilman's coffee cup the first chance I get.*

The thing scrabbled for her, throwing up great gouts of stinking water to splash the brick insides of the tunnel, and Chess hoped her college Latin was up to snuff. *Let's hope the gingko's working for my memory too, shall we?* She drew a deep breath, gagged, and choked out, *"Fiat lux aeternis, in nominae Enomae!"* in a voice that had more Minnie Mouse squeak than kickass confidence to it. Her hand stabbed forward, full of the knife, force bleeding out through the blade in a hot wire of strength that seemed to come from her solar plexus. It was getting easier each time she practiced, but the draining sensation was also getting scarier. *Much* scarier, and much stronger.

Gunpowder flash-blast of blue light, deathlike scream, and she ended up on her back in two feet of stinking water and filth while the thing rained gobbets of already-decaying flesh into the water. The little plips and plops of reeking meat slapping the greasy water made her retch again, her stomach doing its best to engineer a mutiny. *I don't blame it one bit. Stomachs weren't meant for this kind of abuse.*

Just another day in the life of a librarian. My boots are probably ruined. Great.

She coughed and gagged again, trying not to lose everything she'd ever *thought* of eating in the last week. *The books always make this stuff sound so goddamn easy. They don't mention the smell. Or the way getting hit in the face with a tentacle as big around as your thigh hurts.* Her eye was puffing closed, she could feel it throbbing and swelling to almost the size of a baseball.

Wonderful.

Chess swallowed dryly, pleading with her stomach to stay down. The smell of garbage coated the back of her throat, and she probably had gotten some of the slimy water in her mouth. *I don't think it's good for my image to blow chunks all over a . . . what's this thing called again? Either a skornac or just plain Demon-With-Many-Arms. Particularly allergic to a fire-consecrated demon-hunter's knife. One more case where an ounce of research is worth a pound of "oh fuck."*

Dripping, greasy, and filthy, she struggled up to mostly-vertical. Her bag was soaked, hanging wetly by her side; thank God for Ziploc bags. Everything in there likely to be damaged by water was safely in its own baggie. Ziploc was probably the best thing to happen in the last fifty years, along with computerized inventory and truly comfortable shoes.

The muscles in her thighs shook. If she hadn't been suddenly cold from the air hitting her now wet clothes and skin, she might have been—call the newspapers—sweating. Adrenaline lay thin and copper against her tongue and the roof of her mouth; her heart thudded.

"Any more of you assholes out there?" There weren't, of course—the knife's blade had dimmed to a dull punky-blue glow, meaning nothing demonic was near. She wanted to try breathing through her mouth, but the idea that she might *taste* the smell in the air made her gag again.

Christ, Chessie, get a hold of yourself!

As usual, she took refuge in literature. "But soft, what stink through yonder sewer reeks?" Her voice broke, echoing as she waded back through the tunnel, ducking under a pipe right at head-banging level. The water running through here—full of trash and ick as it was, it was still water, and a good friend—would cleanse any lingering foulness from the demon away. *Smart little fucker, going underground. I was stupid to have followed it.* But in the heat of the moment, even a starchy little librarian like Francesca Barnes could get a little impulsive.

"It is the sewer, and the librarian is *really happy* this is all over." A thin, unsteady, hiccupping laugh, and she felt almost ready to face the rest of the screwed-up situation.

She checked her watch in the rippling light bouncing off

the scummy water. *Half-past ten. Good. I might even get some sleep tonight. I'm only a couple blocks from home. Go figure, the first ever demon I kill is right around my humble abode.*

If it hadn't been for the bond issue failing and the loss of the full-time maintenance man—though Stephenson often came around on his days off to do some repairs and heavy lifting, going above and beyond in return for Chess fixing him cups of tea and scolding him about his smoking—she wouldn't have been stumbling around in the basement looking for a spare box of light bulbs. And if she hadn't been stumbling around in the basement, she never would have found the little door and put her hand on the lock.

And I might never have known what was making kids disappear, or been able to stop it. Chess bit back a strained giggle at the very unfunny thought. The urge to laugh was damn near overwhelming. Probably some type of compensation or weird mental crack-up under the strain of facing down her very first demon.

From a dusty library basement to a sewer in six months. *I only have a shiner and an almost dislocated shoulder to show for it. And that was a demon the books called small potatoes. I never want to meet a bigger one.*

She'd reached the end of the tunnel before she felt brave enough to slip the knife back into its sheath and get out a waterproof flashlight, checking her compass repeatedly. *The boys at the army surplus store are getting mighty curious about me, aren't they? Well, I get a discount, I suppose I can't complain.* Chess blew out between her lips. The smell actually wasn't that bad now that she was far enough away from the rotting tentacles. The thing had been living on stray cats and rats—and the occasional schoolchild.

While I don't mind a demon that eats rats—that would actually be pretty useful in Jericho—I draw the line at kitties, even feral ones. And schoolkids. Even feral ones. Call me a softhearted sucker. I suppose if I wasn't, I wouldn't be pulling down forty thousand a year with two college degrees to my name.

After a long time of slogging she found the ladder, sighing in shaky relief. The rusted metal was rough and greasy, and she was glad of the grab in her hiking boots' soles. The maintenance hatch was still open, she rolled out onto the chilly slick pavement of a Jericho City night, blessed city stink taking the place of the thick roil of sewer-stench. For a moment she lay on her back on the concrete, gasping, then it got too cold. Her shoulder throbbed as she pushed herself up to her feet. The alley was small, filthy, and dim, just the sort of place no reasonable woman should ever find herself in after dark.

It didn't take her too long to get home. She made it up the outside fire escape to her fifth-story window, blessing the fact that the little bit of WD-40 had worked wonders on the squeaking, creaking metal. No need to advertise to the whole neighborhood what she was up to.

Chess laid her hand on the window sash and murmured the password. "Nevermore."

She was rewarded with the sound of the lock chucking open. *Two weeks of figuring out that little trick; two weeks of freezing your ass off on your own fire escape is bad for* anyone's *mood.*

The plastic garbage bag she'd laid right under the window crackled as she closed the window and began struggling out of her stinking clothes, glad she'd left the lights off. It took about ten minutes, but at the end of those ten minutes she was able to dump everything in the stackable washer and dryer in her laundry closet. *I am endlessly happy that I don't have to wash my panties in a Laundromat. Never mind that I have to pay a little extra in rent. It's worth it.*

The red eye of her answering machine blinked balefully. Chess pressed the button, then hobbled into the bathroom to pee. *Yet another thing the demon-hunting manuals don't tell you: getting close to death makes your bladder shrink. Maybe it's something to do with electrolyte balances messing up renal function. I'll look it up in the morning. Just one more odd fact to add to my steadily growing store of trivia.*

The answering machine beeped as she sat on the toilet, elbows braced on knees and head hanging. Her hair was wet and filthy. Gooseflesh stood up all over her skin, hard sharp prickles. *I think I'm dealing with this rather remarkably well, all things considered.*

"Chess, it's your mother. Listen, Uncle Bill is in town. Do you want to come over on Saturday for lunch and a hot game of Scrabble? I'll make a pitcher of margaritas. Also, your sister wants her Death Cab For Cutie CD back, and I'd like my Nine Inch Nails collection too. Give me a call, sweetie, I miss hearing your voice. Bye!" Mom sounded, as usual, unremittingly perky. *My mother, the original Pollyanna.*

Chess's older sister was the bright one in the family, having gone to law school and taken a punishing corporate-law job that would make her filthy rich before long. She was already a partner. Librarian was an honorable avocation; their grandmother had been a schoolteacher and education was highly regarded in the Barnes family. But still, Chess didn't earn nearly enough.

I wish I could get paid for hunting down demons. But really, how much do you get paid for almost being strangled and drowned in garbage water before you can consider it worth it?

Next message. "Hey Chess, it's Charlie. Come rescue me Saturday. Mom and Uncle Bill want to murder me with Scrabble. And Mom wants to borrow my Death Cab For Cutie CD. Can I borrow your Charlie Feathers box set? I'll let you hold my Johnny Cash in return. Give me a call at work tomorrow. I'll tell the secretary to put you right through." Her sister chuckled and hung up. Chess made a face at her dirty scraped knees in the dark.

Next message. "Francesca." A piercing childish giggle. "Frannn*cesssssssca* . . . "

Damn phone. It had been doing that a lot lately. *Well, what do you expect when you find a clutch of priceless sorcerous books in a dusty boiler-room basement of a building built in 1906, since the damn city was too cheap to buy a new one?*

Still, Chess loved the old library; its mellow wooden floors, its cranky heat, its moldering shelves and groaning ceilings. Its antique Art Deco elevators—in the twenties, apparently, the citizens of Jericho still cared about their library. She even loved her crammed little nook of an office—as head librarian, she was accorded that one luxury, the office that had been the head librarian's since 1922.

"Frannnnncesssssssca . . ." The voice turned even sweeter, more piping. "Frrraaaaannnnnncesssscaaaaa . . ."

"You know, as a prank caller, you really suck," she muttered. The message ended with a squawk of feedback. Her hair dripped. *I think I'm still alive. God. Really dealing with this well. Chalk one up for me. I'm not in a straitjacket or clawing my own eyes out. This is fantastic.*

Next message. "Hey, girl! It's Bobby."
Chess groaned into her knees. *Oh, please. No.*
"I didn't catch you at work today," Robert continued pleasantly, "and you're not home now. Wow, you've gotten busy. Can you give me a call? I think I have to cancel our date on Saturday and I want to talk it over with you."

Meaning you want to gauge whether or not I feel bad about it. Meaning you want to know whether I know you've been seeing that Cuban piece of trash on the side. Meaning you want to see just how long you can string me along before I get tired of it, wondering if you can drop me first but you're unwilling to give up the sex. Christ I'm glad I made you wear a condom. "Loss of sensitivity" my ass.

Robert made a few more meaningless remarks. She covered them up with the sound of the flush and hobbled out into the living room, wondering just how many messages there were. Then again, she wasn't home in the evenings much anymore, too busy spreading out in a search pattern with a dowsing pendulum to track down the *skornac.*

Another beep. "Chessie! It's Al. Didn't see you at practice today, was worried about you. Give me a call."

End of messages. Chess sighed. Al Brown was the kickboxing teacher at Grant's Gym. He was also a big cuddly giant of a man who seemed to have taken it as a personal quest in life to make Chess the best asskicker she could be. It was kind of sweet; after all, she'd picked him because he looked the meanest out of all the teachers. *Unfortunately, he's so goddamn nice I feel guilty every time I sock him one. Another case of no truth in advertising.*

A long, hot shower helped. Chess emerged in a pink fuzzy bathrobe, her hair wrapped in a pink towel; she carried a small jar that gleamed faintly blue, looking like Brylcreem with glitter. She plopped down on the faded rose-patterned couch and turned the TV on, unscrewing the jar lid. The smell of mint and bitter wormwood exhaled into the apartment, and she took a thick glop of the goo and pushed her robe down, applying it to the spreading red-black bruise beginning to rise to the surface of her shoulder. It tingled and went numb.

"Ah." The sound of her voice, a hurt little cry, bounced off the wall. She sucked in a long breath, flinching as she massaged her shoulder. *Oh, ouch. Ouchie.*

Abbot & Costello was on the comedy channel. Chess

turned it up and dabbed the ointment gingerly around her bruised eye, blinking furiously as tears trickled down her cheeks. The smell was so strong it coated the back of her throat, but the numb tingling was much better than the throbbing pain. *Hallelujah, I'll no longer look like the poster child for domestic violence in the morning.* There would be a little puffiness and soreness, but the shiner would be mostly gone. Tears trickled down her cheeks.

Wish I could market this stuff. It'd be worth millions. Chess stared at the television. Maybe they'd do *Who's On First?* one more time. The tears stopped eventually, she breathed deeply and felt her stomach settle. She'd survived her first brush with a demon and come out alive and only bruised.

She yawned, digging her toes into the rug, and barely lasted another half-hour before dragging herself to bed. *That's another thing they don't tell you about demon hunting: how damn exhausted it makes you.* She fell into her messy, unmade bed surrounded by its stacks of books and piled with blue and green pillows, staring at the framed print of Buster Keaton on the bedroom wall for a full thirty seconds before she passed out. The nightmares, when they came, were expected . . . but that didn't make them easier to handle.

* * * *

The next few days went as well as could be expected, except for a slight lingering headache. The tenuous peace went on, actually, for a whole week and a half.

Chess decided to do some paperwork at the Reference desk. They were shorthanded as usual and she could keep an eye on the checkout counter while she worked. *Really dealing with this well,* she told herself over and over again as she initialed, collated, read, and tried to ignore the way her stomach kept flipping. There was nothing in it; she hadn't managed to eat her toast this morning. It was still sitting on her kitchen counter, precisely placed on a blue porcelain plate.

"Good afternoon, Miss Barnes." Emmylou Pembroke's watery blue eyes glared through her steel-rimmed bifocals. Her graying hair was scraped back in its familiar no-nonsense bun. "I have something *very important* to speak with you about."

Chess set her pen down, her face frozen into the accommodating smile learned in third grade as a defense against bullies. *Oh, good God, what is it now?* She set aside the stack of papers and folded her hands, refusing to look up at Pembroke. Instead, she stared at the old woman's midriff. The Indignant was wearing the blue cardigan and tweed skirt today, and her liver-spotted hands trembled against her tartan bag.

"Won't you sit down, Mrs. Pembroke?" Chess inquired sweetly. "It's so good to see you. May I offer you a cup of tea?" *Or a face-to-face with a tentacled demon in the sewers? I think that would be just up your alley, Pem.*

Pembroke clutched her small purse to her solar plexus as if strangling a small pet dog against her cardigan. "No . . . no tea." She sounded shocked. Relations between Chess and the Indignant had been icily polite ever since the great Barbara Cartland fiasco, with no détente in sight.

After dealing with an octopus-looking demon, Pembroke the Indignant didn't rattle Chess nearly as much. Her shoulder still throbbed a little bit when she reached up over her head, and her face was in good shape despite the tendency of one eyelid to twinge every once in a while, when she forgot and rubbed at it. Her hair didn't smell like filthy garbage water, for which she was *extremely* grateful. Her clothes had lost the smell of sewer after a good two-day soaking in laundry detergent.

Around them, the library dozed in its usual midweek rustles and dust. Chess glanced over, seeing sleek-haired Sharon behind the circulation desk, checking out a stack of romances for a fluffy-haired teenage girl who was methodically placing each paperback in a plastic bag to take home. Sharon's dark, immaculate eyebrows rose as she watched Pembroke sink down in one of the two chairs across from the Reference desk. The message was clear. *Need some help?*

I'll call if I need backup, Share. Chess's wry smile acknowledged her concern. Pembroke, as usual, got right to the point.

"I checked this out yesterday," she began, digging in her purse. Her cheap gold watch flashed, and her earrings, shaped like big plastic cherries, bobbed. Her beaky nose was having trouble holding her bifocals perched on the end, and Chess wished suddenly, vengefully, for them to fall off.

Oh, stop it. She's just a harmless old woman. This is the only happiness she gets from the drudgery of daily life.

Then Pembroke held up a Mylar-coated book. It was a copy of *Huckleberry Finn*.

Chess braced herself. The desire to bray with laughter rose, was suppressed with a violence that tickled her throat and stung her eyes. *Oh, Lord, forgive me. What now?*

Pembroke took a deep breath. "What is this *smut* doing in my library?" she huffed. "Do you know what's in this book?" Her voice dropped theatrically. "*The "N" word*, Miss Barnes! On almost every page! It's indecent, it's filthy, and I wish this book taken off the shelves immediately."

Oh, Christ, help me. I'm about to strangle a crazy old woman who scrubs the floor down at St. Ignatius's. Chess's fingers tightened against each other, she could almost feel her knuckles creaking. The urge to laugh and the urge to throw a paperweight rose hand-in-hand, and she suddenly felt much better. Almost normal. "I've explained to you before that I can't take books off the shelves, Mrs. Pembroke. My job as a librarian is to keep them *on* the shelves."

Her cheeks flushed angrily. "But think of the *children*, Miss Barnes! This—this *filth* was in the Young Adult section!"

What were you doing in the Young Adult section, Mrs. Pembroke? Inspiration struck. "Have you spoken to Father Bruce about this, ma'am?"

The Indignant blinked her watery eyes.

Chess persisted. "You might want to see what he says. I know Father Bruce personally, and would love to hear from him after you talk. We can't take *Huckleberry Finn* off the shelf, but maybe Father Bruce and I can work together to find a list of books you would like better."

Pem was not mollified. "I *certainly* don't want to bring this *filth* to the good Father's attention!" she hissed, her eyes bulging.

It was official. The urge to throw a paperweight at the old biddy's head was winning. Not only that, but Pembroke the Indignant was actually swelling like a poison toad.

Sharon was now done with the teenager and her romance novels, and was watching the scene play out with a worried line between her eyebrows. She seemed even more worried when Chess gave her a tight smile.

That is officially it. I have had enough. Francesca took a deep breath. "Mrs. Pembroke, not a week goes by without you coming to my office or bothering my staff about something you feel is indecent. If this library is such a sinkhole of filth and corruption, why don't you patronize the parish library on Twelfth Street? I'm sure they will have texts more to your taste." Chess gained her feet in one motion. She could feel the little betraying tic in her cheek that meant she was wearing her mother's patented You-*Are*-Aware-I-Am-Potentially-Deadly? expression, the one Mom sharpened to perfection on Principal Bonhoffer when Chess was in tenth grade. Pembroke leaned back in her chair, her face suddenly going cheesy-pale. But Chess simply leaned over the desk and snatched the Mylar-jacketed book from her bony claws. "I will take care of checking this back in for you. I expect your other books will be returned in a timely fashion, and if you are unhappy with our library we will be more than happy to cancel your card. Good *day*, ma'am."

"But I'm not *finished*—" Pembroke began, too late.

Oh, yes, you are. It wasn't politic to annoy the old biddy, she would probably start a letter-writing campaign to get the Head Librarian fired. It was just the sort of crusade that could fill her time effectively.

She's probably just lonely and unhappy, really. But dammit, nobody insults Mark Twain on my watch. Chess marched back to the circulation desk. Sharon stared, leaning against the counter; her dark hair pulled back under a white headband that complimented her tartan skirt and crisp white blouse. She had a green pashmina draped over her shoulders; she was the only person who could wear a pashmina without looking ridiculous. Of course, it could have been because she was a little under six foot tall and model-willowy, with large doelike eyes and a cherry mouth. Despite her obvious physical attributes, she was a good coworker, intelligent, punctual, cheerful, and just occasionally sarcastic enough to be interesting.

Chess carefully didn't slam the little thigh-high swinging door that was more a psychological deterrent than a barrier. It clicked shut, and she crossed to one of the computer terminals. She could feel the French twist she'd trapped her hair in this morning beginning to loosen, and wanted to lock herself in the bathroom to secure it. She also wanted a bacon cheeseburger, with an intensity that surprised her. Of course, she'd skipped breakfast. Again.

"What was that?" Sharon peered over Chess's shoulder.

Pembroke was gathering herself, it seemed. *I hope she*

doesn't want a rematch. I don't think I'd be able to restrain myself. "She had a problem with Mark Twain's use of the Southern vernacular," Chess whispered back. "I told her we could cancel her card any time she wants. Suggested she go to the parish library."

Sharon's cheeks flushed and her mouth twitched. "She's looking." It was a good jailyard whisper, her lips barely moved. "Dear God."

"I know." Chess keyed her code into the computer terminal and checked the book back in, her fingers lingering gently on the cover. Poor Mark Twain, having to put up with *her*. Of course, he probably would have withered her with jolly sarcasm without her ever suspecting. "I have officially defended Sam Clemens's honor. Just call me a white knight."

Sharon's cheeks were pink with repressed laughter. Her eyes sparkled. "Looks like she's hobbling for the front door. Congratulations, Saint George."

Chess made a face at the computer screen, taking a deep calming breath. Sharon snickered and retreated, stepping through into the room behind the circulation desk. The room held a desk and a few filing cabinets as well as the carts of to-be-shelved and a cabinet of circulation-desk supplies, with a coffeemaker and a cabinet full of coffee, coffee filters, tea, and packets of sugar. Share was due for her afternoon cup of herbal tea, and Chess couldn't wait for her to finish. It would be lunchtime when Share finished making her tea, as always. A bacon cheeseburger with lots of drippy, melted cheese sounded good.

The library purred in its afternoon drowse. The smell of paper and quiet hum of computers mixed with the occasional page-turning and murmuring calm voices. One of the library volunteers, Antoine, pushed his cart into the Biography section, white hair gleaming under the lights. He was a retired naval officer, and a good library worker. Another volunteer, Grady, was over in the Fiction section, peering at Chess through his thick horn-rim glasses before he looked back down at his cart. *If it wasn't for volunteers the whole place would sink like a ship. Of course, with the way the maintenance is going, it probably is going to sink like a ship. Right into the sewers. And the Head Librarian might go down with it.*

Other than Antoine, Grady, and a few other volunteers, there weren't many people. There were a few teenagers,

whether skipping school or off for the day, who knew? Of
course, who would skip school in a library?

*Well, other than me. I'm probably looking at some future
class of library-science degree-holders. Yet more bodies
to feed the maw of the library system, working for little
pay and putting up with budget cuts and Pembrokes.* "Lo I
have slain dragons," Chess muttered, leaning against the counter
as she struggled with the temptation to open the book and lose
herself in it. "And lo have I rescued maidens. But lo, oh lo, I
can't for the life of me conquer all the idiocy in the world."

Something tingled against her nape, and she glanced up.
Paranoid. I thought I'd start getting paranoid. Of course,
the kind of things she'd been doing lately, including hunting
down an octopus demon, were almost guaranteed to give one
a fair dose of healthy paranoia as well as intuition. It was a
side-effect often warned about in the books, a strengthening
of the psychic muscles. As well as the inherent risk of thinking
everyone was out to get you.

*Of course, thinking everyone is out to get you is a good
way to stay cautious and undiscovered. You are, after all,
hunting demons, Chess.*

Her eyes traveled along the familiar counter, down the
long strip of polished hardwood floor leading to the steps and
the high narrow foyer, the short blue carpet stretching away
on either side into the stacks. Globe lights descended from the
ceiling, there was a slice of rainy sunlight falling into the foyer.
And someone was coming up the stairs, a sandy-haired man in
a sports jacket and jeans, with a backpack. His hair glowed
mellow under the lights as he mounted the steps. The steps
were hard, having been remodeled more than once, and
everyone's shoes made noise on them.

Everyone's, apparently, except his. He moved very quietly,
striding along, looking around like he'd never been in a library
before. Tall, nice wide shoulders under the jacket, a crisp, blue
button-down shirt, and a pair of wire-rim glasses. Chess set
Huckleberry Finn on the closest cart, sighing when she thought
of the extra work it would take to actually walk over and shelve
it, and turned back to the rest of the library to find that Mr.
Maybe-Hunk had done a Speedy Gonzales and was now right
in front of the desk.

Well, hello. What do we have here? Nice, slightly curly
sandy-brown hair, check. Good cheekbones, dark eyes behind

the wire-rims, a long nose, check. Shoulders nice and wide, waist nice and trim, a little over six feet tall, check. Clean-shaven, check.

Initial hypothesis verified. He *was* a hunk. He looked like every girl's wet dream of an English professor.

Of course, I'm not crazy about sport jackets. But I could make an exception for shoulders like that, I like a man who works out. Hel-lo stranger. Come to get your library card?

His eyes flicked over her, and Chess restrained the urge to push her shoulders back and raise her chin. She wore a perfectly respectable blue sweater over a white dress-up shirt and navy slacks today, along with pearl earrings. It wasn't dowdy—no daughter of Chess's mother would ever *dare* to be frumpy—but it wasn't exactly a cocktail dress either. The way he looked at her seemed to imply he found her a little less than professional.

"Welcome to the Jericho City Library." Chess gave him a wide, bright smile. "May I help you?"

Then her right hip began to prickle.

He gave her a long, considering look, then answered the smile with one of his own. It was a white-toothed, fierce, supermodel-wide grin that actually pushed her back a step, the tingling against her hip intensifying as if she had the knife strapped under her slacks.

As a matter of fact, she did. *Paranoid? Maybe. But facing down a tentacled demon that your entire upbringing says doesn't exist kind of makes you paranoid. Not to mention owning a knife that glows blue whenever anything demonic approaches.* The knife was strapped against her hip, the bulge of the hilt hidden under the length of the sweater. And it had never, ever done this before.

"Hi there." He had a nice voice, an even tenor, but those teeth were too white. "I'm looking for a copy of Delmonico's *Demons and Hellspawn.*"

Her heart started to pound, her palms were getting slippery. "Really? Well, is it fiction or nonfiction?" *It's nonfiction, and I don't think I'm going to take you down into the basement, sir. Who the hell are you?*

He didn't seem to expect that. He blinked, and he didn't lean forward to rest his elbows on the counter. The rare person that didn't lean against Chess's counter was usually too short to reach it. Kids went to the checkout counter in the children's section unless they were lost or precocious.

Silence ticked through the library. Someone coughed over in Biography. Chess tried her best to look interested, disingenuous, and innocent all at once. She could almost feel her cheeks freeze in what Charlie called the Dealing-With-Idiots-Smile. It almost hurt. "Fiction, or nonfiction?" she asked again.

A thin trickle of sweat slid down her back. *Please don't let me be sweating on my forehead, he can see that. I should have practiced this in front of the mirror.* Having a mother who could almost freeze boiling water with a raised eyebrow was far from the worst training for something like this, but how could anyone have found out so soon? She should have practiced more.

Don't be an idiot, Chess. You're dealing with sorcery here. It stands to reason opening the door in the basement, making your tools, learning a few spells, and going out to kill demons is going to get you some damn attention. You screwed up somewhere. Or he's just fishing.

"Nonfiction," he said, finally. His eyes moved over her face, an appraisal not nearly as hard to meet than Mom's eagle eyes. "Delmonico is the author." He spelled, too. Nice of him.

She made her fingers work, woodenly. Tapped to the "author" field, put the name in. Hit the return key. "What's it about?" Tried to sound bright and interested. Her throat seemed coated with cotton fuzz.

"It's a study of the techniques and methods used in classifying and identifying demons," he returned, with an absolutely straight face. His hands were under the edge of the counter, and her nape prickled again. So did her hip. And her stomach was leaping like Lassie on speed.

"Wow." *And it's useful if you cross-reference it with Amandine's* The Four Gates of the Unspeakable, *but you've got to watch out for Delmonico's tendency to give you useless minutiae. Myself, I prefer Gilbert d'Arras, he's far more practical and forward-thinking. Plus he's a better writer. And those diaries I found aren't bad either, even if they are a slow read.* "I'm not seeing it here. When was it published?" *Act normal, Chess. For God's sake act normal.*

"1604. The latest edition was brought out and bound in 1861." His smile widened.

"Ah." Chess nodded sagely. "Sounds like it's a bit too early for our collection. Have you tried some of the rare book dealers?" *I am doing really well with this. Don't get cocky.* The knife now seemed to be vibrating inside its sheath, pressed against her hip and causing a prickling burn against her skin. *How is it doing that? Why is it doing that? For doing so well with research I'm woefully short on practical experience.*

"No. It's a library book." He accented the word *library* slightly, his smile more like a grimace of pain now. The light glittered off the rims of his glasses, a sharp dart that threatened to jab right through her temples and set off a headache.

"Well, it's not in our library. You might want to try the university." Her smile felt like a grimace now, too. "They're very helpful, very nice." *Shut up, Chessie. You're babbling.*

That sparked a long, searching look. Those dark eyes behind the glasses suddenly seemed not so friendly.

"Is there anything else you're looking for?" *Keep a light tone. You do this all day. Don't screw up now.*

His smile widened. "No, guess not. Thanks, Miss . . . "

My God, he's actually asking my name. "Ms.," she said, frostily. "Ms. Barnes. Head librarian. And you are?"

"Charmed," he said promptly, his eyes dropping to her chest. "And Paul. Paul Harrison."

You bag of sleaze. Abruptly she was feeling much less charitable, no matter *how* hunkadelic he was. "I hope the university library can help you, Mr. Harrison." Her tone was now perceptibly unimpressed. Her scalp tingled with unease. He looked very much like Robert, who practically oozed charm when he was trying to get into someone's pants.

Then, mercifully, Sharon appeared. "Chess, I've got my tea, if you want to . . . oh. Hello."

The man's eyes slid from Chess to Sharon. Immediately, assumptions were slid into place and the charm intensified. "Hello yourself," he said cheerfully, changing direction like a champion stunt-car driver. "I was looking for a book."

"Well, you're in the right place." Share did all but bat her long sweeping lashes at him.

Time for a graceful retreat, Chess thought, and took two steps back. "I'm popping out for lunch," she said, to nobody in particular. The scary hunkadelic didn't look away from Sharon, who waved languidly, cupping her mug of steaming tea in one pale, slim hand.

"See you soon," her assistant said, and Chess escaped gratefully. *That was close. That was very very close.*

So someone knows about my library. She forced herself to walk slowly away, her shoes firm and businesslike against the short blue carpet. *I'm going to have to be very careful. But I can't see stopping.*

Not with demons around.

She made it to the door to the stairwell, unlocked it, and opened it calmly. Stepped inside, and began the climb to her office to fetch her coat. She had to stop halfway because her knees were shaking so badly, which was why she hadn't taken the balky old lift.

Someone knows about my library, but I can't stop. Who will keep the other people in the city safe? I can't stop. That thing was taking children. Eating children, for God's sake. It's my job to do something about it.

Maybe I need a few recruits. But who do I know that I can say "Hello, would you like to hunt a few demons" to?

It was a puzzle, and one she suspected would keep her company all through lunch. Who knew? And how could she keep the library a secret and keep hunting demons?

Two

"I'll take the tall one," Paul said, his eyes all but sparkling. "I've got dinner with her tonight. Probably part *sheela*, but the things we do for the Order, right?"

Ryan settled himself further into shadow, hugging the alley wall. "What if she's a Golden?" He had to ask, the place had been a Nest a long time ago. It was built into the soaring lines of the architecture, the glowing outline of etheric force *he* could see but the Malik wouldn't. He could see and hear so much more, any Drakul could.

And all for the price of his humanity. Such a little thing, really. A useless thing.

"There aren't any Golden left." Paul's glasses glinted as he eased them off, slid them into the backpack. As a disguise, they were simple and effective; but anything Other would be able to tell what he was by his smell, the smoky scent of a Order-trained Malik. "But I'll tell you, the inside of that place stinks of sorcery. Absolutely reeks. It's all over the head librarian and her assistant. It's the assistant, I'm betting."

"Maybe both of them?" Ryan's fingers caressed a knife hilt, his black eyes narrowing. *Stuck babysitting a damn Malik.* The demon whispered and chattered inside his head, he ignored it. *If it wasn't for orders, I'd . . .*

But there *were* orders, and good ones, too. He was to look after the Malik, make sure he didn't get into trouble, and take out any demon too big for the other man's training and fragile humanity. Ryan drew back a little further, wishing the sun wasn't up. Night was the better time for him; even though his human part shielded him from the harmful effects of daylight it was still uncomfortable.

"The head's a frosty little bitch. She didn't know anything about the goddamn books. The *sheela*'s the one. Besides, a civvies skin wouldn't have the smarts or the talent to take out a *skornac*. It would take an Other; and neither of them are genetic witches."

You're a skin too, Paul. Ryan shrugged. *Only thing saving you from being a blind skin is the Malik. You poor bastard.* "Guess not." He glanced out over the street. Night came early in winter, and dusk was thankfully gathering in the corners and alleys. The best time, when the sun didn't hurt and the demon in him bloomed, burning through the layers of fragile humanity and turning him into something more. "All right. I'll take the short one, you get the *sheela*." *I shouldn't let you deal with an Other alone, but orders are orders. And on this run you're the boss. As fucking usual.*

"Good deal." Paul's shoulders came up and he blinked. He was a handsome one, and far from the worst when it came to pairing up; there were a few Malik who delighted in ordering their Drakulein around. His habit of chasing women while on runs sometimes got him into trouble, but he at least he wasn't a sadistic bastard. "Stay on the short one, just to be sure. All right?"

"I got it, Malik. Be careful, *sheela* are tricky." *And if you get yourself killed I'll have to put up with training a whole new skin.*

"I'll see you back at rendezvous in the morning." Paul was evidently expecting to have a good night. He eased out of the alley and was soon gone, his sport coat flapping as the edges of his Drakul-laid shielding blurred to make him one with the coming night. Ryan sank back, listening to the slow song of concrete and steel that made up a city. His nose twitched, a little—he could smell the death of a demon, burned flesh and nose-stinging ammonia. A *skornac*, taken down by a non-Malik hunter, in a free city. If there was someone out there looking to tip the precarious balance, they had to be brought in. Questioned. And then invited to join the Malik . . . or put away. And if it was one faction of demons declaring war on another, or the High Ones coming to town, it was even more imperative that the Malik know about it.

Not to mention the sorcery used, a spell that had vanished when the Halston books had—a spell usually only a Golden could use. There had to be a cache around here somewhere, and odds-on someone at the library knew where it was. Melwyn Evrard Halston hadn't been a fool, and had hidden his books in this city. Who better to track down books than someone who worked at a library? Besides, the entire building thrummed with etheric force, and *that* was a recent occurrence. Someone had awakened whatever latent potential lay in the walls.

He waited, leaning against the wall of the alley, practically invisible. The library closed down, lights going off, people shooed out the front door. At seven sharp, a tall, willowy form that had to be the *sheela* came striding out, her faint perfume of lilacs threading through the chill, rainy air. She couldn't have more than a trace of *sheela* in her, just enough to make her tall, sleek, and dangerous. *Sheel* often intermarried with human women; they were fickle but had the gift of manipulating females. Unfortunately, they rarely stayed after the first child, and the human women usually remarried, having enough of the *sheel* on them by then to snare skins with no problem.

This one was probably a granddaughter, and she vanished into a cab down the street. Ryan shook his head, clearing it of the trace of lilac. Being Drakulein, he was rarely susceptible to *sheela*. One more thing to be grateful for, he supposed.

There was one light still burning in the library, on the third floor. He saw a flicker of movement—the head librarian? It was just like Paul to stick him with an ugly woman to follow, even though a Drakul wasn't supposed to get anywhere near a woman that smelled of sorcery at all. Ryan sighed, resting his head against the cold concrete of the building looming over him. *Perfect. If it's the* sheela, *she'll probably join the Order. Be nice to have access to a cache of sorcerous books, though I'm not likely to get anywhere near it.*

No, the Order would only let the Malik researchers near it. Drakulein couldn't be trusted. They were, after all, part demon. No matter that there hadn't been a Drakul traitor in a good three hundred years . . . still.

You're doing yourself no good thinking of this. Just do your fucking job and think on your own time, Orion.

The light went off, and Ryan tensed. He gave her fifteen minutes to get down to the first floor and come out. She didn't.

What's she doing in there? Everyone else left, including the assistant. What the hell do librarians do all day, anyway? Breathe dust and shelve books?

It took a good two hours for her to appear. The front door opened, and she closed it behind her as streetlights flickered on, glowing all the way down the street. Ryan peeled himself away from the wall, peering at her.

Short and graceful, almost lost in a long dark woolen coat very much like his own, the woman locked the door and patted it, proprietary pride evident in the movement. She turned, tucking her keys into her pocket and hitching her bag on her shoulder. Long dark hair pulled back in a French twist, slacks, and the purse, Paul had given a good description; she did seem a little chilly. Very self-contained.

Ryan's eyes narrowed as the woman set off down the steps. She moved well for a skin, as if she'd taken dance. And she seemed wary. Paul was right. She *reeked* of sorcery, in a way the *sheela* hadn't. The way no blind skin should. Sorcery, and a strange perfumed scent that faded in and out, like the smell of violets.

Paul, you didn't let your dick do your thinking again, did you? Ryan stepped out of the alley and drifted after her, calm and quiet. Wouldn't do to scare her, would it? Of course not. Careful and cautious, and this woman never had to know a deadly Drakul was following her. *Should* never know he was following her. The Malik would make contact, if it was necessary.

She walked with her head down, quickly, into the wind. That made her scent unfurl behind her like a banner. Sorcery, water, and the smell of wormwood, a powerful nose-clearing stench as well as that maddening, elusive tang. *Wormwood? Why would she smell of wormwood? And . . . mint? What the hell is this? She isn't witch, she doesn't look like a witch, what is she? What the hell is going on?*

Where was she going?

She turned right, across the wind, her head dropping even further. Her pace quickened. Now he caught another scent under the roil of sorcery and bitterness: water, clean and pure. And the smell of herbal shampoo. She smelled good, at least, under the burning fumes of whatever sorcery had been performed in her vicinity. And what was the wormwood?

He was beginning to think she'd marked him when she ducked into a doorway under a small sign. *Grant's Gym.* She was going to work out. *Where does she find the energy after a day of slinging books around? Where's a window? I want to see this, I want a closer look at her.*

He barely recognized the warning tingle of danger under the thought. He was curious, and so was the demon. *She's female, and smells of sorcery. You're supposed to stay back, stay away. Surely you're not interested in a blind skin? They don't do anything interesting.*

Maybe not. But he wanted to see, and he was supposed to keep tabs on her. There was a handy window, and if he stayed very still, nobody would notice him.

What is she? She's not a witch, but she's been messing

around with sorcery. I'd stake my life on it.
And after all, he just might.

* * * *

She moved in on the heavy bag, hands taped, sweat dripping down her back under the sports bra. Elbow, elbow, fists, knee; the huge hulking instructor said something that was supposed to be encouragement. She didn't even spare him a glance, kept working the bag as if it had attacked her. Her dark hair was in a neat French braid, and her pretty face was drawn into a feral snarl of effort.

Pretty? No, she wasn't just pretty.

Pale skin, her large hazel eyes set above high cheekbones, her lips shaped just right when they weren't pulled back in a grimace of effort. Her hair was dark and glossy, too rich to be called brown, and falling half down her back when it wasn't caught up in a braid or twist. She was short but muscled like a dancer, and moved with a swift economy that spoke of long practice. The bag shuddered under her onslaught and the teacher barked. Sweat flew, and Ryan's jaw felt like it was going to drop. He'd never seen a woman go after a heavy bag this way. The Malik females, researchers and breeders both, largely accepted their place as noncoms. Even the few Malik women who trained for fighting—as exercise, of course—didn't go about it so seriously.

She was obviously a star pupil, top of her class. The teacher was teaching straight kickboxing, but Ryan could tell he'd probably taught this librarian some street fighting. His hypothesis proved correct when the class ended, the teacher suited up in some padding, and the librarian proceeded to kick the shit out of him. Even with the padding, Ryan could see the big guy wince every now and again.

Goddamn. Look at that. He forgot he was standing in the cold, forgot he was supposed to scan the vicinity, forgot everything but watching her move. The teacher, a massive bear of a man, moved in on her, and Ryan winced when she took a fall, probably bruising her hip even though there was matting on the floor. But she simply bounced right up and attacked the padding viciously, striking at groin, throat, clawing, kicking, and generally making Ryan glad he wasn't facing her. He was Drakul, yes, but dealing with a woman this determined would be unpleasant unless he used a bit more of his strength than he was comfortable spending on a skin. Besides, he didn't like the thought of hurting a human woman, no Drakul did. The protective instincts were just too strong.

Paul was wrong. There's more here than meets the eye. And something about that bitter smell of wormwood taunted him. Wormwood and mint, and the smell of her shampoo under that. *I don't think the sheela's the dangerous one.*

But good luck getting Paul to change his mind, now that he'd decided the *sheela* was the one with access to Halston's books. He was the Malik.

Well, he told me to watch the head librarian. I'll watch her. And if I get proof she's doing something she shouldn't, I'll take it to Paul. It's all I can do.

She helped the mountainous teacher take the padding off, smiling and swiping at her sweating forehead with the back of one pretty hand. *Damn, she's cute. Not just cute, but seeing her work a heavy bag is pretty damn striking. I've never seen a woman do that.*

She disappeared into the woman's locker room, and Ryan decided he'd better find a place up the street to watch the front of the gym. It wouldn't do to alert her prematurely, unless Paul had done so already.

Probably. Damn Malik.

No, he was far from the worst. Ryan retreated down the street, finding a convenient doorway. *Who is this woman? She reeks of sorcery and trains like a good Malik at the gym. And what else is she doing?*

It took another half-hour before she came out, calling a goodbye over her shoulder. Her hair was braided back in a thick, damp rope, and she set off down the street at a good clip, long legs in her slacks, her canvas bag hitched up on her shoulder. She seemed a little easier in her skin now, a little more relaxed. The burning smell of sorcery had faded. She'd worked off some adrenaline. Enough remained to taunt him, sliding through his nose and into his brain in a way he should be very wary of. If she triggered his instincts things would get really messy.

Very interesting. Who are you, sweetheart? If I didn't know better, I'd think you were up to something. But you're definitely a skin, you're not even a genetic witch. What's going on here?

It wasn't *entirely* out of the question. Non-Malik hunters showed up every once in a while and were brought in or eliminated. But she looked altogether too pretty and delicate to go running around after *skornac*. She was a *girl*, too. The female Malik did research, the males did the hunting, world without end, amen. Women were altogether too precious to waste, especially female Malik. Besides, hunting would put them in contact with the Drakul, and Drakul tended to get highly possessive over females they protected. Couldn't have a Drakul protecting just one woman when they were supposed to be protecting whatever Malik they were assigned to.

Ryan realized he was trailing her too closely. Not only that, the demon was silent inside his head, focused hungrily on the sway of the librarian's hips. *Librarian? She looks too cute to be a librarian. Don't they usually wear thick glasses and their hair in buns?*

It took a good six blocks before she finally climbed the steps to an apartment building. It was the work of a few moments for Ryan to scale the building next door and take a look from the roof, waiting to give her time to go up stairs or an elevator—no, not on this side, there were no lights on here. He made it to the other side and looked down into the alley, saw a few lighted windows, and his eyes widened in shock.

Bingo. What the hell?

It had to be her window. He could see movement inside. She was probably taking her coat off and laying her bag down; but that wasn't what made him freeze in shock, staring at the squares of glass with warm golden glow leaking out. No, what made him stare was the thin layer of warding along her window, subtle and effective, blended into the physical structure of the building, on the window right over a fire escape. There were a few plants in pots out on the fire escape, hardy stuff like rosemary. He wondered with a sudden vengeance what the inside of her apartment looked like.

Well, Paul did ask me to watch her. So I'm watching her. End of story.

But how the hell did she have warding on her windows? No wonder she reeked of sorcery, she was practicing. But she wasn't a witch, didn't have the smell of incense and caramel-sweet blood that genetic witches had. Self-trained and practicing, and she had access to either a Teacher or a cache of sorcerous texts—and given that they were looking for Halston's library, and this librarian worked in the building Halston had designed, built, and worked from . . . well.

Paul was wrong. Wait until I tell him. He'll never live this down, chasing a sheela while I find the real hunter. But damn, she looks so small and delicate. And I'd be willing to bet that Paul was confused by the sheela. He's only a skin and vulnerable to them.

The demon was still unwontedly silent, settled down and unblinkingly focused on the librarian's window. *What's your name, honey? And why are you going out looking for trouble and training to kick ass? Hmmm? This is a mystery, and I like mysteries. Just call me Nancy Drew.*

The demon was altogether too quiet, a laser-pointed intensity that rarely happened unless he was hunting. Why? The demon part of him generally didn't pay much attention to females unless they were escorts or breeders. Sex was a reward, used to keep the gears running smoothly, and you never saw the same girl twice. Especially if it was a Malik female who had volunteered to breed; the possessive instincts were just too damn strong. It was a good thing the demon inheritance was recessive in females, coming out only in sorcerous talent; otherwise things could have gone *very* badly for the Order.

And the females had their humanity, their *souls*, too; the Drakul males were born without them and trained to disregard the lack.

None of which answered his question: Why was the demon part of him sitting up and paying attention now?

He saw shadows moving. What was she doing? He'd have to get a better vantage point, and there was the fire escape right there. Tempting, tempting, he couldn't see any traps and was halfway down the side of the neighboring building before he had a second thought. Did he want to possibly alert her to his presence?

Dammit, I'm Drakul, I'm more than capable of staying invisible even if she's a talented beginner. I want a look at what's she's doing, and a closer look at that warding on her window. It's my job, isn't it? Business and pleasure, and I haven't had both in a long time. Hell, I haven't even had the latter in a long time.

The fire escape was a surprise, well-oiled and silent, he went slowly and reached the fifth floor ready to be absolutely invisible. He crouched and peered in the window, glad of the darkness that would keep him from being seen if she looked out. But she wasn't looking out.

He could see a slice of her television screen from this angle if he focused just right, playing a sepia-toned movie. That was surprising, but even more surprising was the vision of the librarian, in loose paint-splattered sweats and, with her hair pulled back in a ponytail, bopping around a neat, clean yellow-and-white kitchen. Her stereo throbbed something that Ryan identified, his eyebrows raising, as Oingo Boingo's *Dead Man's Party*. So she was a retro chick.

She'd obviously stretched out and was engaged in dancing while she made herself dinner and the TV screen flickered. *Damn. She can move.* Her ponytail switched back and forth as she sang along, chopping something and occasionally waving a cleaver for emphasis. *Be careful with that knife, sweetheart. Wouldn't like to see you get hurt.* He leaned forward, watching that long, pretty ponytail swing. *How can someone so short work a heavy bag like that? And why didn't Paul think she was involved, why did he fixate on the sheela?*

He got too close, not paying attention. The warding on her window suddenly sparked, pulled into taut singing alertness by his nearness. *Goddamn, that's demon-specific warding! How the hell did she learn to do that?*

But the most amazing thing was her reaction. The librarian whirled, her ponytail floating as she turned with a sweet economy of motion and scooped up another knife from the counter—a knife whose blade glowed a harsh, hurtful blue that drilled right through his eyes and into his brain. He barely had the presence of mind to vanish, his body moving with the ease of inhuman speed and long training, before she ripped her window open and the blue radiance from the knife shone out over the fire escape platform.

Music poured out into the cold air as Ryan hung, his feet dangling and his eyes smarting and watering, from the seventh-floor escape. *Don't let her look up. Christ in Heaven, how did she get a goddamn Phoenicis Fang? Those are extinct. Nobody can make them anymore and none of them are missing. How did she get hold of one? Goddamn, that hurt. Don't let her look up. Look down, sweetheart. I'm not ready for you to see me yet.*

"Jesus." Her voice, under the music. He couldn't hear much under the pounding beat, only that it was female, and low. "Seeing things. I'm really getting paranoid."

The sound of that voice, even screened by the music, made

his skin tighten. Ryan pulled himself up, moving silently, jackknifing to get his feet on the seventh-floor fire escape. He heard her window bang down and the music shut off.

Sorry about that, sweetheart. That was an amateur move, and I'm damn glad you didn't catch me. I have enough to worry about right now.

He waited, crouching on the cold metal of the fire escape, until his sharp ears picked out the sound of her moving around in her apartment. A little while later, the smell of roasting chicken and grilled onions drifted up, distinguishable from the other cooking smells in the building by its smoky tang of sorcery. *Damn, everything she does is covered with that smell. She's practicing.* Ryan carefully, slowly, quietly dropped down to the fifth story again, ready to go over the side and vanish at any moment.

She'd set her kitchen table and stood, irresolute, with her plate in one hand. The television was still going, eerily silent, she'd turned it down all the way. As Ryan watched, the librarian's shoulders slumped. She set the plate down, dropped into her chair, and buried her face in her hands.

Wait a minute. What's this?

Her shoulders shook for a good ten minutes, silently, while the blue-glowing knife lay next to her plate, glittering sharply and almost blinding him. He had to squint, looking past the hard hurtful glow. A Fang was deadly to anything demonic. The only reason why he wasn't crippled with the pain was because he was only *part* demon. *All of the Fangs are accounted for. She had to have made it. But she can't have, the way of making them was lost a long time ago when Halston died. He was the last Golden and old, very old. There haven't been any potentials in five hundred years, the Inkani somehow hunt them down before we can bring them in. Jesus. Why is she crying?*

He watched her get up, leave the Fang on the table, and carry her plate, untouched, into the kitchen. Watched her dump her dinner into the garbage and stand next to the sink, wiping at her cheeks with a napkin. What was wrong?

Hey, what's going on? Why are you crying? Shit. Did I do that? He had to think for a moment before he recognized the tearing feeling inside his chest as guilt. And *that* was something new, too. Why the hell was *he* feeling guilty? He hadn't done anything.

And besides, I don't feel guilt. I'm Drakul.

But it hurt him to see this diminutive woman who could work a heavy bag like a pro crying alone in her apartment, with demon warding on the walls and a Fang sitting on the table next to her. Had she taken on a *skornac*? No way. But still, it was looking more and more like she was a mystery that needed to be solved for the Order. She might even be that rarest of skins, a Golden potential.

And if the Malik pulled her in he might never see her again. He definitely wasn't ready for that. Already he was roused to uncomfortable interest.

I'm going to have to watch you, sweetheart. We'll see what happens.

Three

Two weeks, sleeping badly, and not eating. This is getting ridiculous. Chess turned over, fluffing her pillow, and peered blearily at the alarm clock. The nightmares were getting worse. And the feeling of being watched had only intensified. She hadn't seen the man in tweed anymore, and Sharon had mentioned being stood up for a dinner date. *That* had put Share in a two-day funk of muttering into her teacup and generally moping. It wasn't her usual luck to get stood up.

Not just that, but Chess's family was starting to get suspicious. *Where are you all the time?* Charlie had asked, her forehead wrinkling. *Got a new boyfriend? You never answer your phone anymore.* And then Mom. *Honey, I don't hear from you like I used to. Is something wrong?*

Chess turned over again, sighing. She was almost sure she was being followed, but that was ridiculous. Her knife glowed at odd times; she was beginning to think she'd made a mistake during its creation. But it had dealt with the tentacled thing just fine.

At *that* thought, a shiver went down Chess's spine, and sleep became a total impossibility. She sat up, reached over, and turned on the bedroom light.

"I need someone to talk to," she muttered. "Hi, how are you? I'm Chess. I hunt demons, and I'm having a total fucking nervous breakdown. Why am I acting like a . . . like a *girl?* I can *handle* this."

She looked at her nightstand again. The only way she got *any* sleep was with the knife under her pillow and the Marx Brothers on the TV, curled up on the couch instead of in her bed. Sometimes the feeling of eyes on her was even a comfort. It helped with the crushing sense of loneliness she felt when dealing with everyday people.

On the bright side, Pembroke the Indignant hadn't started her letter-writing campaign to get Chess fired yet, and she hadn't canceled her card either. As a matter of fact, Pem had checked out some Faulkner, and Chess found herself half-smiling when she contemplated the next round of righteous ire that would set off.

Chess scooped up her knife and pillow, and dragged her

down comforter out into the living room. Her windows were dark except for orange cityshine, the alley reflecting the wet gleams from damp pavement and clouded sky. She plopped down on the couch and fluffed her pillow, slid the knife underneath, and snuggled into the warm softness of her couch. A little bit of digging produced the remote, she pressed the power button and was rewarded with the TV's blue glow.

The comedy channel was playing some type of cartoon, but it wasn't Looney Tunes. She switched over to the DVD player and the menu for *Duck Soup* came up. She pressed *play* and was rewarded with a feeling of wonderful release and relaxation. *Man, I love Groucho. Well, I love watching him, I don't think I'd love to date him.*

Even her mother's veiled hints that Chess's withdrawal was *not* making her happy faded in the face of Groucho. Chess felt her eyes closing, she snuggled further into the blankets. She was almost asleep when the faint tapping sounded against her window.

What?

Her eyes opened, heavily. She watched, as if in a dream, her window floating in front of her.

Tap-tap. Tap tap.

Something at her window. The layers of the warding sparked and fizzed, reacting to something, and Chess felt a drowsy alarm. *What's that? I should check that out.*

But she was so tired, and her couch was so warm, and she was halfway through the movie. It would be so easy to fall completely asleep instead of . . .

Chess's eyes closed, then struggled open again. It was now three-quarters of the way through the movie. A fuzzy sense of alarm grew under her skin, a prickling heat roiling down her spine. *Ouch.* She shifted, but it didn't stop, she struggled up to full wakefulness as she heard something like a screech.

Immediately, heart pounding, adrenaline in her mouth, she sat upright, digging under her pillow for the knife. Her answering machine beeped.

Wait a minute, I didn't hear the phone ring!

"Franc*eeeeeessssc*aaaaahhh . . . Franc*esssc*aaahhh . . . " The tinny voice whispered out of the answering machine, and Chess slid her legs out from under the comforter. She was wearing plaid boxers and a *Jericho Warriors* T-shirt. it was going to be awful cold if she had to go outside.

Her knife prickled and buzzed insistently in her hand. She looked down at it, and saw bright leaks of light from the sheath. It vibrated, jarring her wrist. She stepped into a pair of sandals and took a deep breath.

Tap-tap.

Francesca whirled, her hair swinging in a heavy wave, as something dense and heavy smashed against her window. The fire escape screeched violently, metal twisting, and she let out a half-scream as the warding sparked, smoked, and fizzed invisibly. *Oh, God. Oh, God.*

She swallowed dryly, tore the knife out of the sheath, and let the blue glow free.

The thing in the window—red eyes, claws, and smoking, bristling hide—scrabbled frantically at the glass. The blue light touched it, lashed smoking weals in its skin, and it screeched, a falsetto squeal drilling right through Chess's head.

She screamed, lifting the knife, *if that thing comes in here I'm going to have a hell of a fight on my hands. I'm not even* dressed! The thought flashed through her head and was gone in a millisecond. Then the impossible happened.

Another hard impact, more screeching metal. *Everyone in the building's going to be up by now,* she thought, and something hit the thing from above. She had a confused impression of motion, and everything fell away from her window.

Chess's jaw dropped. *That was someone else! Holy fucking shit, that was someone else falling on the thing from above!* Her heart leapt into her throat, started to pound, and she looked around for her coat. *Down in the alley. Someone's fighting that thing down in the alley. If it's another demon hunter, they'll need backup.*

Exhaustion forgotten, she bolted for her closet. Fifteen seconds later she had her coat and her keys, and was out the door, running swift and silent down the hall. It would be a miracle if nobody called the police. Whoever was out there was going to need all the help they could get, after falling five stories with a hungry demon. It would be a miracle if there was anything *left* of them to rescue.

She ducked into the utility stairwell, the one that would give out onto the alley below, and barely slowed down enough to round each corner. Her sandals almost went flying, and she had to remember to stuff her keys into her left coat pocket before she hit the door giving out to the alley with everything she had, the knife suddenly shining like a star in her hand.

The alley was clean except for the Dumpsters, and dark except for the glow of the knife blade. She skidded out into it and stood, her chest heaving and her hair falling into her face. She smelled a breath of smashed rosemary; her plants were probably gone. *Should have tied my hair back, no time . . . a fall from my window would put them right about . . . there. But I don't see anything, I—*

"Look *out!*" Someone smashed into her from the side, her knife went flying, and her head hit the side of a Dumpster with a hollow *bong* that might have been funny if it hadn't hurt so fucking much.

Snarling. Ripping. Sounded like dogs fighting, low hideous growls and tearing sounds, another hollow boom as something else hit another Dumpster. It was cold, her boxers were getting soaked and her legs were wet. She was lying in a puddle. Her head swam. *My knife. OhmiGod my knife, where's my knife, some help I am!* She made it to her hands and knees, her head ringing, roaring in her ears. The knife was easy to see, glowing like a star, she scrabbled for it. She'd lost a sandal, the concrete hurt her bare foot. She made it to the knife and scooped it up, pushed herself unsteadily to her feet and turned back to the end of the alley.

Two shapes, one low and feral, another tall and broad-shouldered. The knife's light picked out a black knee-length coat, flapping as the man—had to be a man, it was too tall and broad for anything else—moved two steps to the side with eerie fluid grace, between her and the thing. The thing snarled, scrabbling against the pavement, red eyes fuming and the smell of it hitting her suddenly. Burning hair and ammonia, the stench of a demon, she recognized with a flare of relief.

Baltiriaz. Burning hair and cat piss, that's distinctive, it looks like a dog with red eyes. Okay, I've read about this. What's it vulnerable to? Think!

It was hard to think with her head pounding and her shoulder rippling with pain. Her knee felt scraped, a thin trickle of heat slid down her shin. Her coat dripped against her calves. *Did I dislocate my shoulder? How could he survive a five-story drop? Think, Chessie! Think!*

D'Arras, referring to the *Baltiriaz*, called them Dogs of Darkness; Aventine Carlyle said they were allergic to sunlight,

as most demons were. But *Baltiriaz* were incredibly sensitive
to any kind of light, not just sunlight.

Light? Fiat lux, let there be light. She raised her knife as
the other figure locked with the dog, growling, snarling, spitting;
she had no time to wonder how a hunter was getting that close
to a demon and still standing upright. "*Fiat lux,*" she whispered,
"*In nominae Eunomines et Brigid, fiat lux,* so I command,
so it shall be, give me *light!*"

The disorientation of working an act of sorcery without
preparation and patterning hit her, her empty stomach rising in
rebellion. Thank God she had nothing in it. The feeling of vital
force bleeding out of her solar plexus intensified. Her knife
turned red-hot for a moment, the power pushing out through it,
then light burst over the alley in a brilliant flash, rich golden
light.

Sunlight, a flood of it, as if she'd pointed a high-powered
yellow searchlight down the alley.

The *Baltiriaz* made a grunting, snuffling, howling sound of
absolute pain, and the other hunter descended on it. There was
a squeal, cut short, and a sickening crack. *Holy shit, I think
he killed it. That was quick.*

No sound but distant sirens. Chess blinked, coughed,
goosebumps the size of small eggs pushing up under her skin.
Is it dead? Her eyes watered, stinging furiously under the
assault of the light. "Is it dead?" she whispered.

"The light." The other person's voice, dark and low, a man's
voice, rough and strangely breathless. "Goddamn, girl, shut it
off."

She let the spell go, light bleeding away. Her eyes stung
and she was temporarily blinded as darkness returned. The
smell of a dead, stinking demon roiled. "Are you all right?"
Her voice broke. She shivered, the knife blade jittering, the
blue glow helped. She felt cold, and suddenly very, very hungry.
Scrambled eggs, steak, bacon—*I need protein.* Her shoulder
throbbed, and her head felt like a swelling pumpkin on a slender
stem, huge and bruised and painful. "Thank God. I wasn't
sure . . . thank God."

"Christ." He backed up, footsteps sounding lightly on the
wet pavement, and she was suddenly aware that she was in
her jammies and her coat, one foot bare and already hurting
from the cold concrete, her hair wet and messy and bruises
puffing up on the side of her face. *Ouch. Cops are coming,*

*and this thing stinks. It's raining. And who is this man? I
just ran out here, this entire place smells like demon . . . oh,
God, what have I gotten myself into now?*

He made a quick movement; she could barely see it in the
darkness. "You weren't sure? About what?" There was a
sparking, sizzling sound, and the smell thankfully shredded. He'd
done something to clean the air. *I want to learn that.*

"If it really was a *Balteriaz.*" Her voice sounded thin and
high next to his. She glanced back over her shoulder, saw
twisted metal blocking the entrance to the alley. "Who the hell
are you?" The sirens were even closer. The big shape of the
man slumped, and he exhaled as if hurt. "Are you okay?" She
sounded like a little girl, all breathy and ridiculous. The ground
seemed to shake underfoot.

He turned around, and she saw dark hair, cut short, he
was much taller than her. He clutched at his shoulder as if he
was hurt too, and lights began to flick on overhead. Her
neighbors would be wondering what the hell was going on.

"You're hurt." She coughed, dug in her pocket and brought
out her keys. Her head pounded thickly, she was having trouble
enunciating clearly. *I think I've got a concussion. Ouch. I
wonder if the salve will work on that?* "I have something
that might help. Come on."

"You shouldn't trust me." He slumped even further. "Go
back up to bed, little girl."

"You fought off that thing," she pointed out. "You can't be
all bad. Come on, the police are coming."

"I could care less about the *police.*" But he stepped away
from the space where the thing had died, and she saw smoke
rising. There was no stench, and for that she was grateful.
"Jesus, you're bleeding."

She lifted her right hand, almost poked herself with the
knife before she could make her fingers work to spin the hilt so
the blade was tucked against her forearm. It still glowed, not
as brightly but still dappling the walls of the alley with blue
shadows. "Something's still out there," she whispered. "Come
on." She jingled her keys. "Hurry. I don't feel so good."

He came closer, and she saw the pale dish of his face,
painted with dark blood down one side. Scalp wound, probably
messy, but he was holding his left shoulder as if that hurt too.
She couldn't see his eyes, only that they were dark, blazing
holes in his face. "I mean it," he said, hoarsely. "You shouldn't

trust me. I could be anyone."

"You're a demon hunter." Her tongue seemed incredibly thick, incredibly clumsy. "I'm Francesca Barnes. I live up in 5D, and the square key with the blue rubber shield will open that door right there. You're going to have to carry me." Darkness was closing in, starting at the edges of her vision and clouding across her eyes like steam. "I think I'm going to pass . . . "

The last thing she heard was his curse. She didn't even remember hitting the ground. Or maybe he caught her, but Chess was out cold.

* * * *

Softness. Warmth.

Chess groaned. There was a cool cloth on her forehead, and something poking into her side. Her knife, almost certainly. Someone's fingers pressed gently against her wrist, taking her pulse.

Her eyes fluttered open. Closed just as quickly as light struck through her aching head. "Ohhhh, *owwww*." She dragged in a deep breath, smelled something wonderful: toast. And . . . eggs? Damn. *I'd love to wake up to breakfast already made. But does it have to be when I feel like this?*

"Just lie still," a deep, male voice said. No hoarseness now, he sounded actually amused. "You'll be fine. Took a knock to the head, your shoulder's badly bruised, and your knee was ground up a bit from the concrete. I've done what I can to patch you up."

"Argh." She could barely manage to squint, the light was so painful. "Phone."

"What?"

"Phone. Work. Call in." *There is no way I'm making it in tomorrow. Today. Whenever it is.* The pain was incredible, Biblical, titanic.

"I called for you. Spoke to someone named Sharon, her number's right by your phone. Told her I was a neighbor, that you had a bad case of food poisoning and I was looking after you." The amusement didn't leave his tone. "You seem pretty organized."

If you only knew. "Born that way." *The salve.* "Bathroom. Go into the bathroom, look in the medicine . . . " She had to stop, take a deep breath. "Cabinet. Blue jar, kind of sparkly. Bring me?"

"You got it." He paused. "I'll be right back."

Of course you will. I doubt you're looking to steal my TV or ravage me. You seem like a nice guy. She took a deep sniff. Yes, it was definitely eggs. Her stomach growled. Go figure, she was finally hungry. And all it took was a dog-demon and another hunter. *What about the demon's body? It's raining, and he did something to get rid of the smell.*

"I found it." His voice came from very close, startling her. Her head was pounding so bad she hadn't heard him approach. "What do I do with it?"

"O-open it up. P-put some on my head. And my sh-shoulder. Use some yourself." *Agh, I feel like I've been kicked in the gut. And the head. Not to mention my shoulder. Holy shit. I shouldn't have gone out there, but what else could I do? God. At least we're both alive.*

He cracked the lid on the jar. The pungent smell of the ointment filled the air. "What is this stuff?"

"Old recipe." She hissed in a breath as he dabbed some on the aching sore spot on her head. "Good for you. Ouch."

"Sorry." The amusement was gone. He did sound sorry. Very sorry. He sounded, in fact, like he was almost frantic with worry, in a very contained sort of way.

"Don't be." It stung, but the pain began to bleed away. He pushed the torn neck of her T-shirt aside, spread more of the ointment on her shoulder, his fingers gentle. "It almost got in my window. Hate to think of cleaning *that* up." The stinging, calming feel of the ointment seemed to clear her head, make it easier to talk. "The cops. Did they—"

"Came by. I pretended to be your boyfriend, did a convincing just-woke-up act and said you were sick with food poisoning." He dabbed a bit more ointment on her forehead, trying to keep it away from her hair. "They're blaming it on kids fooling around with the fire escape. Just glad nobody was hurt, they said. You're in the clear."

She felt a draft of cooler air as he pushed the down comforter up, exposing her knee. He paused. "Is this safe for your knee? You've got a good scrape there."

You took care of everything. Wow. "Put it on. It'll sting, but that's better than what it feels like now." She was rapidly beginning to wake up. Her eyes opened, she blinked furiously, tears trickling down her cheeks from the smell and the stinging of the greasy goop. Her apartment swam into focus, shelves of books, the framed print of Saint Michael and Satan just a collage of blurry reds and taupes, the greens and browns lost. "Hi. I'm Chess."

"Beg your pardon?" He began pasting a thick layer of the salve on her knee with finicky delicacy. "Would you look at that. It's taking the swelling down already. What's in this?"

"You don't want to know. I'm Chess. Francesca Barnes. You are?" *I want to at least know your name. And are those eggs I smell?*

"Ryan."

Is that a first name or a last name? She waited for more, he didn't give any. She blinked away the tears and found thin early-morning sunlight coming through the windows, her apartment taking on its familiar sharp focus. She was on her couch, her television was turned off, and her knife was a comforting hardness against her hip. And the man was . . . well.

Black hair, cut short, with blue highlights showing in the weak gray sunshine. He wore a black T-shirt, straining against nice broad shoulders. He crouched by the side of the couch, looking intently at her knee as he smoothed the ointment on, his touch butterfly-delicate. His profile was severe but very nicely balanced—aquiline nose, strong jaw, nice chin—and his charcoal-fringed eyes were so dark she could barely see where the iris ended and the pupil began. His hands were much larger than hers, and she could feel calluses rasping as he attended to her knee. There was a healing slice across his own forehead, and his shoulder seemed to be much better, though his T-shirt was torn and flapping, crusted with dried blood. He wore a pair of dark-blue jeans, and dark socks; his hair was mussed as if he'd run his hands back through it damp and made it stand up in soft spikes.

Her mouth went dry. *Wow.*

The faint scowl of concentration he wore was even more attractive. He looked very serious, and Chess's heart thumped against her ribcage.

"Hurts?" he asked, giving her a dark glance. Those eyes were deadly, really. He looked *very* serious. Very concerned.

He's cute. How the hell did he survive a five-story drop like that? She found she'd stopped breathing, hastily inhaled and almost choked on the thick smell of mint and wormwood. "Little bit. Not bad." *That's a damn lie, Chess. But oh well. I got rescued by a hunk. Though technically, I suppose I*

could have just left him out there. That wouldn't have been very nice, but I could have done it.
Yeah, sure. "So, Mr. Ryan. You got a first name?" *Or a last name? Or should I just call you yummy?*
One corner of his mouth curled up slightly. "Just Ryan, sweetheart. Short for Orion."
What a moniker. And if you stick around we're going to have to talk about that "sweetheart" bit. "Orion. The Hunter." She tried to nod sagely, winced as her neck reminded her she'd been thrown against a Dumpster. "You made breakfast?"
He shrugged, dropping his eyes and finishing his ministrations to her knee. "Yeah. Needed a protein load after last night. I can pay you for—"
"Pay me? You saved my life. We're pretty even." *I must look like I've been hit by a truck. Nice first impression, Chessie the Demon Hunter, who goes out in her jammies to fight the denizens of the dark side. Crap.* "So you . . . you know about them."
"About what?" He capped the jar deftly, tendons flickering in his wrist as he tightened the lid.
Um, are we even speaking the same language? "About . . . demons."
The half-smile dropped from his face. "I'm Drakulein," he said sharply, as if she'd just insulted him. "I'm a hunter. The question is, what the hell are *you*? How did you get that knife? And what the hell have you done with my Malik?"

Four

She blinked at him owlishly, and Ryan was suddenly shaken with the urge to grab and *shake* her. He was in a fine stew of frustration. His Malik was gone, and he'd spent a further five worthless days trailing this skin, who didn't seem to have the faintest goddamn clue what he was talking about. And *that* meant Ryan had miscalculated. Paul's disappearance was linked to something else, and while he'd spent days shadowing this woman he'd probably lost track of his Malik for good.

It didn't help that he'd shown his hand too soon. He'd felt the Dog tracking her as she went on her round of work, gym, grocery store, and home; the house she'd visited turned out to obviously be her family. Then, seeing the wards crackling and smoking after repelling the demon's initial attempt, he'd simply flung himself thoughtlessly down after it, causing a whole hell of a lot of noise and attracting the attention of the authorities.

The trouble was, he hadn't stopped to rationally consider any of the consequences. Thinking of her inside the apartment while that thing came for her had damn near blinded him with red rage. He'd heard her bail out of the building behind him with that damn Fang, pain blurring and buzzing into his nerves, and he'd moved to protect her instinctively. The demon in his head hadn't fought him; as a matter of fact, the hard fiery alien part he'd inherited as a Drakul had snarled with possessive rage, spurring him on.

And *then* he'd lingered here and taken care of her, as if she was his Malik and not Paul, who at least deserved a Drakul who would look for him. But he had no goddamn leads, the *sheela* that the head librarian worked with was too damn scatterbrained to be any threat. Not to mention the fact that Ryan had tracked down Paul's dinner reservation at a tony North Side restaurant. A few careful questions had elicited the troubling news that the *sheela* had shown up, waited for three hours for his feckless partner, then left in high dudgeon. The head librarian had looked like his best bet . . . but she was obviously clueless. He had shaken her awake every hour, checking her pupils' dilation and working what limited healing sorcery he had possession of, and the worst part of it was, he'd actually been . . .

Well, *frightened.* He was getting awfully attached to this librarian with her obvious love of books and her practice with the heavy bag, not to mention her habit of dancing while she made dinner. Watching her for so long had given him a much better sense of her, and she wasn't like the usual brain dead skin. For one thing, she had fantastic taste in music. He hadn't heard a bad song yet.

Now the way she was staring at him told him he'd made a mistake.

"My Malik," he said tightly. "Tall guy, wears glasses, asked you about Delmonico's *Demons and Hellspawn.* You know him. He had a dinner date with your friend, and didn't show. Didn't show at the rendezvous either. Where the fuck is he?"

Her eyes were extraordinarily large, and very dark. He could see the flecks of gold and green in the hazel as she stared at him as if he were speaking a foreign language, her pretty mouth ajar with shock. Her hair fell over her shoulders, tangled and rumpled, and her torn T-shirt and boxers had been soaked with rainwater. He hadn't tried to get her into anything dry, but he'd wondered if he should. She stared at him, one hand creeping out to touch the hilt of her knife. He was fairly sure he could fend her off, especially in her injured state, but he wanted information and her help, and the best way to get that was by being . . . well, charming.

Too bad the charming half of this partnership was gone.

The thought of Paul charming his way around this woman called up a hot nasty flare of emotion he didn't want to examine more closely. Ryan decided to try again. "Look." He tried to make his tone as soft and cajoling as possible. "I don't want to hurt you, and I don't want to frighten you. It's very important that I find my partner, and you seemed like the best bet I had of finding him. You have no idea what kind of trouble could come down if I don't track him." *The Malik will eat you for breakfast, sweetheart. You won't know what hit you if they decide you're a threat.*

"You've been following me." She reached out, and he controlled the urge to twitch away as she plucked the jar of ointment from his fingers. "Get out."

"What?" *She didn't just say that, did she? Not very grateful. But she's smart, she's put two and two together and come up with me following her. Probably even suspected it, she's been edgy for days now. That was a stupid move, leaning against her wards like that.*

"I don't know what books your partner was talking about, and I don't care." She was lying, and if she hadn't been so hurt she might have actually pulled it off. Her pupils dilated, and her fingers curled around the hilt of the knife. She had turned deadly-pale, the bruise on her forehead stretching up into her hair suddenly standing out heavy and glaring against the chalky tone of her skin. That alarmed him more than he liked to admit. "Get out. Get *out*."

"I saved your life," he reminded her. *And you don't know it, but I'm going to save your life again. The Malik will kill you if you don't join them. They will follow you until you slip up, and they'll find wherever you've hidden those books, and they will take them. If you're not part of the Order, you're part of the problem, and they are very good at solving problems.* "You could at least hear me out before you do anything hasty."

"How do I know you didn't sic that thing on me?" She tensed, putting her hand with the jar down as if she was about to push herself up to standing. "Get the *fuck* out of my house or I'll—"

He grabbed her shoulders, shoving her back down on the battered, rose-patterned couch and wincing inwardly when she flinched, letting out a soft sound of pain. *Great, you big dumb Drakul. Just perfect. Scare her even more.* "Or you'll what? Call the cops? Tell them I'm a big bad demon hunter? I *saved your life*, and I'm *Drakulein*. I don't sic demons on people." He felt his lips pull back in a wide, humorless smile; she had no idea of the depth of the insult. "I am of the Order of the Dragon, a knight of the Balance, and it's because of people like me that ordinary skins can walk around safe at night. You found a cache of sorcerous books, you're relatively bright and you have some talent. You've started messing around with things you don't understand, fine. But if you don't start listening to me you're going to end up in a world of hurt. You can take that to the bank, sweetheart."

Her eyes flashed at him. "Don't you fucking *dare* call me sweetheart," she hissed. "Get your hands off me and get out of my goddamn house!"

"No." *You're not Malik, I'm not bound to obey you. And if I leave you alone, you'll get yourself killed.* "I'll make you a deal, librarian. You help me find my Malik and I'll overlook your screwing around with demons. How about it?"

Color began to flood her cheeks. She was even prettier when she was angry, despite her tangled hair and the bruise on her face, which was rapidly starting to look much better. Whatever was in that oily goop was evidently worth its weight in gold. "I don't *screw around* with demons. I *hunt* them. Where were you when that octopus thing was eating schoolkids, huh? Well? Where were you? Spying on someone else?"

Schoolkids? The skornac? His hands gentled on her shoulders. She'd actually damn near dislocated one of them and he didn't want to add to the pain. "Wait a second." *Damn, her eyes are pretty. Look at that, her eyebrows are perfect, and when her eyes light up . . . Keep your mind on your goddamn work, Ryan.* "Kids? Octopus—a *skornac* was taking humans?"

The change that came over her face was alarming. She bit her lower lip and nodded. "I f-found out." The color started to fade from her cheeks, and he suddenly had the horrible idea that she had indeed gone out and killed a *skornac* all by her lonesome. The thought managed to turn his knees to jelly. He was glad to be actually on his knees and braced against the couch. "It started with r-rats, and then moved to c-cats and kids. F-five of them. The newspapers thought it was a . . . a human. I knew better."

"Wait a second. Just hold on one goddamn second. Don't tell me you . . . " He searched her face. She didn't look half as angry now. As a matter of fact, she looked like a woman reliving a nightmare, and he had the sudden uncharacteristic desire to smooth her hair back from her face and say something soothing.

"I caught a glimpse one night as it took a . . . a victim. He was n-nine . . . I bought a knife and researched all the demons I could, and I followed it." She was ashen instead of pale now, her skin taking on a tint he didn't like one bit. "Then I researched some more, finished consecrating this—" She held up the sheathed knife. It was a long, double-bladed beauty with a plain, high-quality hilt; the blade was a good six inches long, a thin line of glowing blue between the hilt and the sheath. "And I tracked it down by using a dowsing pendulum. I caught sight of it, it went underground, and I followed it into the sewer and k-killed it."

Ryan let go of her shoulders. He sat down, hard, on the

hardwood floor and stared at her. Cold sweat prickled on his back. *She's either incredibly fucking lucky or very, very talented. Either way . . . Jesus Christ on a pogo stick, she killed a skornac. On her own. She should have had a Drakul there to protect her. She should never have been allowed near one of those filthy fucking things, she's lucky to still be alive.*

Not to mention that if the *skornac* had been taking humans, something was very, very wrong here. This was a free city, not policed like a Malik town was, but an uneasy border between the Inkani in the far south and the Malik territories to the colder north. Each enclave of Others here was supposed to operate by its own rules, and the Inkani weren't supposed to spill out into its pressure zone. But this was a keyhole city, and if the Inkani took it they would likely take a large chunk away from the already-stretched-thin Malik.

And the skins would suffer.

He would have to look around and see what was going on. A *skornac* taking humans *could* be a freak occurrence, like winning the lottery was a freak occurrence.

Or, far more likely, it was the Inkani, the hellspawn themselves and their human dogs, trying to expand.

If it was the Inkani, she was looking at a very short lifespan indeed without a Drakul's protection. And Paul was either hunkered down somewhere waiting for Ryan to find him, or he was messily, painfully dead.

He stared at her, a small, tangled woman who had flung herself out into the dark alley last night as if she could protect him. A woman who said she had managed to consecrate a Fang, though he was sure she had only *found* it, since all the Phoenicis were gone. But the knife *was* evidently new, it wasn't an antique. How could he explain that?

Her wrists were thin, she barely reached his collarbone, and even though she was hell on wheels against a heavy bag, she wouldn't have a chance in hell against a combat-trained Malik, let alone even a *small* demon.

"You need to get out of my house," she said finally, as he stared at her, his jaw suspiciously loose. "I don't like being spied on and lied to." Her chin lifted stubbornly, and Ryan realized he was in very deep trouble. The thought of her facing down a *skornac* made the inside of his chest feel curiously leaden and cold.

Come on, Ryan. Use that tongue of yours for something constructive. What would Paul say? "I was just being cautious, not spying on you. You know all about being cautious, sweetheart. You played your cards so well Paul doubted you had anything to do with the missing books. You found Melwyn Evrard Halston's library, didn't you? And once you figured out what it was and that it was for real, you didn't tell anyone. You just quietly went about making some ritual implements and went chasing after a fucking class-3 demon. *That* wasn't very cautious, but females get a little impulsive, I'm told." *Whoops. That didn't come out right.* "Imagine you didn't know about any of this. What would you have said if Paul came up to you and announced he was a demon hunter and suspected you of knowing about a cache? If you didn't laugh at him you'd call the cops and have him hauled to the funny farm, if they could catch him. We had to be sure." *Not to mention the fact that killing that skornac's made you a target. If we found you, the Inkani can find you too. If they find you you're dead. And I'll be damned before I let that happen.* "You made a lot of noise and mess killing that thing, and you've attracted a lot of attention. Like it or not, you need me."

That gave her chin an even more defiant tilt. The ashen tone to her cheeks was going away, thank God, and he was beginning to recover from the feeling of being punched in the gut.

Beginning to. Thinking of what the Inkani would do to her made the feeling threaten to come back. "I don't need you," she informed him haughtily. "I'm doing just fine on my own. And quit calling me that. You may address me as Ms. Barnes."

Keep dreaming, sweetheart. You're only doing fine on your own because nobody's found out about you yet. You've got some damn good protective coloration, but that won't save you. "Look." He had to work for an even tone. "You don't understand what you've gotten into here. I got that thing away from your window and you helped me kill it. Good. We can make a good team. I have to find my Malik, and I'd hate it if the Inkani got their claws in you. I can teach you how to fight more effectively, and you can do me the honor of trusting me. I won't ask where the goddamn books are." *Besides, if you join the Order, they'll have it out of you sooner or later. You're talented enough they'll cut you some slack.*

Especially if Ryan explained it to them the right way. He

couldn't lie, but he could shine the most positive light on her actions.

Christ, what are you contemplating? You're can't get emotionally involved with her. You're a Drakul, and they won't even let you do so much as sniff her hair. Keep yourself under control.

Too goddamn late for that. He knew, with miserable certainty, that he had committed a grave sin and allowed himself to get attached. It would be deathly hard to fight his instincts and let her go into the Order, let her be whisked away, vanishing into the Malik. And if they guessed he'd gotten possessive over her . . .

She again stared at him as if he were speaking a foreign language. He wanted a closer look at the gold flecks in her eyes, but didn't dare move. "What's Ankeny?"

"Inkani," he corrected automatically, hearing the strange accent in the word as if for the first time. "They're the upper echelon of demons, the people that have made deals with them in return for privilege and power. The Order—the Malik and Drakulein—are the people that keep them in check, fight them off, and keep the rest of you skins from becoming slaves."

"Skins?" she whispered. At least there was no more of the *get-out-of-my-house* stuff. But she was alarmingly pale again, and he began to worry that he should have fed her before questioning her.

"People with no sorcerous ability. Humans. The people we protect." He was beginning to feel a little less woozy. If Paul was still alive, he was likely to stay that way, having found a good bolthole; if he wasn't, there was nothing Ryan could do about it now. The Inkani were bad, but he'd fought them before, and with this little prize to bring back to the Malik he could probably escape a black mark on his record. He could handle this.

Maybe. With a miracle or two he might even be able to pull this one off.

"I'm a . . . a skin?" Her eyebrows drew together, and she put aside the jar of sparkling ointment, on a teetering stack of books. A few reference texts about old bookbinding, Carlyle's *The French Revolution*, a few herbals, and a battered leatherbound Mark Twain, *Tom Sawyer* and *Huckleberry Finn* in one package. Odd, but he'd come to expect that from her.

"Not any more," he said shortly. "Now you're a Malik

recruit. Congratulations."

She pushed the down comforter—dragged off her bed, he thought, seeing it was blue like the rest of her bedroom—away. The boxers rode up, exposing very interesting legs, sleek and smoothly muscled, the horrible scrape on her knee already looking much less serious. Her toenails were painted with crimson polish, and there was a smear of dried mud on her left ankle. Add to that her torn T-shirt, slipping down and showing a slice of her bruised shoulder as well as the top slope of a perky C-cup that most definitely wasn't trapped in a bra, and he suddenly found it a little difficult to breathe. "That's an honor I can do without," she said, dryly, and he recognized the tone as "professional".

He knew enough from watching her to guess that meant trouble, especially with the way her shoulders went back and one eyebrow arched, the equivalent to a cobra's hood spreading out or a mama bear's warning growl. *Uh-oh.* "Look, sweetheart—"

"I've had enough," she interrupted, making it to her feet and wincing as more aches and pains became apparent. "I'm going to the bathroom and I'm going to get dressed. Then I'm going to have some breakfast. We're even, you yourself said so. You can go looking for your friend and I'll take care of my library. I *don't like* being spied on, and if your friend Paul hadn't been such an arrogant idiot he might have had better luck. He quit paying attention to me and spent his time flirting with my coworker and *then* proceeded to stand her up. I don't think much of either of you. By the time I finish in the bathroom I expect you to be gone. Lock the door on your way out."

Goddamn it. What part of this do you not understand, woman? He made it to his feet in one swift motion, a little gratified when she flinched. *I don't like scaring you, but I will if I have to.* "I am not going anywhere." He folded his arms and glared at her. "You're going to help me find my Malik, and I'm going to keep you alive long enough to figure out how to keep the Order from making a mess of your life. Because they will, sweetheart. You have no idea."

"I don't think much of your Order and I think even less of you." Her eyes lit up with what he recognized as incandescent fury. It made her even more beautiful, and he wondered how Paul could have ever thought her less than stunning. Or even been *attracted* to the *sheela* with this woman around. "Nobody tells me what to do, and nobody's going to try to steal my library! Where were all the rest of you when I was taking care of it? I've done all the work and now you want to ride in and take the credit. No, *thank* you! Where was your goddamn Order when I was hunting down the—*ulp!*"

He didn't mean to, but he almost knocked her off her feet. His arm locked around her throat, not tight enough to cut off her air but tight enough to pull her back against him. She struggled and raked at his forearm with her short fingernails, also tried stamping on his foot. But there were advantages to being Drakul: enhanced strength wedded to quicker reflexes, reinforced bones and superior musculature. Besides, she'd taken a hell of a beating and was in no condition to fight him.

Time to put this in terms you can understand. "I don't want your goddamn library," he said in her ear, getting a good lungful of her. She smelled, even after last night's dip in alley water, of clean herbal shampoo and that maddeningly elusive warm, fresh golden scent that made it difficult to concentrate on what he was saying. "As far as I'm concerned, the Order won't hear about your books from me. You're just talented enough to have picked up a lot of this as you go along. What I *do* want is to find my Malik and keep you alive, sweetheart, and if you make it difficult for me, I'll make it *much* more difficult for you. Trust me, you don't want that. Since I'm prepared to play it nice and easy, I suggest you do the same."

She even tried to elbow him, but the fight gradually went out of her. She went limp. He could almost feel her vibrating with fury nevertheless. "Deal, Miss Barnes?" *I kind of like this, having her struggle. She's so damn bossy. But I like that about her too.*

One last frantic burst of effort, then she sagged exhausted against him again, and he had another problem—he was starting to respond. Starting to?

No, he already had. His skin flushed with heat and the demon part of him—suspiciously quiet for too goddamn long— roared into life. He had to clamp down on his control, trained into him harshly the instant the Malik found him, and hope she didn't notice that the man holding her still was not only shaking slightly and sweating, but also sporting a serious hard-on.

Without a Malik around to remind him of his duty, he was about to get very attached to this bossy little librarian, and that wasn't something the Order would look kindly on at all. If his

instincts were triggered things could get messy indeed.
If? It's too goddamn late. I'm in too deep already, and this has barely gotten started. She's mine. Nobody knows it yet, but she's mine.

"Bully," she said harshly, and he hoped he wasn't choking her. "You're nothing but a big *bully*, and I hate bullies."

"You were pretty glad to see me last night. Do we have a deal, librarian?" *If she moves, if she leans back or even tries to struggle . . .* The world narrowed to a single thread, Ryan fighting to stay perfectly still, perfectly calm, controlled. *I am Drakulein. I am of the Order of the Dragon. I do not force myself on women, nor do I hurt them. I am Drakul.*

The mantra helped, but only a little.

"Fine." Her voice broke. "Deal. Let go of me."

I don't know if I can. But he did. As soon as her feet touched the floor she scrambled away from him, pausing at the edge of the living room, in her bedroom doorway. The bathroom had two doors, one to her room and one to the short hall leading to the kitchen, but she was probably instinctively retreating to the place where she slept. "Don't ever do that again," she said tonelessly, rubbing at her throat with gentle fingers.

Though he knew he hadn't come close to choking her, he still felt a sharp spear of that new, aching feeling. Guilt. "Don't give me reason to." He earned himself a glare that could shatter a clock face. "I'll make you breakfast. How do you like your eggs?"

"You leave my kitchen alone. I'll make my own damn breakfast." And with that, she vanished into her bedroom.

Perfect. I managed to handle that in a spectacularly bad way. But she's agreed, and she's decent, so she'll probably live up to it. That, however, was the least of his problems. He had to find his Malik and find out what the Inkani were up to. And then he had to figure out how to stay as close to her as possible, for as long as possible.

I'm in trouble, and if the Order finds out I'll never see her again. His throat went dry, and he retreated to the dining room, where he'd left his weapons and his bag. *What am I thinking of? I'm contemplating something very dangerous. Let's hope I come to my senses sometime soon.*

But he heard the shower gurgle into life, and his entire body seemed to vibrate with tension, kicking up a notch. It was too late. She'd triggered some of the worst and deepest instincts a Drakul had, and he was in the biggest mess of his life, without the faintest idea of how he'd gotten there.

Five

He didn't listen to her, of course, and had a plate of scrambled eggs and buttered toast for her as soon as she appeared, showered, in clean clothes, and feeling marginally more able to handle the situation. He hadn't done her toast right—Chess preferred it just lightly toasted, and he'd damn near burned it—but she was so hungry she didn't care. He had even made coffee, and it was little consolation that he'd managed to do *that* right. The coffee alone was strong enough to eat a silver spoon.

By the time she finished the first piece of toast—made tolerable by a liberal layer of strawberry jam and frequent gulps of coffee with cream—she was feeling much better. The ointment, reapplied after her shower, had worked its sorcery, and she was well on her way to simmering with fury. It was only eleven o'clock in the morning. If she was at work she would be shelving for a little bit before lunch. The rain had blown itself out, now the windows darkened when a cloud went over the sun and brightened when it came back out.

"So the Malik are human, but they've got sorcerous talent. They're like sorcerers. What are . . . Dragool?"

"Drakul," he corrected. Settled on the other side of her table, his black eyes focused on the wickedly-curved, sharp-looking knife he was oiling, he looked far more deadly than he had this morning. His profile was harsh, especially when he was concentrating, and he didn't treat the knife with the same delicate care he'd used on her knee. Instead, his eyebrows were drawn together, and he looked almost distracted but still . . . well, lethal. Muscle moved in his arm as he lifted the knife, eyeing the blade critically, and her heart began to pound. He had a black bag with a flap and a shoulder strap; it seemed to hold a lot of odds and ends he probably needed for demon hunting, like her own bag. "Drakulein. The Order of the Dragon. In 1431 the original order—meant to fight against the infidel in Eastern Europe—was expanded. One of Sigismund of Luxembourg's vassals was a Malik, a kind of medieval demon-hunter. He got a secret charter from Sigismund, who was King of Hungary. Then he started finding men with demon blood."

"Demon blood?" She almost forgot to eat, this was so

interesting. But she was absolutely *starving* and took another bite of toast and contemplated more coffee. *I have a big, tall demon hunter sitting at my kitchen table. Whoa.* She was beginning to feel almost charitable toward him, despite him dangling her from her throat and spying on her.

"Whether by rape, by trickery, or through bargaining, Others have been breeding with humans for a long time. Not all of them have tentacles or are foul-smelling dogs. Anyway, the children of those unions usually had lots of sorcerous talent and the changes in bone structure began at about that time, we think. We're not sure. Sigismund's vassal laid the foundation for the Order. When Sigismund died, the human Order of the Dragon—"

"Wait a minute. Dracul." She made the connection. *The 1400s, Order of the Dragon, Eastern Europe. Oh my God.* "You mean like Vlad Tepes? As in—"

"He wasn't one of ours. He was part of the human order, just a warlord in Wallachia." But he looked pleased that she knew her history. He set the knife down, and his eyes settled on her. They were so *dark*, iris blending into pupil, it gave his gaze a piercing intensity she wasn't sure she liked. "Anyway, that was the start of it. When Sigismund died, the human Order went into decline, but the Malik and Dracul . . . we stayed. We had to. Demons were everywhere, feeding on the chaos wars left behind, and we had a hard time clearing out territories so people could sleep at night without worrying about the sounds they heard outside. There were outbreaks, of course, but after 1607 we were largely in control of things. I'm Drakul, my father and mother both had demon blood. Gave me some trouble when I was young, I could do things ordinary kids couldn't. I learned early and well to be circumspect; but my mom couldn't handle the demon in me coming out. Neither could anyone else, and I got labeled a runaway and a juvenile delinquent." His mouth turned down bitterly at both corners. "Then the Malik found me. I haven't looked back since."

"So you're . . . part . . . " Her mouth was dry. She took a hurried gulp of coffee, scorching her tongue. *Ouch. So that's why he moves so fast and why my knife's been acting funny. Why didn't any of the books warn me about this? I thought he was human. Like me.*

"Part demon, lacking a soul. Scared of me yet?" He gave her a bright, sunny smile, the tips of his white teeth showing, his eyes cold and dark.

Yes. Of course I am. I saw you move last night. Too fast to be human, and you survived a five-story drop onto concrete. My God. "No. If you mess with my library, I'll find some way to get rid of you." She popped a piece of toast into her mouth, chewed, and took another drink of coffee. It was too hot, but she needed the caffeine. "So you lost the guy in tweed—Paul."

"Yeah. He didn't meet me at the rendezvous, and didn't meet your friend. That means something's wrong. It's not like Paul to miss a dinner date. He thinks he's a goddamn Casanova." He slid the knife back into its sheath and took something else out of his bag. It looked like a coil of copper wire. The shoulder of his T-shirt was still torn and crusted with dried blood, and her conscience suddenly gave a hard twinge.

So he'd been watching her because he suspected her of having something to do with the disappearance. He'd still intervened, getting that *thing* away from her window. She'd been too exhausted to recognize the danger. He deserved a little slack, even if he had practically manhandled her in her own home. "Hey, take your shirt off."

That managed to get a reaction. He looked steadily at her, his jaw gone hard as stone and his eyes hard, closed-off, and almost feral.

"I mean it," she persisted. *I'm offering you an olive branch, you bossy jerk. Take it, why don't you?* "I've got some T-shirts left from an ex-boyfriend. One of them will probably fit you. I'll wash the one you're wearing and put it in my mending. No reason for you to go around all bloody."

He still stared at her as if she'd just informed him there was something unspeakable in his cornflakes. Chess sighed. "Fine. Forget it. So you want me to help you find this guy Paul. All right. Where do we start?"

"Nightfall." He looked back down at the table. "If you've got an extra shirt, I'll take it. I can mend this one, but it would be nice to have it washed."

"You could probably use a shower, too. It was pretty dirty and wet out there last night." *And I ran out in my pajamas. I haven't even looked at my coat yet. If I bled on it I'll have to take it to dry cleaning and wear my camel coat . . . dammit. And if I'm out all night I'm going to drag at work tomorrow. Lovely.* "So this . . . Order. You'll keep them away from me and my library if I cooperate?" *I've admitted to having the books.* Her heart rose to her throat, she swallowed hard. Whether she liked it or not, she had to trust him now.

He shrugged. "The Malik aren't likely to believe you took out a *skornac* on your own, so they probably won't believe you found a cache the Order's been trying to find for over a hundred years either. Halston was Golden, he had a falling-out with the Order and hid his books. He's part of the reason why this is a free city. I'll have to figure out who to blame the dead *skornac* on and figure out . . . " He blew out a long, frustrated breath, looking far less scary and far more human. "I'll do my best, sweetheart. I promise."

Again with the sweetheart. "You can call me Chessie," she offered, taking a forkful of egg. "Everyone does. No more of the sweetheart stuff, okay?"

"Sorry." He didn't look sorry. He kept rummaging in his bag, taking little things out, reorganizing. It looked like a nervous tic, but she couldn't imagine him nervous. "Look, there's something else."

"Huh?" Her coffee had cooled, and she took down half of it in three gulps, waiting for the caffeine to hit her system. *I am dealing with this really well,* she thought for the fiftieth time, and felt like it might actually be true. She had a bloody bully of a demon hunter sitting at her kitchen table, and he didn't look like he minded the books stacked on the other chairs and on the unused end of the table. He hadn't gone looking through her bookshelves yet, but she was feeling charitable. He didn't look as if he minded the clutter or her collection of Charlie Chaplin memorabilia.

The scrambled eggs weren't bad either. Neither was his coffee.

And he knew about demons. She could *talk* to him. Just the thought was enough to make her feel relieved.

"You want to be careful." He stared at his left hand, lying spread on the table. "Drakul . . . well, we have instincts. And they're not pretty."

She waited, but he said nothing else. "Instincts? What kind of instincts?" *This doesn't sound good.*

"Don't run," he finally said. "If I grab you and tell you to stay still, stay *still.* I've got a reason for everything I tell you to do. Can you agree to do what I tell you, at least for the time being?"

She finished her eggs, almost feeling her blood sugar level rise back up from the basement. All things considered, for being flung against a Dumpster and possibly given a concussion, she felt pretty good. Except for the deep bruising pain in her shoulder and the way her eyes refused to focus fully for a long time. Not to mention the headache pounding behind her temples, and the aching in her leg.

Yeah. Pretty good. "Is it . . . like a cat? If you dangle string in front of them, they'll chase it?"

"Kind of." He looked like he wanted to say more, shook his head. "I've been hunting demons for a couple decades. I'm the expert here, and I don't want you getting hurt like last night. Okay?"

I never thought a man telling me what to do would be even remotely acceptable. "Decades? All right. For now, you're the boss. When it comes to demons, that is." She nodded, her freshly washed hair sliding forward over her shoulders. "I generally work much better when people explain why they want me to do something, though."

He looked relieved. "I'll pretend you're a new Malik. I've trained a bunch of them, shouldn't be that bad. But it's very important that if I tell you to be still, you *freeze*. Got it?"

Why? "Why? I mean, why's that so important?" *And it's going to be really damn hard to stand in one place if there's a demon around, buddy. I'll either want to run or take it on. I don't do well with doing nothing.*

"It just is." His jaw set again and his eyes glittered. "Trust me."

What the hell. Why not. "All right. For now." She yawned, patting her mouth delicately, like Sleeping Beauty. *I should call the library.* "I need to call in to work, make sure everything's okay, and I should do some laundry if I'm going to be home today."

"You should rest." His eyes dropped to the table. "Tonight's probably going to be a little stressful."

You know, when you say that, I bet it means something totally different than when I say it. "All right. After I put a load of laundry in and call the library, I'll take a nap. I feel like I've been thrown up against a Dumpster." She managed a weak smile. "Why don't you go get cleaned up and I'll dig out a new shirt for you, to start with?"

He looked up, and there was something in the darkness of

his eyes that made her heart do a triple backflip. *Well, I suppose if I had to have a total bully of a demon hunter sitting at my kitchen table, he's not so bad.* Her smile quickly grew more natural, and he searched her face as if wanting to be sure she meant it.

Then he offered his right hand over the table. "Sounds good. Partners?"

She took his hand. It was much bigger than hers, callused, and very warm. "Partners. Just don't boss me around." A couple of halfhearted shakes, and she pulled her fingers away, pushed her chair back, and made it to her feet. Her knee twinged, and her bed started to sound really good.

"I'll do my best," he muttered, messing around with his bag again. Chess decided that was good enough, and carried her dirty dishes into the kitchen. *How much worse can this get? But if I'm going up against another demon, having someone like him on my side is far from the worst help I could have.*

The trouble with being intelligent was that logic always had another link in the chain ready. *Always assuming, of course, that he's really on my side.*

* * * *

"Hey." A hand on her shoulder, a gentle shake. "Hey, wake up a little, sweetheart."

We're really going to have to negotiate something else for you to call me. Chess blinked, trying to wake up. *Wait a second, who are you and what are you doing in my bedroom? Oh, yeah. Right.* "Murph. Go 'way." She sounded slurred and exhausted.

Go figure. I was just getting comfortable playing possum.

"Someone's at your door. Sounds like a man."

"What?" Now she could hear the knocking. Three knocks, then two, a familiar pattern.

Oh, no. Could this get any worse? "It's Robert," she managed, waking up a little more and propping herself up on her elbows. The light through her window had turned gray again, more rain. And the angle the light was falling through the door told her it was afternoon, the blue of her comforter and the rug making her room look filled with sky. She'd been asleep for a while, just passed out. Buster Keaton gazed sadly at her from the print on her wall. "Crap."

"Who's Robert?" Ryan stood by the side of her bed, sliding his hands into his pockets. The only shirt big enough to fit him was a black, long-sleeved NIN T-shirt she'd used for sleeping in after breaking up with Martin the Mexican Bandit, as Charlie had called him. He filled it out better than Marty had, his broad chest framing the logo nicely. *Wow. He looks really good in that.*

More knocks on the door. *Great. Wonderful. Perfect.* "Soon-to-be-ex-boyfriend," she managed, sliding her feet out from under the covers and rubbing at her eyes. "Just a *minute!*" she called, loud enough that Ryan jumped a little. "Sorry," she mock-whispered. "He's a real jerk, I've been trying to get rid of him."

"Want help?" And, wonder of wonders, the demon hunter gave a lopsided, very amused smile. He'd combed his short hair and taken a shower, the slice on his forehead was gone as if it had never existed.

She wondered if he'd used the salve or if being part-demon made him heal faster. *Curiosity, my besetting sin. I should be scared of him, he's a big bully. But I haven't slept this well in weeks.* "Where would we hide the body?" She yawned, stretched, and reached for her robe. She'd chosen a long-sleeved T-shirt and a pair of boxers to sleep in. Her hair was probably sticking up every-which-way, but she was long past any need to impress Robert. *Did you get tired of that Cuban piece of trash, Rob?* "He's been cheating on me with a waitress named Carmen. Plus, he only tips ten percent." She struggled into her pink fluffy robe, tying the waistband with a savage jerk. "Anyway, I'll get rid of him. Just hold on."

She shuffled out into the living room just as he knocked again. "I'm *coming!*"

God, I sound irritated. I was dreaming. Wasn't I? I think I was dreaming.

She didn't hear him, but when she glanced back over her shoulder from the hall Ryan was right behind her. "I'll handle it," she mouthed, and he nodded, but his dark eyes were gleaming. "Who is it?" she called.

"Baby, it's Robert." His voice was muffled by the door. "I called the library, they said you were sick, so I decided to come by and help nurse you." She could almost hear his eyebrows raising.

You sleazy son of a bitch. I just got tossed into the side

*of a Dumpster last night, but you think I have food
poisoning, and you want sex? Oh, I am SO ready to be
done with you.* "I'm not in the mood for company," she hedged.
"I feel really sick, Rob."

"I'll make you some soup. Chicken soup. All right? Open
up, baby." Rob's tenor voice was smooth, cajoling. He was
trying to charm her. Again.

Too bad she didn't feel charmed.

She slid up to the door, unlocked the two deadbolts, flipped
the lock in the doorknob, and opened the door a crack, peering
out.

Rob's fair blond face greeted her. He wore his beret,
perched on his expensive, artfully-mussed haircut. His shirt
was open a little, his coat hanging wetly on him, and he wore
jeans and a pair of Testoni loafers. He was also carrying a
bunch of daisies, probably yanked from someone's window
box.

You jerk. He'd been nice while he lasted, but she had so
many other things to worry about now it wasn't even funny.
Besides, the sex wasn't *that* good, especially if he was dipping
his wick elsewhere. "Robert." She tried to sound sick, succeeded
in sounding exhausted. "I'm not in the mood. Go away."

He held up the flowers, offering his most charming smile.
The one that made his blue eyes twinkle. "Come on, baby. Let
me in, I'll play doctor."

Goddammit, I said no. Chess took a firmer grip on her
temper. "I said no."

He stepped forward, still smiling, and Chess's stomach
flipped. "Open up, Chess. You've been avoiding me, I want to
know why. I'll make you some soup, we can talk."

*I am not in a talkative mood. I have a demon hunter in
my house and my life has just sped into the Twilight Zone.*
"Go talk to Carmen," she said, and watched his face fall. He
slid right into "pretty repentance" without even missing a beat.
Very slick, he must have done this before.

"Carmen was a mistake, Chessie. You know that." He
used his most cajoling tone, spread the fingers of his left hand
against the door, and pushed. Chess, caught off-balance,
stepped back. Her heart hammered. He was acting a lot more
aggressively than she'd thought he was capable of. "Let me
in."

What happened next surprised both of them. Ryan's fingers

curled around the door and he pulled it back, opening it further. He had also stepped forward so his chest brushed Chess's back, looming over her. "Who is it, sweetheart?" His tone could best be described as "combative," and Chess had the distinct pleasure of seeing Robert turn cheese-pale, his right hand with its cargo of stolen flowers drooping back to his side. "Who's this?"

Chess found her voice. "It's Robert." *I sound uncomfortable. What a surprise, I feel pretty damn uncomfortable. Would he just have pushed past me if Ryan wasn't here?*

Then the demon hunter slid his right arm around her ribs, resting his chin on her head; she was short enough that he could do that. He was very warm, the heat of him working through his T-shirt, her robe, and her own shirt. Her heart hammered in her chest as if she was facing down the *skornac* again, but it was—wasn't it?—almost *comforting* to feel his arm around her and his solidity behind her. "Oh, yeah. Your friend. Nice of you to come by and check on Chess, but she's really sick. She should be in bed." He gave the last two words far more significance than they merited, and Chess felt heat rising to her cheeks. *Oh, fucking hell. I'm blushing. Lovely. But I wanted this guy gotten rid of, didn't I?* "I took the day off to take care of her."

And how Ryan managed to inject that chauvinistic sense of possessiveness in the last four words was beyond her. It was probably a testosterone thing. As it was, it sounded very caveman. *Me Ogg, take care of woman. Grunt. Snort.*

Robert stared up, his blue eyes narrowing. "What the hell is this?" he demanded. "Chessie, who the hell is *this?*"

The totally inappropriate desire to laugh like a maniac rose in her chest and was ruthlessly strangled. "This is Ryan. We've been spending some time together." *And you can make whatever you like of that statement, Rob. You will anyway. What, you think I belong to you? Not even if you weren't a cheating asshole. I belong to me.* "Do me a favor and pay the person whose garden you burgled for those flowers, okay?"

"You *bitch*," Rob hissed, and Ryan went tense behind her. "You fucking *bitch!*"

"I think you'd best shut your mouth, friend." Ryan's tone was even, soft, and merciless. "Or I might decide to shut it for you. You want this guy around, Chessie?"

At least he didn't call me "sweetheart." She watched all the color drain out of Rob's face. She didn't blame him, the sense of cold danger exhaling from behind her was enough to make Chess want to wriggle away. But she stayed still, watching Robert and glorying in a not-very-nice feeling of satisfaction. "No," she said finally. "I don't ever want to see his face again." *Go back to Carmen, you arrogant jerk.*

Ryan eased her back, his hand still on the door. Then he pushed it. It swung shut with a decisive click, and he reached forward, flipped both deadbolts loudly, and clicked the lock in the doorknob.

Well, that was easy. Chess sighed. She waited, but he didn't let go of her. Robert stood there for maybe ninety seconds, she heard the smack of the flowers hitting her door and his heavy footfalls as he stamped away.

"Well," she said finally, when she heard the door at the end of the hall slam. "One problem out of my hair, at least. Thanks." She moved as if to step away from Ryan, but his arm tightened. "What? Let go, it's okay. He's gone."

He didn't move, and Chess tried to step away again, reaching down and grabbing his wrist, trying to peel his arm away from her ribs. "Hey. Leggo. Come on."

"You'd better stay still." The chill, soft tone in his voice hadn't altered, he sounded thoughtful, and very very dangerous. "Just for a second. I wasn't ready for that."

What? "What weren't you ready for? He's just a jerk. A two-timing jerk, I might add. Nice touch with the voice. Very cavemen. Let *go* of me."

He did, so suddenly she stumbled, almost falling against the wall and barking her elbow a good one. *Ow!* "What the hell—"

Her shoulders hit the wall, Ryan's fingers sinking in. He held her at arm's length, her back against the wall and her hip pressed into the little rubber thingie that kept the doorknob from bashing a hole in the drywall. "I *smell* like you." He sounded distracted now, too. Cold, dangerous, and distracted, a bad combination. His hair stuck to his forehead—was he *sweating?* His eyes were half-closed, and a muscle in his cheek twitched madly. "I think it's the shirt. Dammit."

"What?" *Oh, Christ. What the hell is this? Is it a demon? Not during the day, no; at least I don't think so.* "What's *wrong* with you?"

His hands were shaking. His fingers didn't hurt her, but he held her still. Her hair fell in her face and she wanted to brush it away, didn't dare move. "Instinct," he muttered. "Triggered it. Hard to think. Just . . . stay still."

Uh-oh. He said they weren't pretty, these instincts. Does he want to hurt me? Oh, Lord, it's a fine time to wish someone else was here, even Rob.

"Talk to me," he said hoarsely. "Please, Chessie."

At least he didn't call me "sweetheart." Things are looking up. "About what?"

"Anything. Keep talking and *stay still.*"

Are you kidding? I want to brush my teeth, and I have to pee, and I want to go back to bed and forget about all this. Goddammit, Rob, of course you would come by and ruin everything. I was just starting to like this guy, too. Note to self: don't let mean old demon hunters help you get rid of old boyfriends. It only ends in disaster. What am I supposed to talk about? Her mouth was dry, and for once in her life Chess couldn't find a single goddamn thing to say.

His eyes closed. He *was* sweating, and she didn't even try to move. "Talk . . . to . . . me." Now he sounded pleading.

Books. Let's talk about books. "My favorite book of all time is *Jane Eyre.* But I suppose *Huckleberry Finn* is the one I love the most. Twain was a genius, and the layers of symbolism in the book are just amazing." The back of her throat tickled with the urge to cough; she settled for clearing her throat. "The river, for example. It can mean freedom or slavery, life or death and destructiveness, depending on which part you read. For symbolism, though, it's hard to beat poetry—Emily Dickinson. Baudelaire, who just happens to be the best there is at symbols right next to Rimbaud. But my favorite is Yeats. In particular, *Sailing To Byzantium.* When I hear it read, say, by someone with a British accent, I just get shivers." *I'm running out of things to say, help me, God. What's wrong with him?*

He leaned in, his eyes still closed, and actually sniffed her hair, taking a deep whiff. *This is the strangest thing that's happened to me lately. And that's saying something. He's smelling me. Why?*

His fingers loosened. She took a deep breath. "Other poets." Her voice sounded thin and breathless. "Shakespeare, for one, though I'm not really a fan of Elizabethan. I actually really like Marlowe, what little I've read of him. I hope you're okay. This is the weirdest thing I've dealt with in six months, and that's *really* saying something. Thanks for helping me get rid of Rob, but if I'd known it was going to do this to you I would have just let him bang on the door until he got bored. That or called the cops." Another deep breath. It was damn hard to breathe with a big dark-eyed hunk of man in a NIN T-shirt looming over her. Even if he *was* shaking and pale, sweating and slowly, slowly letting go of her shoulders. He hadn't hurt her, but he was still standing too close. Way inside her comfort zone. And smelling her hair didn't help either. It felt too goddamn intimate. "Don't hurt me. Please." *For God's sake, Chess, you just faced down an octopus demon and the best you can come up with is "don't hurt me?"*

"Last thing on my mind," he said, through gritted teeth. "Hurting you is the *last* thing on my mind. Don't worry."

I am not comforted by that in the least. "Can I move now? I want to go to the bathroom."

"Slowly. Very slowly." His hands fell away from her shoulders, curled into fists. "Then you'd probably better go back to bed. Couple more hours before dusk hits, that's when we'll get started."

I don't want to go anywhere with you. "Yeah, sure. Like I can sleep now." She edged along the wall away from him, toward the bathroom door. "Are you okay?"

He looked a little better now, his shoulders coming down and relaxing, his eyes still closed but his jaw not clenched nearly so tight. He nodded, his hands curling loosely into fists. "I won't hurt you, Chess. I just wasn't prepared for that."

"Prepared for what? Rob's a jerk, but he's just an old boyfriend. I know he's a sleazebucket, but even librarians have needs. And he got me tickets to a Rolling Stones concert." The half-laugh she attempted fell flat. *I'm trying to justify my taste in boy-tarts to this man. What the hell am I doing?*

"I don't care about him." The dismissive tone convinced her. "I just had a hard time with him threatening you. Go on, I'm okay now. I'm just going to breathe for a bit. You go do what you need to, get some rest."

Chess shook her head. "Fine. Great. Perfect." It took all her self-control to keep moving one slow step at a time instead of bolting. "He wasn't threatening me. He's a big coward." *Keep talking, Chess. Keep him occupied.*

"Just go, sweetheart. I'm okay now."

She got to the bathroom door. "Quit calling me sweetheart." She shut it behind her, locked it—like that would keep him out, but it made her feel better—and slumped, trembling, against the counter, flipping on the light and exhaling shakily. *Wow. I never want to do that again. He sounded fucking dangerous. What have I gotten myself into? I should have left those books alone.*

But she hadn't had any choice, had she? It was as if the library had *chosen* her, and she'd felt compelled. The books needed someone to take care of them, and finding out about the existence of demons had cemented her responsibility to do something. He said she had a lot of talent, and there were people out there fighting to keep the innocent safe.

And any chance she'd had to walk away from this had fled the instant she'd run across the *skornac* feeding on the dead body of its nine-year-old victim. Nobody could see something like that and be unaffected.

Chess let out a shaky sigh. She was flushed and shaking, her hair tangled and tossed every which way, and she saw her eyes flicker nervously in the mirror. *I look scared to death.*

What a coincidence. I am.

Six

Darkness was beginning to fill the windows as Chess slid the strap of the bag over her head. She pulled her hooded sweatshirt down over her hips, then adjusted the bag until it settled to her satisfaction. The Fang's sheath rode on her right hip, the bag on her left, and her hair was braided severely back. She wore old jeans and a pair of hiking boots that had seen better days but looked very comfortable. She was altogether too quiet, and Ryan didn't blame her. He hadn't meant to frighten her.

But dammit, the woman simply didn't know when to stop struggling, and the feel of her against him, leaning back and accepting his touch, had severely strained his control. Watching her sleep and wearing a shirt that smelled of her skin didn't help either—some of the deeper Drakul instincts were tied to scent. He could smell himself on her, and her on him; the mix was teasing and tempting. Not to mention the sudden chemical drift of fear coming up from her when the blond man had tried to push open the door. Her fear could trigger one of the deadliest rages known to the Drakul, the reason why they were kept so carefully segregated from Malik women.

I've really done it now. I've gotten attached to her. Far more attached than I should be. But who wouldn't? Look at her.

She bit her lower lip, digging in her bag. "Ziploc," she muttered, the light from the fixture over the kitchen table touching the dark sheen of her hair. "Finest invention since comfortable shoes. God, I hate this part."

It was the first thing she'd said since he'd awakened her at dusk. He hadn't touched her, merely stood in the doorway to her bedroom and called her name softly until she'd stirred, yawning and flushed and looking absolutely . . .

That thought didn't help his frayed control. *Stop it. You know it's just instinct. Leave it alone. You're Drakul, you swore an oath, and your Malik is out there somewhere.*

"What part?" He risked asking the question, wanting to distract her a little. If she got tense, he'd be tempted, and that would be hard on both of them. He had already had a hard time with seeing her in boxer shorts and that shapeless robe again. She'd made more coffee, then kitted herself out with such swift efficiency he was sure she'd been out patrolling for demons much more than she'd let on.

"Anticipating." She blew out a long breath, closing her eyes. "Where are we headed?"

"Ferne Street." He shrugged into his knee-length wool coat. It was dry by now but would soon be wet if the rain kept up. "There's a club down there, we can get some information, see what's happening."

"Ferne Street?" The glitters of gold in her hazel eyes suddenly flared, and he found himself taking a step forward. The color had drained from her cheeks. "You're kidding. I can't go down there, that's dangerous after dark!"

For a lone woman, yes. You'll hunt down demons but you're scared of getting mugged? Nice to see you have some *sense of self-preservation.* "You're with me," he reminded her. "I won't let anything happen to you." *Anything that a Drakul can prevent, that is. If we run up against a full massed company of Inkani you'll have to run while I hold them off. But that's not likely to happen, sweetheart. I'm going to take very good care of you.*

He slid the stiletto up his sleeve, checked the gun in his shoulder-holster—now *that* had turned her an interesting shade of chalk, too. For such a stubborn, bossy little lady, she certainly seemed to be frightened of the oddest things.

She slid her hands into the front pocket of the sweatshirt jacket. The dark navy blue would meld with shadows, and her jeans weren't likely to give her away. Her hair was dark, the only thing she'd have to worry about was the paleness of her face and hands. "What if you have another attack? Of your . . . instincts?"

What if, indeed. A curious idea stopped him, and he stared at her for a long moment. "What do you think?"

"I think you might slip up and hurt me," she replied baldly. "If I touch off anything demon in you, that is. You might even get me into trouble and leave me there tonight, if you think it'll find you your partner. I don't have any real reason to trust you, other than you getting that thing away from my window and nursing me through a concussion." Her jaw set stubbornly, her eyes flashed, and he took another step toward her.

Is that what she thinks? She had no idea, and it was probably just as well. "They're not hunter's instincts, sweetheart," he informed her. "You set off an entirely different set. Just remember to do what I tell you, I'm going to treat this as if I'm training a new Malik. I won't let anything happen to you." *Besides, a little bit of uncertainty's good for you. It'll make you manageable, for a while at least. And I am finding that I like you manageable almost as much as I like you being bossy.*

"Wait a second." Her chin looked particularly stubborn now, and he wondered again what had possessed Paul to think of her as the less-attractive option. Of course, the thought of anyone else finding her attractive made the demon growl in the bottom of his mind, but he could live with that.

Couldn't he? *I'm thinking of betraying the Order and tying myself to a human female. They'll put me down like a rabid dog.*

"Exactly which instincts are we talking about?" She stared at him as if he'd grown another head.

Get it, another head? Not funny, Ryan. Get your mind on business and keep it there. "Different ones. I won't throw you to the wolves, either. I promise. Now come on, it's time to go."

"I'm going to be hashed at work tomorrow," she muttered grimly, but followed him to the door. He would have preferred to take the fire escape, but it was still a mangled hunk of metal down in the alley. And she couldn't handle a five-story drop like he could.

Yeah, you probably are going to be tired tomorrow. Human endurance isn't all it's cracked up to be. "We'll make it an early night, it's just a recon run. If Paul's still alive, he's dug into a good bolthole and waiting for me to find him. He has enough sense to stay hidden." *Though he's likely not alive if the Inkani are in town. He was likely caught the first night when he went to prepare for his fucking date. I knew his dick would get him into trouble.*

Of course, I'm a fine one to talk. Christ. I'm contemplating throwing my life away for a librarian.

But she's such a good hand with a heavy bag. And she actually came down into the alley in her pajamas to protect me. Me.

It was the kind of thing that could warm a Drakulein's heart. If he could be said to have a heart, that was.

"Fine." She didn't sound happy, but she let him go out into

the hall first. He'd cleaned up the daisies and tossed them from her living-room window, wanting to get them away from her but not wanting to leave her apartment even for the moment it would take to walk to the garbage chute down the hall. Ryan checked the hall, then motioned her out.

"Safe enough. Now, what are the rules?" *Just one last time, sweetheart. So we start off the right way.*

"Don't talk to anyone, stay behind you, don't grab your right arm." So she *had* been listening. "If you tell me to freeze, freeze; if you tell me to run, run and come back here, wait for you to show up. If you stop and look like you're listening, *stay behind you* and don't talk." He could feel her gaze on his back. "Have I forgotten anything?"

"Nope. Especially if we get separated, come back here and wait. Think you can remember that?" He led her down the hall to the stairs, falling into the old familiar habit of listening to the footsteps behind him. Her footsteps where a Malik's should be, but she hadn't been taught to step only where he did. That didn't matter tonight, but he would eventually have to train her to do that, as well as induct her in a few Malik soreceries . . .

What the fuck am I thinking? I can't do that, they'll . . . Christ, I'm already in over my head. I might as well.

"I'll try." Her tone was dry and unamused. "So which instincts, exactly, am I triggering? You might as well tell me."

I don't think I want to. He contented himself with saying, "Protective instincts. We'll take a cab."

* * * *

Neon slid wet and slick against the pavement as he held the door, scanning the street. She got out of the cab, he slammed the back door, and the yellow car took off. Chess glanced around, her shoulders coming up. Even with her hiking boots, the top of her head barely reached above his collarbone, and he was suddenly, exquisitely aware that she was also much slighter than him, her shoulders slim and her hips narrow, her ribs delicate and so fragile. The mix of smells—hers lighter and clean with its edge of something he couldn't identify, his own dark and tainted with the burning scent of *demon*—was powerfully attractive, and would mark her as his. It was a protection for her; not a very good one if they ran up against the Order, but still a protection. There was something a little off about her smell, though, as if the human was wearing away and something else showing, something golden and smelling of spice.

Maybe it was just his imagination. Of course she would start smelling good to him; pretty soon her scent would start to have an aphrodisiac effect.

Pretty soon? That's yesterday's news. His eyes slid over the street again. Bars and nightclubs, mostly, one liquor store with barred windows and a steady stream of customers, and a good crowd. The last of the sunlight left the sky, he could *feel* it go, and his full strength roared back through his bones and veins. Day wasn't good for him.

No, he was a night creature. Strength returned, strength and full sensory acuity. He welcomed it even as his shoulders tightened a little and the familiar burning cold of the demon inside him rose to the surface. He took her elbow and inserted them both into the stream of people on the sidewalk, careful not to squeeze her arm. "You're right not to come down here alone." He bent down a little so she could hear him over the noise of the crowd. Throbbing waves of music poured out of nightclub doors; the bars all blinked with beer signs in the windows. Across the street, the hookers strutted; there was a sloping hulk of tenements and cheap hotels one street over where most of them probably lived. Traffic had slowed to a crawl, both because of the pedestrian crowd and because cars kept pulling over on the other side, disgorging passengers or picking them up. A police cruiser poked halfway out of an alley two blocks up, and his sharp eyesight picked out two Chinese takeout cartons as the cops inside ate, watching the street action.

If Paul was here he'd be checking out the hookers. I don't have to stand guard at the door while he "takes a break" anymore. A hard delighted smile tilted up the corners of Ryan's mouth. He let go of her elbow, but matched his steps to hers. She was supposed to be behind him, but in a crowd like this he could easily lose her; he moved as if herding her. Nobody jostled him, of course, his pheromones would give him some space even when the skins around him were unaware.

"This is a bad part of town. People get killed down here. There was a stabbing just the other day, I read about it in the paper." She didn't sound afraid, thank God, but she did slow down. He had to bump into her to get her going the speed he wanted, matching them to the crowd's pace.

"I'll look out for sharp objects." He kept scanning the street. Lots of skins. The smell of alcohol and desperation, sharper musty smells of other drugs, sweat and peppermint, and strained, quick sex spilling through the air. The demon part of him shivered, liking this collage of scents. Good food, good fuel, good hunting here.

Not hunting tonight. No breath of Malik, but plenty of the faint smoky tang of Others. *Sheela* and *sheel*, tall and graceful and passing for human, looking through the bars and nightclubs for their next partners. There was a stocky man in a trenchcoat who had a breath of stone and cold wind on him, a stonekin probably come out for the beer. Others, too, sliding through the crowd or crouched in the shadows; one that looked like a bag lady pushing a shopping cart and mumbling to herself was actually a *slinharik*, its cocoon wrapped tightly against the chill and the fleshy sensors on its high cheeks quivering as it scented him.

As they passed the cop car, she tensed but her stride never faltered. "Do you have trouble with the police?" she asked as they passed a bar with pool tables inside, the clack of balls striking each other sounding through the window's rippled glass.

"No." *They can't catch me, and even if they catch me they can't hold me. That's a benefit of being Drakul, resistance to cold iron; it doesn't trap me the way it traps some of the Others.* "I sometimes get taken in if we're chasing an infiltration in the police department. That was only once or twice though. I have to remember not to break the handcuffs, and to pretend that the beatings hurt."

"Really?" She glanced up at him, her eyes wide and dark, and he was surprised by a flare of proprietary sweetness. She sounded breathless, but they weren't going very fast. He could almost hear her pulse, sensing the tide of blood in her veins, and was willing to bet that his own pulse and respiration were beginning to match hers.

I am in so much trouble now. Why did I do this? Paul only told me to watch her, not get involved with her and sign my own death warrant.

But the memory of her slumped at her kitchen table, her face in her hands and her shoulders shaking, rose in front of him. She had faced down a *skornac* on her own. He was involved with this because from the moment he'd seen her dancing in her kitchen and waving a cleaver for emphasis, it had been too damn late.

"Cops don't bother us much. There are Malik cops, and sometimes the Inkani buy a few officers just in case." He eased her around the corner onto Malvrell, the bars that lined this street were seedier the further they got from the main drag. "We're almost there."

"Great." She sounded thrilled. "Can't wait. Perfect neighborhood."

"Be careful." He couldn't impress the importance of those two words enough on her. "This is an Other bar."

"Other?" She looked up at him again, her dark braid swinging; little jewels of rain clung to her hair since it had tapered off to a drizzle. She had long legs, and kept up a good clip, he only had to shorten his stride a little.

"Anything other than human. All demons are Others, but not all Others are demons. They'll smell me on you, shouldn't bother you." *But if they do, I'll stop it quick enough.* "Just follow my lead. And—"

"—be careful," she finished. "I'm not *stupid*, Mr. Ryan."

How did I get to be Mr. Ryan? "Far from, sweetheart." He knew it would irritate her, couldn't help himself. "You're too smart for your own damn good. That's why I keep reminding you. Here we are."

Three concrete steps down to a yawing, off-center wooden door miraculously not drifted under paper rubbish, and he put his hand up to push open the door. A faded, peeling sign above the door proclaimed the *Shelaugh Taverne*. "Stay close," he warned, and pushed.

The door swung and creaked open, a draft of warmth and cigarette smoke bellowed out. He herded her into the sudden thick noise of a jukebox playing Warren Zevon at high decibels and conversation trying vainly to be heard over the top. Cigarette smoke, alcohol, copper tang, and the smell of Others, nothing off, his ears took everything in and decided it was a normal night. She stepped in and he loomed behind her, making the point before anyone thought to ask. *Subtle, Ryan. Way subtle.*

There was a gaggle of full *sheela* at the bar, with bell-like voices and long bright hair. He squired Chess over to a small table in a defensible corner. "Drinks?" he asked over the hubbub.

She shook her head, her eyes moving over the whole place. She looked very calm for someone sitting in the middle of a clutch of *definitely Other*, from the red-skinned man in the corner drinking from a shallow black bowl to the woman whose small black dog sat on the bar, watching her toss peanuts that somehow were shelled when they landed in her coppery hands. There were warty, gray-skinned stonekin too, taking down beer at a prodigious rate and paying with silver pieces; the shadowy corners were full of strange shapes with bright eyes. The breath of *alien* exuding from this place would keep the skins away; normal people had a positive genius for ignoring what they didn't want to see.

He left her at the table, elbowed his way to the bar and got two whiskey sours, leaving the tip and a single silver piece laying on the shipwrecked, rollicking oaken monstrosity of the bar itself. Then he forced his way through the crowd back to the table and scooted into the booth next to her, testing the table—not secured to the floor. Good. He made sure his back was to the wall and ran a practiced eye over the crowd. His coming had already been remarked, and the presence of a female with him too.

Well, I've come this far. I might as well go all the way. Let them come. It was empty bravado, but he felt a fierce sense of relief. Nothing he could do about it now, he was committed to a course of action. There was a certain relaxation in that realization.

"Here." He edged one glass toward her, across the sticky tabletop. "Won't be long."

"What's going to happen?" She eyed her drink as if she expected a coconut palm to spring forth from it.

"Someone will bring me that silver piece on the bar, and we'll talk. Go ahead, drink that. It'll relax you." *I like the thought of you relaxed.*

The thought was amused and completely reflexive. Yes, he was fucked for sure.

"What's in it?" Still distrustful, she touched the glass with a fingertip, condensation beading up on the surface.

"Whiskey and calf's blood."

"You're kidding."

I am. Though you can get that here, the sheel *like it.* "You're right. No whiskey."

She actually laughed, and he had to stop himself from smiling. *She liked my joke. Paul wouldn't have asked what was in it, he just would have taken it down while eyeing the sheela. Where the fuck is he?*

It didn't take long. One of the stonekin wandered over, his tread heavy and Ryan's silver piece in his paw. *"Nagàth,"* he said, in a voice like stones rubbing together. He lowered himself in the chair with its back to the room. "Wondered when show."

"Been busy." Ryan's tone was easy and polite, but his hand came down over Chess's wrist. If she decided to move or speak, the stone might get twitchy. They didn't know what to do when a female not of their species talked to them. "Word?"

The stone shrugged, his skin creaking. He had a fat, wart-starred face and broad yellow teeth, a mark of handsomeness among his kind. His shoulders were broad but hunched, and his legs powerfully built but not for speed. His shirt was rotting, black cloth, fine-woven and thick. "Malik, then no Malik. Bad. Black smoke rising."

"Guess so." Ryan's stomach turned over once, hard, then settled. The music suddenly seemed too loud. *The Inkani are in town, and Paul was seen. Someone knows something.* "But the moon always comes out." *And the sun, too, but mentioning sunlight is rude. After all, the Phoenicis potentials were mostly killed during the Long Dark and we haven't been able to save any since. They were closely allied with the stonekin.*

The logical extension to that thought came circling back, and he realized it was bothering him. *So how did the woman sitting right next to me make a Fang, then? It doesn't make sense, she was very specific that she found the instructions, bought the knife, and consecrated it.*

The stone wasn't looking at him. Instead, his flat yellow eyes had come to rest on Chess, who looked back, seeming only mildly surprised though her pulse beat frantically in her wrist. Ryan could *feel* her heart racing, his own pulse was starting to pick up and follow hers. "Hey," he said sharply, wanting the stone's eyes on him. "She's with me. Keep your eyes in your own head."

The stone didn't look at him. *"Shaala non grigh,"* he rumbled, staring at Chess, whose eyes had grown very round. "Sunlight come again soon. Listen, know, understand."

What the fuck? "She's mine," Ryan repeated. "You have something to say, talk to me."

"Grigh non vakr." The stone's eyes flicked contemptuously over him, and Ryan readied himself for combat.

It wouldn't take much to turn this whole place into a goddamn free-for-all, he didn't want to do it, but he would if the stone made any move on her. But why? Stones didn't attack humans unless the humans came across a mating or a kenning, they were one of the few non-carnivorous Other species. "No *taillaki nagàth; emmikah vakr.*"

Did he just say what I thought he said? "You're sure? You're absolutely sure?"

The stone shrugged, his skin moving with a sound like a leather jacket creaking. "Saw Flights in old day. Know smell. Gold under skin, soft to win."

Christ in a chariot-driven sidecar, this is the last straw. Paul, if you're not dead, I'm going to kill you myself. The thought was only halfway joking. His hand gentled on Chess's wrist, and his eyes moved up and over the interior of the bar. They were getting a few looks, but none out of the ordinary. Maybe this wasn't going to be as bad as he thought.

Just as he thought that, the lights died. *All* of them, and all at once. The sudden sharp smoky smell of sorcery bloomed and Ryan's skin seemed to shrink two sizes as the demon in him stretched, feeling the company of others of its kind.

The Inkani had arrived. And he had to get her out of here. All of a sudden saving Paul didn't matter so much.

Saving the only Phoenicis potential in five hundred years was the only thing that mattered. And Paul, the brainless pudding, had overlooked her to fixate on a *sheela* and probably gotten himself killed.

Seven

It wasn't so much the death of the lights as the sudden screaming that sent Chess's pulse into the stratosphere and made her brain fuzz into uselessness. The whole place descended into chaos; even the neon had died and it was dark like a wet bandage pressed against the eyes. She actually swallowed a scream, her wrist slipping out from under Ryan's hand as she snatched her hand to her mouth, and felt the table slide away from her, heard tinkling crashes as glass broke. Scuffling sounds, fists meeting flesh, and an absolute chaos of motion and throaty yelling swirled through the air. It sounded like the mother of all barfights happening during the mother of all blackouts, and Chess was glad to be mostly out of the way.

A stray breeze brushed her cheek. *"Chess!"* Ryan yelled, and the thing that had been sitting across the table from them— it looked like the illustration of a Tolkien troll, only in living color and with warts festooned with hair—made a scraping, creaking noise like a boulder breaking apart during an earthquake, with a high squeal of stressed stone.

Chess slid off the booth and hit the ground, undeniable instinct blooming just under her skin. She had to get *away*, it wasn't safe for her here. Whatever the troll had said to Ryan, he'd looked at her with eyebrows raised and chill appraisal on his face. Then the lights had died. And the screaming started.

How do I get myself into these situations? I'm lost in a fairy tale. Why do they call them fairy tales, when there aren't any fairies in them? Troll tales. Giant tales. Witches and gingerbread tales. She almost choked on a mad giggle and heard a deathly screech, too high and sawing to be called a scream. It spiraled up into falsetto and ended in a wet gurgle.

A deathscream. There was no mistaking it. She'd thought they were fictional inventions until she'd killed the *skornac*. *Well, what do you know, art* does *imitate life. I'm living my reading material, oh God.*

Shuffling footsteps. *"Chess!"* Ryan sounded frantic, but she couldn't make her legs work to push her back up. It was so *dark*, a cold that filled the marrow of her bones with ice and lead, and along with the darkness came a sudden chilling certainty that there were demons in the blackness. And that they were looking for *her.*

Light, she thought incoherently. *I made light last night, I could do it again. But then they'd see me and they would eat me.*

How wonderful. She had reverted to about three years old, huddled in her bed and terrified of the dark. But there were good reasons to be afraid of the dark, weren't there? She'd just found out how good.

A hand closed over her shoulder and she screamed, lifted bodily up from the floor. Her legs seemed not to be working properly. *I'm dealing with this as well as can be expected,* she thought, *the books never mentioned trolls or elves or women who look like they're half-swan. Or the bartender with four arms. And Ryan just acts like it's normal. Well, of course, I am the one hunting demons after finding them in books, but this is . . . this is . . .* Her brain reeled as a large hand that smelled of sun-warmed rock clamped over the lower half of her face. If Chess had had a stuffy nose she would have suffocated. Someone was carrying her as if she was a limp piece of cabbage.

I am a limp piece of cabbage, she thought, and the urge to giggle madly rose again, was squashed more by the hand over her mouth than by an effort of will, and died hysterically away. The blackness had gone strangely fuzzy, and she had the odd urge to simply curl up in a ball and let the world do what it would without her.

Shock. She was in shock. The trolls and the tall beautiful women giggling at the bar, the bartender's many arms, and the hairy thing in the booth next to theirs with eyes like flat red coins and a puglike snout . . . she was definitely in shock. Where was Ryan? He'd promised. *What, like I can't take care of myself?*

But the fey asskicking courage that had carried her through killing the *skornac* seemed to have deserted her.

As if on cue, his voice rose again. "*Chess!*" He actually screamed, a battlefield shout that tore through the rest of the noise in the air. The person carrying Chess didn't even pause, and she wondered blankly if she should try to struggle.

And I was doing so good at kickass. But her brain seemed to have stopped giving orders. There was only so much a girl could take, after all. And the swimming weakness in the dark seemed to have penetrated down to her bones. She felt like jello. Warm jello, even.

"*T'haik nagàth*," whoever was carrying her rumbled.

The troll. I'm being carried off by a troll. The thought struck her as eminently hilarious, and as the screaming reached a fresh pitch she began to giggle, a high terrified sound.

"*Francesca!*" Ryan yelled, and she felt a swimming loose satisfaction that he was using her name before she passed out. Again.

* * * *

She surfaced as if through a great quantity of very clear water, and heard a rumbling voice. "*Varakhin nagàth; il vakr maig.*" It sounded like oily dirt being stirred, pebbles clicking against each other, with a faint but distinct note of far-off heavy machinery.

What the bloody blue fucking hell? Chess blinked. She lay on her back, under something soft and *on* something soft; she was covered with a great quantity of what felt like heavy downy blankets. It was dim but not dark, and she saw a great sheaf of hanging threadbare velvet, ragged and blue, with huge moth-eaten holes in it. Up at the top was a sunflower in what looked like heavy massive beaten gold. She stared at it for quite some time before realizing the dancing dim lights she saw out of the corner of her eye were candleflames.

There was a scraping squeak as if a door had closed, and a low murmur. She blinked again, lifted her hand, and felt gingerly at her head. No, she hadn't been hit in the head again. What had happened? All she remembered was darkness and the horrible screaming. The cold, spilling up her arms and legs.

And Ryan yelling her name. *What instincts? Protective instincts. He sounded frantic. Where the hell am I? That's a cliché, isn't it? But really, where am I?*

She pushed herself up on her elbows. Thin blue silk sheets slid away from her body, her bag lay right next to her, her knife jabbed her hip before she sat all the way up. She winced, reached down and readjusted it, sat up all the way. Ryan. Where was he? There had been demons—maybe the weird Ankeny thingies—and she'd passed out. *That* had never happened before, but she was tired and had been thrown against a Dumpster, not to mention had a part-demon hunter dangle her like a rag doll and threaten her. No wonder she was feeling a little less than frisky.

It felt so cold, she thought, and shivered.

The room was low and small, and made completely of stone. The ceiling looked like one sheer blank piece, so did the walls; the floor was flagstones carefully fitted together. There was a table, festooned with wax drips and holding lumpy homemade candles. Chess blinked and rubbed at her eyes. *Did I get carried off to a troll's castle? I'm not a princess.* The thought was accompanied by a screaming, dark well of hysteria she didn't much like. Where was Ryan? He'd promised to watch out for her, had the demons caught him?

I don't care if he manhandled me, I can talk *to him and he'd tell me what was going on. At least, I think he would; unless the troll told him something that radically redefined his idea of partnering up with me. What did the thing say to him? He seemed to understand it.*

There was a lopsided, rough wooden door, and she slid her feet out from under the silky sheets and layers of motheaten velvet. Everything was ragged and lumpy except for the flagstones and the sheer rock walls; she wondered where she was.

Her head hurt. She rubbed at it, gingerly, and sighed. The chill from the darkness faded, and she rubbed life back into her fingers and took a deep breath. *I am going to be really tired at work tomorrow.*

That was a comforting thought, and one she decided to keep with her as she stood, unsteadily and ducked through the strap of her bag, settling the bag itself on her hip and fiddling with the strap so that it passed directly between her breasts. *Thank God I'm wearing a sweatshirt. Where am I? And how the hell can I get out of here and back home? Everyone out of the pool, I'm done.*

Just then, the door scraped open, and she looked up. Her jaw threatened to drop.

A troll stood in the door. This one was squat and wide, powerfully built, with a wide face so scarred with warts it looked like smallpox. It wore a threadbare black silk tunic that met its horny gray knees, belted with a bit of rough hemp cord. Its shoulders hunched, and its broad bald head gleamed. Its shoulders touched the lintels on either side, behind it she could only see darkness.

Chess swallowed. *Oh, my God.*

The troll's yellow eyes regarded her mildly. Then its massive gray lips parted, and it made a sound like rocks shifting, rubbing together in oily dirt. The sound turned, lowered itself, mutated into words at the very lowest audible range. *"Vakr danath illyanar,"* it thrummed. Its teeth were broad, and yellowing; Chess could also see little bits of something stuck between them.

The troll obviously expected some kind of reply. Chess gathered herself. *Well, this can't be any worse than trying to get vitals for a library card from a Russian immigrant.* "I'm sorry." She pitched her voice low, soothing. "I don't speak your language."

The troll actually nodded sagely, as if that was expected. "Come," it rumbled. "Come now. *Grgath* take."

Come now? Take where? What? "I'm . . . supposed to follow you?"

It nodded slowly, still smiling broadly. *"Vakr,"* it said. She was getting used to the way its voice seemed to shake her bones, thumping against her chest like the subsonic beat in a nightclub. "Come. *Davr 'zing."*

Sing? I doubt you want a rousing rendition of Hungry Like A Wolf, *but I could probably come up with some Dylan for you. Or some Kansas. How about* Dust in the Wind? The lunatic urge to laugh spilled through her chest, she strangled it. It was one thing to fight a tentacled thing in a sewer. It was *totally different* to be standing in a room she was beginning to suspect was underground facing a troll with huge yellow teeth and hands that looked like they could tear her apart. *Don't trolls eat young women? That's what all the stories say. Ryan, for God's sake, where are you?* "You want me to sing?" She heard the disbelief in her voice, congratulated herself on not screaming.

"Come." The troll beckoned. Its long blunt fingers didn't have claws, thank goodness. Chess took a few nervous steps forward.

I really don't have much left to lose at this point, she realized. "Ryan." Her voice cracked in the silence, she could almost hear the hissing of the candleflames. "The . . . the man I was with. Is he . . . "

The troll shrugged. *"Nagàth."* The rumble filled the room, made Chess's scalp crawl as if the hair was trying to stand up. Goosebumps stood up hard on her arms, spilled down her back. "Drakul." The one word was loaded with the rumble of rocks down a mountainside, the preface to a landslide. He didn't sound happy.

Chess's hands flew up instinctively. She stepped back, hoping she hadn't just pissed off a thing that looked like it could debone her with no trouble at all. "I'm sorry," she whispered. "Really, I'm sorry. Forget I said anything." Her voice sounded very light and breathy compared to the troll's rumble.

Yellow eyes widened, stared at her. She stared back, trying vainly and desperately to think of something, anything, she could say to return this situation to normal.

Normal. Yeah. A troll. Underground. A bunch of candles. Bars full of things that shouldn't exist. God, help me out here. I think I'm going into shock.

He beckoned again, this time very carefully and slowly. "*Vakr* come with," he rumbled. "Safe with stonekin." He nodded his broad hairless head, and Chess was suddenly struck by the fact that he resembled a very old bulldog Mrs. Flatbush down the street from her parents used to own. The dog, almost blind and with its teeth worn down to nubs, had been almost pathetically grateful for a calm voice and a gentle pat on the head. Mrs. Flatbush had run all his food through a blender, he couldn't chew it anymore. He'd been called "Killer" in his youth, but all the neighbors had taken to calling him "Old Glory."

Chess dropped her hands. *It can't hurt,* she thought. "All right. I'll come with you." She pitched her voice low and soothing, as if she was talking to Old Glory again. "Just take it easy with that voice, huh? It's a little scary."

He backed out of the door as she stepped forward again, her boots slipping a little on the smooth stone floor. The air smelled leaden and dead down here. The troll's bare four-toed feet spread to grip the stone. She followed cautiously, stepping out into darkness broken only by the gleams of a heavy brass candelabra held by another troll.

Outside the door was a vaulted stone passage, floored with the same fitted-together flagstones. The walls were smooth as glass, she was glad the almost-invisible seams between the stones on the floor gave her some traction or she'd be slipping all over like a cartoon character skating. Both trolls were massive, green, and watched her with disconcertingly mild, wide yellow gazes.

I am not cut out for this. She managed a smile that seemed likely to crack her face. "Okay," she said, heard her voice fall flat in the close, choking confines of the tunnel. "I guess I'm all

yours, guys. Where are we going?"
                    * * * *
Chess soon found out she was *way* underground, deeper
than the sewers, and that the second troll-thing seemed unable
to speak much English. It held an ancient brass candelabra in
one thick, horny hand, and she saw warts marching along the
back of its neck, each decked with black hair. The first troll
had vanished down another corridor into the darkness, shuffling
and making a deep *hoom*ing sound that even now reverberated
through the air. Every once in a while they would pass arches
yawning up to the left or right, some with a faint gleam of
golden light far back in them, each resounding with that
humming sound. It sounded like there were a whole bunch of
singing trolls in this labyrinth, and the sound worked its way
through her bones, shaking tension and her headache away.

It shuffled ahead of her through the fluidly-curving stone
passage, its back hunched under a frayed black shirt, and she
wondered if it was the one from the tavern. Her hiking boots
made shushing sounds against the flagstone floor, each rock
fitted together with exquisite care. She had to go carefully
with one hand on the smooth cold wall or she'd slip. The tunnel
began to slope sharply up, no doors on either side, and she was
breathing heavily by the time they reached the end and a set of
stairs through an arch carved with flowers and beautiful,
strange runic lettering she wanted to examine more closely.
"Excuse me," she managed politely. "Excuse me?"

The troll stopped. "Thank you," she began, unsure of
whether that meant it was listening or if she'd just committed a
grave breach of etiquette. "Look, can you take me up to Tenth
Street and Argyle? That's close to my house. I'd really
appreciate it."

The troll made a snorting sound. "*Nagàth ilmesto.*" Its
voice was like rocks dropped into a pool, chill and plonking.
"*Tang vakr.*"

Gesundheit, she thought. "I'm sorry, I don't understand
you. I apologize." She deliberately made her voice soft, not
almost-yelling like people sometimes did when they spoke to a
foreigner.

"Following," the troll said. "Danger for firebird."

"Firebird?" *What the hell does Stravinsky have to do
with this? Have I been stuck with a troll that loves classical
music?* She dragged herself back into the present with an

effort. The books also didn't tell you how your mind jagged from place to place when confronted with the absurd, things your life hadn't prepared you for, violations in the reality you grew up into, leaving behind fairy tales and sorcery. *If I wasn't such an avid reader of speculative fiction, I might well be stark raving mad by now.*

"Firebird. Knife, gold, soft, smell good." The troll ruminated on this for a moment, then said, "Yew!"

Yew? You? Oh, my God. "Firebird? You mean I'm the firebird? Someone's following me?" *Give Chessie a prize, she catches on quick, don't she? Ryan, you'd be proud. Why am I thinking of him?*

"Drak'ul. Follow Firebird. Black smoke too." It still didn't turn around, but its shoulders slumped. "Take firebird secret way, no follow."

Gee, that's mighty swell of you. "I'd like that." She cast a nervous glance behind her—nothing but the yawning maw of blackness that was the rest of the tunnel, the candles flickering and failing to dispel the darkness. "Thank you." *Jesus Christ, I'm in a tunnel with a troll. An actual tunnel and an actual troll. I'm getting the idea Jericho City is a lot weirder than even I suspected. I wonder if there are Others living in every city?*

It certainly seemed likely. On *both* counts.

"Up," the troll grunted, and set off up the steps. She began to see how its odd, awkward legs were actually perfectly suited for tunnels and stairs. He stopped every once in a while to let her catch her breath. *I'm in good shape, but damn, these are killer. My ass is never going to be the same. Stairmaster, eat your heart out.* He said nothing else, but she began to hear a deep thrumming, a subsonic noise that rattled her bones and made her a little less sanguine about being on a narrow set of stairs with a troll that smelled like leather and sunwarmed stone.

At least he didn't smell like she'd always imagined trolls would smell. Though those warts were something else.

He says the Drakul are following me. Is it Ryan? Why did the lights go out? Was it them? Only it was demons . . . but he said the Drakul were part demon. She suppressed a shiver as the walls turned from stone to crumbling brick, the candleflames beginning to dance in drafts as other passages opened up on either side, galleries and halls of darkness. The pale candlelight was not at all comforting, even though the humming noise—almost definitely coming from the troll—was pleasant, kind of like a sonic massage. And there on the stairs, with a troll in front of her, Chessie had another deep urge to laugh maniacally.

Eight

He heard the sound of the key in the lock and made himself a shadow, unbreathing, almost unthinking, melding with the darkness. It was the long, dead time of early morning, right about half past two, the dark thick and absolute before false dawn began to creep up through the cracks of night. The knife was steady in his hand, and the beginnings of combat-sorcery tingled on his other fingers. Blood dripped into his eyes, warm salt stinging; his shoulders both hurt and his wrists were bracelets of agony. His knee was destroyed too. He'd taken a bad shot, and the shirt she'd given him was going to be a rag, useless, slashed, and bloody. He felt bad about that.

Another lock unlocked, the faint sound loud to his Drakul senses. He heard only one heartbeat, as familiar to him as his own by now.

The door opened, a slice of golden light from the hall outside appearing. "Hi, honey, I'm home," she whispered, and stepped inside, closing the door and locking it. Two deadbolts, thudding home, then the lock on the knob. The smell of stonekin hung on her, stonekin and Inkani; she still smelled of the demons that had attacked the Shelaugh, the demons he'd thought had taken her.

Rage brought him to his feet, the knife thudded into the wall in the kitchen as he went through the arch into the hall. His fist slammed into the wall over her shoulder, the combat sorcery spending itself uselessly, his body pinning hers. He dropped his head, inhaled deeply, taking in her scent. Yes, there was the taint of the Inkani, but she hadn't been touched. The smell of stonekin was much stronger. Under it, the smell of her shampoo and the taint of demon, his own smell, very strong; another Drakul would recognize it on her. The smell of Inkani was just a faint fading tang under the smell of the night outside. She was safe, they hadn't gotten close to her.

And under it, the fresh golden smell starting to wear through her human camouflage. He should have noticed it first off, but he'd been confused. It was true.

Holy God, it was true.

She screamed and struggled, then he had his bloody right hand clamped over her mouth, glad he'd gotten rid of the knife.

"Stay still," he rasped. "Just fucking stay still, woman, if you know what's good for you." *Because if you don't I'm going to drag you into the bedroom and add another reason for you to fear me.*

She went limp, leaning against the wall, and he inhaled the smell of her hair again. It calmed him as nothing else could. *Mine. She's mine, and here.* Her lips moved slightly against his palm—was she praying? Gasping for air? The sharp chemical smell of fear smashed through her scent, his body tightened one last time, pressing against her. She probably couldn't breathe, he had her pinned. She was alive.

He buried his face in her hair. *Calm down. You're scaring her. Calm down, Ryan. Come on. You're better than this. You can calm down, you can calm her down, check to see if she's wounded, find out where the stone took her. And above all, just fucking calm down.* A deep breath, all the way down into the bottom of his lungs, a soothing, pleasant burn working into his skin as the wounds started to heal, now that he was relaxing. Now that he was sure she was still alive.

"Are you hurt? Tell me, are you hurt?" *I sound just one short step away from murder. What a coincidence. I feel just one short step away from doing something very, very bad. If they hurt her . . .*

One slow shake of her head, very slow, as if she was afraid to move. No. He didn't smell any blood on her, either. That was good. If she was hurt he might become unmanageable.

Christ, she doesn't have a clue how to manage me, either. Have to teach her, and soon.

"Good," he murmured. "Very good. Now, were you followed?"

She shook her head, slowly. Then, deliberately, she shrugged. The movement made her breasts move, pressed against his chest, and he swallowed a hot flare of desire. *You're frightening her. Stop it. Calm the fuck down.* "I'm going to take my hand away from your mouth," he said softly. "And you're going to be quiet. I'm on a hair-trigger right now, sweetheart. I won't hurt you, but it could get *very* uncomfortable for both of us if you set me off. I am *not* thinking clearly right now, I was out of my fucking mind worrying over you; I've become very fond of you in my own little way. You don't mind, do you?"

A hot wetness touched his right hand. Tears? Was she

crying?

Christ, if she's crying I've really fucked up. "Forget it. Now, you're going to be quiet, right? No sudden moves, no screaming. All right?"

There was a long pause, she took in a small shuddering breath. She was so *soft*, he wanted nothing more than to touch her skin again. More of her skin, more of her. Wanted to press forward and press his mouth on hers, wanted to feel her breath against his as her lips opened, wanted all *sorts* of things. And he was very close to simply taking what he wanted, instead of keeping his self-control.

It's official. I'm a danger to the Order. But she's not just human, is she? That doesn't make it right, won't stop them from trying to put me down before I can explain. If they can catch me.

She nodded slowly, her chin dipping. Yes, the wetness touching his hand was tears. She was weeping.

The discovery broke the shell of rage, introduced something softer, something better, even though it broke his heart. He relaxed a little bit, his hand loosening. "I'm sorry. I didn't want to scare you. It's been a rough night." He tried to speak softly. He relaxed further, peeled his hand away. She sniffed, a slight hitching movement. "You okay?"

Her voice was so calm he almost missed the trembling of panic underneath. "No, I'm not okay. What the hell happened back there? I woke up underground. And there were more— more of them—"

"Inkani?" His left fist relaxed a little, fell away from the wall, but he still leaned into her. She couldn't wriggle away. "Are you hurt?" *She's not hurt. Thank God, she's not hurt.*

"N-no. T-t-trolls." It caught in her throat. "They l-let me go. The t-troll said I was being f-followed, that he would t-take me a safe way, without being f-followed."

"Trolls? Oh, stonekin." *There were Inkani there; they pulled back because of a stonekin counterattack. That makes sense. A stonekin brought you Below.*

"Big g-green t-trolls." Her voice broke. "He said I was f-f-followed."

"Maybe you were." *By who, though? And the stonekin took you Below. Bless them and their worship of the sun.* "The Inkani was there at the tavern. My Malik's gone and I haven't reported in. I've been a bad boy."

"H-he said black s-smoke." She swallowed dryly. He heard it, and he had the sudden incomprehensible desire to bury his face against her throat and taste the salt of the sweat springing up on her skin. The trembling in her and the harsh chemical spill of her fear tore through his control, left him shaking too.

He did, did he? And so he took you down Below. I thought you were already trussed in an Inkani cell, sweetheart. "They don't like Inkani." He pushed himself back, away from the wall, his body aching with the need to press against hers. "They were hunted in the dark days; the Inkani put them in slave coffles to build the dark castles. There are still places underground where the blood of stonekin can be seen on the walls."

"That's horrible," she whispered. "The d-d-demons . . . I thought they'd killed you, I thought you were g-gone—"

I'm not going anywhere, sweetheart. "Tell me everything. Everything." *If the Inkani followed her, they're watching this place. But I sense no other demons here, all is as it should be. Did the stonekin cover her tracks and buy me some time? That's most likely. I owe them.*

"Can I . . . can I turn the light on? And get changed?" The fear in her voice hurt him somehow. Did she think he was going to hurt her?

I might without meaning to, if I get clumsy. And I'm covered in blood and guck. "I don't look so good. I ran across some trouble." *I went fucking insane thinking they'd taken you, sweetheart.* Relief unloosed his muscles further. She was alive, she was *here*, and nobody else had touched her. Everything was fine, for right now at least. "I think I've ruined this shirt." He reached over, flicked the light switch. She flinched, blinking up at him, and the horrified expression on her face was equally gratifying and frustrating. *I know I look like hell. You don't have to look like that.*

"My God," she whispered. "What *happened* to you?"

"Inkani." He shrugged. "They attacked the tavern. The stone must have dragged you out while I slowed them down, exactly what he was supposed to do. Only I thought an Inkani had taken you. I went crazy." He was still standing too close to her, could feel the heat from her body brushing his. He was on the fine edge. It wouldn't take much to push him over. "The thought of them hurting you . . . " *Christ, I'm in deep.*

She blinked. Her hair was mussed out of its sleek braid,

but she was otherwise unharmed. There was dampness on her shoulders and her hair, from the rain that was now beginning to sweep restlessly against the window. The gold flecks in her eyes glowed as her gaze went down his body, taking in the blood and the ripped clothing, the dark stain over his smashed knee that was starting to twitch as it healed. Strangely enough, right now the pain didn't matter as much. He tried to pull himself up straighter under her scrutiny, as if she was a Malik choosing a new Drakul. "Good God," she whispered, her lips shaping the words, and he stared at her mouth. "You look *awful.*"

"Thanks." One corner of his mouth tilted up slightly. He stared at her lips. *I'm about to do something I shouldn't. But if I'm going to be damned, I might as well earn it.*

"You said to come back here and wait for you. What were you doing sitting in the dark?" She shifted her weight, as if she wanted to slide along the wall away from him. He put out his left hand and braced it next to her shoulder, stopping her.

"Waiting. For the Inkani to come rifling through your apartment, looking for the books. I was going to trap one, make it take me to you." *I didn't think you would come back. I thought they had you and when the red haze cleared I was standing in the middle of a bunch of dead Inkani and had to jump to get away. Never dreamed a stonekin had you. Bless them and their worship of the sun.*

"*They* want my library too?" That sparked indignation. But she was still trembling, and her eyes were wider and darker than he liked. Shock. She was in shock. Just because she was so calm outwardly didn't mean she was dealing well with having most of her assumptions about the nature of the universe whacked away from underneath her.

"Not anymore." His voice hurt his throat. "If they find out exactly what you are, they'll want *you,* and not just for party games. They have a use for you, sweetheart."

"Don't call me—" Her eyes flashed, and he lost the battle with himself.

He leaned forward. His mouth trapped hers, his tongue sliding in. She tasted like sunlight, the harsh light that hurt even as it warmed him. She also tasted soft, and of the mint toothpaste in her bathroom, still lingering in her mouth. Her breath mingled with his, the flavor of night and stonekin and some taste that was uniquely hers. Fire slid down his back, roared through his nervous system. He was damn close to dragging her into her pretty blue bedroom before he finally broke away, pulled her away from the wall, and closed her in his arms, smelling her hair again. "I can explain," he said into her hair. "I can explain, but first I need you to tell me exactly what happened. Everything, all right?"

She didn't say anything. She simply shook as she cried into his shredded shirt. He stroked her hair and shifted his weight, easing his shattered knee as it healed. He should have questioned her, demanded to know exactly what happened, pushed her until she told him everything. Instead, he held her. Everything else could wait. *Nobody's going to take your library, sweetheart. And they're sure as hell not going to take you, not if I can stop them. The Order has no goddamn idea how important you are. They might not listen to the stonekin, or the stones won't tell them. And if the Inkani find out, they will take you and use you for their Rite of Opening, and you'll beg for death before they're through. It's up to me to keep you alive until we can show the Order what you are.*

* * * *

Later, as the gray of false dawn began to take its first breaths in the east, he watched her. The strength of nighttime began to fade as the demon inside him went to sleep with the sun's rise.

Chess lay on her side among the scattered pillows, breathing deeply, the flush of sleep high in her cheeks. Ryan smoothed the blue comforter down, glad he'd washed his hands at least. He didn't want to get blood on her blankets. He stood by the side of the bed, staring down at her long dark hair spread over the pillow, one small hand flung out, loosely cupped and holding only darkness.

She hadn't been happy, repeating over and over that she just wanted to go to bed, that she was finished with it. But she'd told him enough that he'd heaved a sigh of relief. The stonekin knew what she was, and had saved her, not even requiring payment for passage Below. Ryan had been seen publicly with a woman right before all hell broke loose, and he'd run in time. The Inkani might suspect what she was... and if the Malik caught wind of Ryan with a woman all hell would break loose.

Doesn't matter. She's a potential Golden. There haven't been any surviving potentials for five hundred years, why now? And why did Paul not notice? His fingers itched to touch her hair, smooth it away from her face. She'd actually *clung* to him, wrapping her hands in his shredded shirt and refusing to let go, sobbing. All things considered, she was a lot more resilient than a lot of civilians faced with their first Inkani attack. Crying was better than screaming and beating your head against the walls, as sometimes happened when a skin came face-to-face with the night side.

He closed his eyes, breathing her in. *I am in a deep hole, and it's getting deeper by the second. She's one of the Golden, and I'm attached to her. Too attached to her. I let my instincts get involved, but what the hell was I supposed to do?* The image rose, again, of her sitting lonely at her kitchen table, crying into her hands, dealing with facing a *skornac*, something she should never have had to even *see*. There was so much lonely bravery in that image a lump rose in his throat. She was far braver than any of the Malik he knew. What had it cost her to know these things existed and bear that knowledge in absolute quiet, going out to defend the children of her city with only a Fang and her wits to protect her? Then to mislead Paul, and face a Drakul with her chin held high and her eyes flashing?

I have to call in. Tell them what she is. They'll send a whole division to protect her if need be, bring her in and give her anything she wants. She'll be as safe as it's possible to be.

Especially with *him* protecting her. Would they let him stay with her? Not bloody likely . . . but if she insisted, maybe, just maybe . . .

You're only fooling yourself. His fingers itched, ached, he wanted to touch her. *You're a liability, you've broken Rule Number Two for a Drakul. But your duty as one of the Order is to protect the Golden.*

He had to call in. The chill voice of logic told him the more Malik around her, the safer she was. She shouldn't have to deal with this alone. She should be watched, taught, protected, allowed to fully come into her own as a Phoenicis. *Call in. Tell them I'm protecting her because she's something we haven't seen in five centuries, a way to drive back the Inkani and reclaim some of the cities. Call in and tell them I'm obeying the precepts of the Order, protecting her. Don't mention that I've let myself get tangled in a knot over her and abandoned my Malik. But someone saw Paul, the stone said as much. And now I've been linked to her, and the stones know she's . . . God. What a mess.*

She made a soft sound, curling more tightly into herself. And damn him if he didn't want to shuck off his coat and his torn-up shirt and sink down next to her, share her space, slide his arm over her and hold her. Share her warmth like the animal he was.

More trouble than you need, Drakul. Call in. Bring in reinforcements. Take your punishment if you have to, but call in. Keep her safe.

He let out a soft, frustrated breath. A thin edge of light from the nightlight in her bathroom gleamed in her hair, showed the curve of her cheekbone. Why did that make the inside of his chest feel like it was cracking?

He stood there for a long time, struggling with himself. Call in? Of course. In a minute. As soon as he could pull himself away from standing here, watching her sleep. She looked so peaceful, and she needed her rest. She wasn't like a Drakul, able to go without sleep or food, using inhuman endurance. He'd handled her clumsily from the very beginning, accusing her of having something to do with Paul's disappearance and generally behaving like a big, dumb, brainless Drakul. It would be a wonder if she wanted anything to do with him after that little display in the hallway—

The phone shrilled.

He actually jumped, adrenaline smashing through his entire body. Chess muttered and rolled over, the T-shirt she hadn't bothered to change out of pulling down and exposing pale flesh. *What the hell?*

She reached for her bedside table blindly, and grabbed the phone as it started to squawk again. It was a pink plastic Princess phone, he felt grimly amused by that as she fished it up and struggled with the receiver. "Mph." The sound of her voice, slurred with sleep, brushed against his nerves. He should have been there on the bed beside her.

Down, boy. She doesn't understand, just do your job for right now. We'll figure everything else out later.

"What?" She sounded irritable, and exhausted.

He heard it, coming through the phone, tinny and eerie, stretched out by distance. "Fran*cessssss*ca . . . " Her name, spoken in a long, tinkling, dragging whisper.

"Franc*eeeessssss*ca . . . ."

"Oh, for God's sake," she muttered irritably, "find someone else to prank call. I'm busy."

His knee pressed into the bed, making the springs creak. He ignored her soft cry of surprise. He grabbed the phone, lifted it to his ear, and felt his throat swell as the subvocal growl escaped him. He heard a faint tinny squeal, then it disconnected and a dial tone echoed. Ryan dropped the phone back in the cradle. He was suddenly aware he was right next to her, she pushed herself up on her elbows, blinking at him as he lowered himself down to sit on the edge of her bed. The framed print of Buster Keaton watched them both with sad, knowing eyes.

"Does that happen a lot?" He pitched his tone low, very soothing, the last of the growl dying in his chest. "Chess?"

She slumped back onto the bed, pushed her hair back from her face. "Guess so. Couple times a week, since I found the books." She sighed, a long sleepy sound. "I didn't know you were there."

Poltergeist activity. She must be breathing sorcery into the air. She's farther along than I thought. "Was watching you sleep." That was, at least, the absolute truth.

"Aren't you tired?" Her eyes were closing, he could see it in the dimness. Of course, he was a night creature, wasn't he?

And she was a Golden. The Halston books had triggered her potential. She had been breathing in an air freighted with another Golden's sorcery, and using the books he had collected. No wonder. Even if she'd had only the smallest shred of *potential* that atmosphere would have strengthened and triggered it. He would be willing to bet, though, that there wasn't just a small shred of potential in her.

"Not tired." *I have to tell her. As soon as she wakes up tomorrow.* "Go to sleep, Chess."

"'Kay." And she turned over, the blanket pulling away from him.

Her breathing turned deep and even again, as she dropped back into slumber without any trouble. He thought about it, then reached over and clicked the switch on her alarm clock to "off." She didn't need to get up in the morning, she needed her sleep.

Ryan braced his elbows on his knees, hanging his head. Someone knew about her. The Inkani would find out soon.

And he had to call in, report what he'd found to the Malik and get them looking for his skin.

And he had to face the fact that he'd let his instincts attach themselves to a woman who had not the faintest idea of how to handle a Drakul, let alone her own potential as a Golden.

Christ, what am I going to do?

Nine

For some reason, her alarm didn't go off, so it was her mother's phone call at noon that woke her up. "Chess? Honey, are you all right? Sharon said you ate some bad Chinese. Have you stopped throwing up?"

"Mmh?" Chess blinked at her clock and at the fall of weak winter sunlight coming in through her bedroom window. She hadn't even pulled the curtains last night. "What time is it?" *I sound dazed. I feel dazed.*

"It's noon, sleepy. She said you had a neighbor helping you. Are you all right?" Mom was in the kitchen, Chess could hear splashing water. Washing dishes, which was a sure sign of Mom's worry. There was an indistinct murmur in the background—Chess's father. "Be quiet, Brian, I'm asking her! Sweetie, are you all right?"

Chess winced, yawning. Her head hurt, and so did her shoulder and her ribs; deep bruising, she suspected, from being tossed into a Dumpster. The salve could only do so much, even though the swelling had gone down and most of the surface coloration was gone. *I should feel grateful I didn't break a bone.* "Better," she managed. "What's Dad doing home?" He should have been at the college, teaching.

More water splashing. "Oh, he's got the sniffles, and it's Friday. His students needed the time off, so I got stuck with him. Should I bring you some soup and your Connie Frances CD?"

Oh, Christ, Mom, I can't wait for you to meet this guy. He wears my T-shirts and gets them all soaked with blood; he screams my name in crowded bars and gets between me and hell-dog demons. Oh, and he's part demon too. A real winner. "No, Mom, I'm still feeling a little squidgy." Her voice was husky, probably from last night's screaming. She *sounded* sick. "I feel really bad, and I like to be alone when I throw up."

"Are you still throwing up? Maybe I'll send Charlie over," Mom waffled. Chess could hear the battle between "motherly concern" and "leave her alone to rest."

"No, Mom. I'll be fine, I'm okay. I'll call you in a day or so when I feel better, you can cook me chicken and garlic. How

about that?" *And by then I might have a good way to explain
all this. Sure. If I have a miracle and a couple of lexicons.*

"Sure, honey. You call if you need *anything*, and you keep
covered up and away from drafts. Drink plenty of fluids. Do
you need groceries?"

"No, Mom." Her throat was full. Her mother was worried,
and Chess *had* been withdrawing lately. *Well, I've been
chasing demons at night, and that kind of eats into my
energy level.* "I'm fine."

"All right, sweets. Go back to sleep. Call me if you're still
throwing up tomorrow." Mom hung up reluctantly, and so did
Chess. She met Buster Keaton's eyes from behind the glass,
and wondered why her apartment was so silent.

Then she picked up the pink handset and dialed again. She
loved this phone, it reminded her of Mae West. *Come up and
see me sometime,* Mae's throaty voice whispered, and Chess
actually smiled.

"Jericho City Library, Emma speaking. How may I help
you?" Yet another unremittingly-perky voice. Chess could see
Emma's round face and flyaway golden hair.

Chess cleared her throat. "Em? It's Chess."

"Good Lord, you sound *awful.* Don't worry about a thing,
Sharon opened and I'm manning the Reference desk. It's Friday,
and we've already had a visit from Pembroke the Indignant."

Chess's heart plunged. She heard the familiar sounds of
the library behind Emma's voice: paper, the murmuring quiet,
and a soft voice—probably Sharon's. *"It's Chess,"* Emma
stage-whispered. *"She sounds terrible."*

"What did old Pemmican want?" Chess asked. *I do sound
terrible. I wonder how much of it is hunting demons and
how much is just me?*

"Just to return some Faulkner and to leave you a fruit basket.
The damn thing looks older than the Mayflower—the fruit
basket, I mean. Though Pem's close. Guess you won her
crotchety old heart." Emma giggled, a carefree sound. "Connie's
been asking for you, something about budget meetings, and
Loren wants you to look over the new catalog. We caught a
pair of teenagers making out in the Biography section; there
was a bra on the floor. And the downstairs toilet needed plunging
again. All in all, a normal day." There was a series of soft
muted beeps, the phone was ringing again. "Oh, and some guy
named Paul was in here for you. Very dishy. Share wouldn't

talk to him, gave him the cold shoulder. He left his number."

What? Chess struggled to sit up, reaching for her journal. The pen skittered away but she caught it. "Hang on, let me get my pencil." It was an old library joke, and Emma laughed again. "Give me the number?"

Em did. "Do me a favor and don't call anyone, you sound like Kathleen Turner. Go back to bed and drink lots of liquids, okay? Don't eat Chinese no more."

"I'll put it in my day planner. I'm sorry, Em." *No, the first thing I've got to do is get the demon hunter off my couch. At least, I think he slept on my couch.* Chess took a deep breath. She smelled something wonderful, something magnificent, something fantastic.

She smelled coffee.

Well, now she knew he was in her apartment. *Bless him.* And then she remembered his body pressing against hers, and his mouth; he'd kissed her. Shoved her up against the wall and kissed her, real he-man style. *I should be furious over that. Okay, I'm furious. We're going to have a little chat about how to treat a woman like a human being instead of a china figurine. Or a rubber doll. Or something like that.*

"Now you stop that right now," Em's voice fairly crackled. "You haven't taken a day off for good behavior in three years. No *wonder* it took Chinese to do you in. Grady won the office pool, his bet was two years."

Grady? Oh yeah, the volunteer with the thick horn-rim glasses. There was a betting pool? "I don't want to hear this," she mumbled. "Thanks, Em."

"Go back to bed." Emma was actively giggling by the time she hung up. That was Em, always sunny.

Except for those three days a month, that is. She laid the phone down, collapsed back into bed, holding the journal. She coughed, closed her eyes, and blinked again. The sunlight falling across her bed was welcome, *very* welcome; the rain had stopped for a while. The coffee-smell got stronger, and she began to hear little sounds of someone moving, as if he was making noise for her.

Just as she thought that, he appeared in the door, his eyes half-closed against the bright light. His hair stood up in soft blue-black spikes, and his eyes seemed to look right through her. He'd managed to repair his original T-shirt, and his jeans were clean, looking like they hadn't been all ripped and bloody last night. "How are you feeling?" His tone was soft, conciliatory. He leaned against the doorjamb, hunching his shoulders as if he wanted to appear smaller.

Fat chance. He was too damn *big*, and now that she knew how fast and strong he was, no amount of hunching his shoulders could fool her. Not when she could still feel his mouth on hers and taste the night sliding against her tongue.

She held up the journal, sinking down into the warm comfort of her familiar bed. "Your friend Paul stopped by the library. He left a phone number." *Now you can go rescue him. And stop manhandling me. And maybe I can start to forget what it feels like to be trapped underground with a troll. Or forget what it's like to lay in the dark and listen to screaming.*

And just maybe, just maybe I might forget what it's like to have a half-demon hunter kiss me. Although I might not want to forget that. That was, I daresay, the only good thing about this whole damn chain of Twilight Zone events.

The room turned utterly silent. His eyes fastened on the journal. "When?"

"Yesterday, Em said." She dropped the pen and tore the page out of her journal, dropping the small book next to her on the bed. "You want this?"

He shrugged. Muscle moved under his shirt, she wondered how he'd mended it. "As soon as you're ready, we'll go collect him."

What? "What? I thought *you* wanted to go get him. He's your partner."

Ryan folded his arms, his jaw setting. He looked dangerous in the weak sunlight, muscle moving under his T-shirt. "You're coming with me. We'll collect Paul and call in, and—"

"Wait a minute. I found you your partner. That means you can keep him and your Order off my back. Right?" *And keep them away from my library.*

Though how much I want to keep this up, I just might have to re-evaluate. Stinky things in sewers are one thing, but trolls in tunnels under Jericho and demons that feel like I'm in an ice bath are something else. You guys hunt these things, and I just got shown how much of an amateur I am. I need to reconsider this. She stared at him, not liking the way he was looking at her. "Right, Ryan?"

"We have to talk." He peeled himself away from the door and paced softly across the floor.

No shit we have to talk. Chess struggled to push herself up to sit, pulling her knees up. "Can it wait? I want a shower. And about a gallon of coffee. And some fresh clothes wouldn't hurt either."

"Just a second. There's something I need to explain to you before anything else." He lowered himself down on the end of her bed, his profile presented with harsh lines, his nose a bit too long, his jaw too strong. But still . . . she liked the look of him. "I frightened you last night. I'm sorry."

Well, goddamn, he apologized. Miracles do happen. Though you didn't exactly hurt me. You just shoved me up against the wall and kissed me. As a matter of fact, you kissed me so hard I can still feel it in my toes. "You need to stop pushing me around," she managed. Come to think about it, he hadn't *ever* hurt her, unless you counted when he'd shoved her out of the way in the alley, throwing her up against the Dumpster. "I don't like it."

"I'm sorry," he repeated. "Look, I'm Drakulein, I'm part demon. That means I . . . I have a set of very strong instincts, most of which help to keep me alive." His eyes were fixed on his upturned palms, held loose and cupped in his lap.

"Protective instincts," she supplied. Her mouth tasted like morning and her eyes were sandy, and she felt muzzy as she always did after sleeping too long. But hell, she'd *needed* it.

"We're segregated from women with sorcerous ability because we can . . . we can become attached. Very attached. The longer we spend with them, the more . . . cemented the instincts can become. They're triggered by scent, mostly; and if I go off I *need* your help. If you scream, or struggle, or become afraid, I might drown. There are a couple things you can do—"

Wait just one goddamn cotton-pickin' second. "Hold on just one second. I don't even *know* you, I'm not even—"

His fingers twitched. "I'm sorry," he repeated, cutting her off. "The Golden usually have one or two Drakul bodyguards. It's not as bad as it seems. I'll be careful, I just need you to understand a few things."

She opened her mouth to protest and stopped, a curious thought occurring to her. She'd asked him to help her get rid of Robert. He'd screamed her name in the dark when the awful cold had spilled through her body. *And let's not forget the thing he got away from my window. Just tore it—and the fire escape—away. He carried me up here and took care of calling work and the police. And he was here in the dark last night, all bloody and beaten-up. Waiting.*

And all she'd been able to think of in the troll-tunnels was, *what's happened to Ryan?*

It was official. She was about to do something really stupid and girly. *Oh, God, I'm going to regret this.* "Like what?" Her tone, flat and ironic, surprised even her. *I have the worst taste in men. What is it about this guy? I like him, even if I don't understand half of what he talks about. This is so goddamn crazy.*

"Like when I ask you to stay still, it's because it helps *me* stay calm. If you're frightened or hurt, it may make me unmanageable. If you stay calm, move slowly, it will calm *me* down. If I hold you still, it's because I want to make sure I don't hurt you. It . . . reassures me."

"Stay calm." *I sound like an idiot.* "Calm you down. Reassure you." *What if I'm half out of my mind with fear because I'm being chased by a fucking demon, huh? What about that?*

"Just imagine I'm a big wild animal. You don't want to give it a reason to get nervous, do you?" His fingers tightened again, curling into fists. "I'm sorry. Really, I am. I shouldn't have allowed it to happen."

"You're not an animal." For a moment she wondered why she said it so fiercely; then she realized that it *bothered* her, the way he seemed to consider himself such a second-class citizen. What he'd told her about this Order pissed her off. And the way this Paul had treated her hadn't impressed her either. "You're not an animal," she repeated, a little more softly. "You're a *human being*, dammit. So you have these instincts. Are you saying you're going to . . . do what? Hurt me? Try to . . . um, eat me?"

"No." His eyes squeezed closed, but the tension left his shoulders bit by bit. "It means you have your own Drakul. I have something else to tell you, too."

He looks like he's expecting me to start screaming. Chess reached out, her hand very pale and visibly shaking. She touched his left hand. His back was to the window, and the sun brought out blue highlights in his hair and the shadow of charcoal stubble on his jaw. He was a very nice-looking man, now that she looked at him.

Her fingers touched his knotted fist. She curled her hand around his much larger one, as far as she could, that was. He was pale as she was, but his skin was a different texture. Rougher. *If you're part demon do you have the same equipment men have?* She bit back a ludicrous giggle. *Shut up, Chess. Quit it. Sure, your hormones are all in a stew, he's a nice guy and he smells good, but for God's sake. He's part demon. And you don't know a damn thing about him.* "In a minute. First of all, are you going to try to take my books?"

"What?" Now his eyes opened, he turned his head and looked at her as if she'd just made an embarrassing bodily noise. "Of course not. I'm telling you I've thrown away my entire fucking life and tied myself to you. If the Order finds me before I can explain to them you're a potential Golden, they'll put me down like a rabid dog. They can't have Drakul getting territorial, we're the muscle of their war. We start protecting only our homes and families and pretty soon the Inkani will pick us off one by one, and the skins won't be able to play at having their nice safe little world—"

That's the biggest load of crap I've ever heard. "Nonsense." Her fingers tightened, she would have driven her nails into his hand but didn't dare. "That's *bullshit*. I think you'd fight even harder and *find* ways to cooperate, especially if the women had anything to say about it. My mom wouldn't stand for any territorial crap, you can be sure of that."

"It doesn't matter if you see it that way. That's the way the Malik see it." His shoulders slumped.

"And I can't say I'm too impressed with them." She heard the sarcasm in her own voice, sighed. "All right. So what do you have to tell these guys to make them leave you alone?" *And not so incidentally, leave* me *alone?*

"That you're a Golden, Chess. You're damn close to a full Phoenicis already, unless I miss my guess." He kept his eyes closed. "I should have recognized it, *Paul* should have recognized it, but we didn't. There hasn't been a potential for five hundred years; Melwyn Halston was the last one to achieve full power. When he broke with the Order he retreated here from Vienna and his squad of Drakul kept the Inkani out for a good half-century—"

Halston? Like the Halston who built my library? "Century? Melwyn Halston was borne in 1826 in London, he moved here in 1851 and—"

"Paper. Paper to mislead people. Melwyn Evrard Halston was the last Phoenicis. When he was finally killed by a Viperi Inkanus he was nine hundred fifty three human years old—"

"You're crazy." She let go of his hand and pushed the comforter back, struggled free of the sheets. She must have thrashed during the night. "I need a shower and some coffee before I can deal with this. Just . . . try not to hold anyone up against the wall while I'm in the bathroom, okay?" Chess stalked around the bed, patting at her hair and feeling the tangles in it, wincing each time her fingers found a fresh one. *I'll have to douse it in conditioner and spend some time working everything out, dammit. And he's not done yet, he'll probably have some new and stunning news to give me. Perfect. Wonderful. Lovely.*

His hand shot out as she paced toward her dresser, closing around her wrist with warm, hard fingers. Chess stopped, looking down at him. His eyes were open, his face shadowed by the sun coming through the window on the other side of the bed. "I'm Drakulein," he said quietly, but with a harsh edge she'd never heard in his voice. His dark gaze never left her face. "Are you afraid of me now?"

She tugged against his hold, gave up. "Of course not," she snapped. "You got that thing away from my window, you nursed me through a concussion and dragged me to the weirdest bar I've ever seen in my life, then held me up against the wall and kissed me. Not to mention you got rid of Robert. All in all, if you can stop calling me little nicknames and shoving me around, I think we'll get along just fine." Her breath caught in her throat as his thumb drifted across the underside of her wrist, a gentle touch, his calluses scraping. "Let go of me."

He stared at her for a long moment, his eyes turning even darker. "You treat me like I'm..." He sounded like he had something caught in his throat too. "Like I'm not . . . tainted."

Oh, God. "You don't have any control over who your parents were," she managed in a curious husky voice that sounded nothing like her usual brisk self. "And you're . . . I mean, you're not very polite, but you're on the right side. Aren't you?"

A single brief nod, his chin dipping. *He needs a shave. Why the hell am I thinking of that?*

"From now on, it's *your* side I'm on. Trust me." He looked

absolutely serious. "Please?"

His fingers loosened, and Chess pulled away. "We're partners, remember? I'll get ready and down some coffee, and then we'll go collect your dude. You're probably wanting to bring him back here, right?"

"Maybe. Depends on what shape he's in when we find him." There was no levity in his tone.

"You know, you have a really comforting way of putting these things." *It's the funniest thing. I don't sound amused either.* She took a deep breath. *Okay, first things first. Shower. And coffee.*

Ten

He called the number on the scrap of paper she'd left in her bed, but nobody answered. He recognized the number, of course; it was the cheap room Paul had gotten for them, the rendezvous. It simply rang endlessly. The sound of water running in the shower—and her occasional breaking into tuneless singing—mocked him.

You're a human being. We're partners, remember? And she'd said it so lightly, as if it didn't matter at all.

Sunlight came weak and weary through the windows, clouds massing in the north. He could smell more cold rain on the way, and her entire apartment had started to smell like him, too. Like a lair, his scent mixed with hers, a powerful calming weight in the air. He'd just told her the worst thing most Malik women could think of—a Drakul's possessive instincts tied to her, him shadowing her footsteps and tainting the air—and she acted like it was no big deal.

And she was a skin, for all her potential. Just a skin. And yet she'd trained herself, going out to hunt a *skornac* and dealing with his presence and the Inkani attack with far more presence of mind than he'd seen in plenty of Malik trainees. And now, she treated him just like anyone else.

Just like one of her skin friends, maybe. But that's good enough for me. Better than I deserve.

She would need food, and he still had things to tell her before they set out. It was already past noon, they might be out past dark if Paul was out chasing tail instead of staying in his bolthole and waiting for Ryan to find him.

But I've already wasted time following her around. Only I can't really call it a waste of time, I was here to protect her and that's what matters. Paul will be impossible, but once he understands he'll do his best. He might even try to charm her.

He had to breathe deeply through the red flare of rage that called up. If he was even thinking of attacking his Malik, it was further along than he'd thought.

Why had Paul not answered the phone any other time he'd called in? Why hadn't Paul been at the rendezvous? Was it just coincidence, them missing each other, or had the Malik been holed up somewhere else, waiting, unable to go back to the rendezvous?

By the time she was out of the shower and halfway through breakfast, pouring herself more coffee and humming to herself as she checked her demon-hunting bag, he was in a fine stew of controlled impatience. She had several powders and different items sealed in Ziploc bags, an idea so practical and simple it approached genius. Her Fang lay set-aside on the table as she buttered more toast and poured some apple juice, cheerful and unconcerned. Her hair, drawn back in a sleek braid, was even darker with water, and he smelled her shampoo. She'd changed into a long-sleeved gray T-shirt and another pair of well-worn jeans. He wondered when she wore the slacks and conservative skirts he saw in her closet.

Christ, I've gone poking through her closet like some weirdo. But her clothes smell like her. I smell like her, now. The thought sent a bolt of something hot and gold through him, the demon turning over uneasily at the bottom of his mind. Night was coming, and with it, his full strength. All he had to do was wait.

She muttered to herself as she pulled a small plastic tub out of the bag and shook it. "Salt," she said. "Blessed salt. Very useful. You have no idea how many little jars I have of this stuff, some with wormwood, some with angelica, some with charcoal—"

"With charcoal?" He raised an eyebrow, folding his hands around his coffee cup. The warmth sank into his hands and added to the funny light sensation in his chest. He could imagine sitting here across this table with her, as night pressed against the windows; could imagine her cooking dinner and singing along with the music while he watched. He could imagine watching television with her, watching the light play over her face as she laughed.

I'm turning into a fucking Leave It To Beaver rerun. Control yourself, Ryan. For God's sake control yourself.

"For consecrating a fire," she replied, in her *don't you know that?* tone. "Repels *mnyar* and *skornac*, but those tentacled fuckers like to stay underground in damp places, the books say. Hard to light a fire down there."

"A Drakul could," he heard himself say. "There's a simple spell; flame's easy for a part-demon. Wonder if it'd work."

Her eyes grew round. He saw that the gold flecks were

becoming more pronounced, giving her gaze an eerie bright quality. "You think? Where can we test that?" She sounded, actually, *excited* at the prospect. He even heard her pulse speed up, could smell the lightening of her scent. And damned if he didn't feel a blurring pleasant glow at the thought of making her happy.

Easy, Ryan. Steady down. Don't get her all upset. "Not anyplace around here. Maybe later. Right now we've got other problems."

"Right." The excitement left her face, and he cursed himself for reminding her. "All right. What's this golden thingie you keep talking about?"

Dammit, where do I start? "They're special." He looked down at his coffee cup, wishing there was an answer in the thick black brew. She seemed to like his coffee, at least. "We call them the Golden because that's what they are, gold. The stonekin call them *vakr*, which is their word for sunlight. In the old days, before Christianity, they were usually sacred to the sun gods because of the way they worked their sorcery: they deal with light and they're pretty damn inimical to the Inkani. I've heard that it makes sense, the demons would naturally call out a counterbalancing response in the human race, like any prey taking on aspects to defend itself from a predator. Anyway, the Golden, they're Phoenicis." He took a deep breath, smelling her. She kept fiddling with her bag between bites of toast. "Certain people are born with a . . . potential to become Phoenicis, a kind of avatar, I guess. The potentials are triggered by self-defense during a demon attack, by being around other Golden, or by working sorcery. You're powerful, and when you reach your full potential there will probably be a fair number of demons you can get rid of just by taking on your mantle. But before then, you're vulnerable, and you need training. I'll teach you what I can, and the Order will send a full division if necessary—"

He knew it was going too smoothly, but her interruption still surprised him. "Wait a second. I don't want anything to do with your Order. I told you that." She pushed the Fang into the bag and closed the flap. It was a relief. Even the thing's presence made him uneasy, the demon in him recognizing something hostile to it. "They'll try to take my books."

He heard the possessiveness in her tone and winced slightly. Phoenicis *did* get territorial over their Nests, and she probably unconsciously felt the library—built by another Golden and used as a home of knowledge ever since—to be *hers*. He didn't blame her. "They'll just *guard* your library, and probably help you with funding and things like that. You don't understand, with a Phoenicis to wake up other Golden, we can begin fighting back instead of just defending the cities we've taken. We can begin to push back the Inkani, we can—"

"No." Her chin jutted out stubbornly. "I don't care, I don't want anything to do with this Order. I have to deal with enough supercilious assholes at work." Her eyes swung up, met his as her fork paused in midair. "But . . . they'll try to hurt you if I don't play along with them, right?"

Christ, she's too quick. Dammit. "I'm a danger to them," he said slowly. "If they let me go without punishing me, it will set a bad example for the other Drakulein."

Her eyes glittered. "That is the most ridiculous thing I've ever heard." She jabbed at her eggs with her fork. "Those *bastards*."

"They're not all bad. They're fighting the Inkani. It's serious business, Chess." *Holy Christ, I'm sticking up for the Malik. Damn. Who ever would have thought?* "All things considered, they're the lesser of two evils."

"So was Hitler, in the beginning," she mumbled. He pretended not to hear. Her profile was beautiful, severe and classic like an old statue; her eyelashes swept down, veiling that disquieting gold-flecked gaze. "So you think I'm one of these Goldie thingies."

"The stonekin told me you were. Last night, in the Shelaugh."

"The sheloff . . . oh, yeah. The bar." She nodded sagely, took another bite of toast. "Any chance he could be wrong?"

Not bloody fucking likely, since he took you underground. They don't take humans underground; even the Malik are there only sometimes as allies on sufferance. "No chance, sweetheart."

She didn't protest the nickname, for once, staring at her plate. That managed to disturb him. She was taking the news a little *too* calmly, after all. He didn't trust this sudden docility, just like he didn't trust an Inkani treaty.

"I think he was wrong," she said, and pushed herself up from the table. "We'd better get going. It's already afternoon."

"He wasn't wrong," Ryan said to her bent head as she

scooped up her plate and silverware. She was, at heart, a neat little soul. He watched her wrist, bent at just the right angle to display maximum vulnerability. If the Inkani got their claws on her . . . "I can smell it on you. I could when I met you, but I didn't know what it was. You're a Golden, Chess. And I'm going to protect you."

"Would you still 'protect' me if I wasn't useful to this Order of yours? Or if your own ass wasn't on the line?" Her dark head shook once, sharply, side to side. "No, of course not. We're business partners, Ryan. And as soon as we pick up this guy of yours, I guess we'll see which side your bread's buttered on."

Wait a second. What the hell? "Chess—"

"No." She turned away, stalking into her kitchen. "Give me a couple of minutes, and I'll be ready to go."

What the hell? What did I do now?

He didn't have the faintest clue.

* * * *

He couldn't drive, and she didn't have a car, so it was an agonizingly slow bus ride and then down to the subways, managing to make him uncomfortable. If he'd been on his own he could have used rooftops and alleyways, the secret back routes of the city, but she was in no condition—or mood—to be clambering up the sides of buildings and leaping from roof to roof, even if she could have kept up with him. He could have carried her, but what would be the point, other than enjoying the feel of her?

No, they took the subway. And she was monosyllabic, staring out the window and biting gently at her lower lip, evidently deep in thought. She wore another sweatshirt jacket, this one a deep maroon and zippered up the front, its hood resting gently on her slim shoulders. The train bulleted around a bend and her center of gravity shifted; she actually leaned into him. Though there were empty seats, they both stood—Ryan preferring to be on his feet in case of attack and her . . . she probably didn't want him looming over her. He didn't blame her.

I don't blame her for any of this. Even though she found the books, woke up her potential, killed a fucking skornac and got me into trouble. No, the books probably called her, if what I was told of potentials is true. She probably doesn't even know why she found them, probably felt compelled. And now she's frightened, I haven't given her

any goddamn reason to trust me other than dragging her
to a tavern the Inkani just happen to decide to attack while
she's there. He glanced up at the map and looked down at her
sleek bent head. "Next stop," he murmured, and her shoulders
hunched. She'd heard him.

Why had she suddenly withdrawn into herself? Was it
something he'd said? Probably. He had no gift for handling
females, like Paul did. Hell, Ryan barely had any idea of how
to *talk* to a woman, she seemed mercurial at best and stubborn
at worst, when she wasn't so bloody foolhardy and brave it
threatened to drive him right out of his head.

They emerged onto Harkness Street, and even though it
was during the day she shivered. The sun was sinking, it had
taken them much longer than he'd thought. "Not far now," he
said, wondering why she didn't have a car. It didn't seem like
the right time to ask.

"Maybe you should go up alone," she said suddenly. "If
you're this guy's partner, he might not be too happy to see me.
Especially if you're not supposed to be around a . . . female."

"You're coming with me. Once Paul understands, you'll
have two protectors instead of one. I'm no coward, but the
more Malik around, the safer you are. Even if you don't want
to talk to them." *They'll wait. Hell, for a Golden they'll fall*
on their knees and beg. And she trusts me, I have to be
careful. Not do anything stupid.

Harkness Street was in the Vietnamese district, and the
crowds here didn't make eye contact as Ryan towered above
them, occasionally touching Chess's shoulder to direct her. The
smells of *pho* and baking cream puffs, strange spices and
laundry steam, permeated the air. Vegetables spilled out of
sidewalk booths, and a little girl in a red jacket, her black hair
cut straight across her forehead and falling in an unbroken
sheet down her back, pointed at Chess and asked her mother a
question. Chess had turned pale, and her steps slowed.
Frustration and annoyance boiled under Ryan's ribs. He'd been
gentle, he'd been careful, he'd been as kind as he could.

Maybe she was having second thoughts about hanging
around a Drakulein.

He guided her to a door tucked between an apothecary's
shop and another grocery, this one with colorful paper pennants
for sale under the awning. The clouds were beginning to show
up in earnest, and the temperature was dropping even through

the sunlight. The door was glass, marred with spiderweb cracks as if someone's head had been rammed into it, and Ryan began to feel uneasy. That hadn't been there before.

The door opened, and he crowded Chess in. The noise of the street fell away. A narrow tiled hall, indifferently-carpeted stairs at the back, they'd rented this room from a hard-eyed Vietnamese woman and paid in cash, weeks ago. Ryan sniffed cautiously, and didn't like what he smelled.

Paul's scent, of course, familiar as his own breath. And over that, the red roil of bloodlust, of fear, of dark purpose, and a fading tang of demon. Not Drakulein, but another type of demon entirely. Maybe a *brilnac*, it smelled wet and disgusting, like fur left to rot with potatoes in a dark corner.

"Upstairs. Second floor." He had to move forward, herding her. She went reluctantly. The smell of her fear and adrenaline began to come in waves, and he tried not to breathe deeply. Little shallow sips of air, the scent spiking across his hindbrain and hiking his pulse to match hers.

She climbed the stairs in front of him, trying to move quietly. When they reached the narrow sloping aperture that gave way to the second-floor hallway, he slid around her and took the lead, going slowly and glancing back when she paused. "Stay with me." He didn't like the way her eyes were now ringed with white. *Dammit, woman, what's wrong with you? Why are you afraid if you're with me?*

Still, her fear was only normal. Maybe she could sense the presence of demons, too, if she was far along the path to becoming a full Phoenicis. If she could . . .

As soon as he drew near the door he could smell something else, too. Blood, violence, and a copper scent he recognized.

Death. *Fuck. Oh, holy fuck.*

He turned back, sliding a knife out of its sheath. "Stay here," he whispered, and pointed to a spot right up against the wall, where she wasn't visible from the stairs or at risk from flying wreckage if any of the doors burst open. "Right here."

"I thought I was supposed to stay with you," she whispered back, fiercely.

"Don't fucking argue with me. Stand right there and *don't* move." His tone brooked no disobedience.

Her eyes glittered, but she moved. She stood where he'd pointed, and her chin lifted a little, mulishly defiant. Spots of high color stood out in her pale cheeks, she set her jaw and glared at him. Even that glare made her look adorable.

We're going to have a talk about your attitude, sweetheart, just as soon as I see what's behind Door Number One. He eased up on it, moving soft and deadly. No pulse behind it, but there could be a masking-spell; sometimes the Inkani got a little tricky like that.

Paul, I hope you got out of here in time.

If he hadn't been with Chess he would have come in through the window on the fifth floor and come down. Her perfume was beginning to fill up the hall, her heartbeat accelerating even more as he reached down and tested the doorknob, barely realizing he'd made the habitual ward-movement to blur his fingerprints.

It was unlocked.

Oh, dammit. Dammit.

The door swung wide, and he studied the room, the bed in the corner Paul had slept on, the chair in the opposite corner Ryan had stood guard in for at least a week while they canvassed the city for signs of the *skornac*'s killer. The tiny sink and counter for a hotplate, the narrow bathroom off to one side. The smell boiled out and he heard Chess moving. There were no demons here.

Not anymore.

A man's body slumped across the bed. Blood had splashed in a high arc up the peeling wallpaper. The little room was close and full of the stench of death and spoiled Malik sorcery; no window because this was a bolt-hole, a rendezvous point. His throat had been slashed, a quick and messy job. He wore a brown leather jacket and unbuttoned jeans, a dark green T-shirt. His head lolled obscenely over to one side, his face pointed toward the door. Below his chin the wide grimace of his cut throat opened, grinning huge and horrible.

There was another body on the floor, a human woman in a tight skirt and high boots, the perfume and hairspray she'd worn while living turning into a cloying reek. Her neck had been broken and her shirt was off, her torso glowing pale in the dim light from the overhead lamp.

Goddammit, Paul. You couldn't go a night without a female, could you. You stupid, stupid . . . Wait a minute. Just wait one goddamn minute.

Relief welled inside his chest. *That's not Paul.*

"What is it?" Chess, at his shoulder.

I thought I told her to stay back! He reached out to push her away, to shield her from this unlovely sight, but she looked past him and gasped. Her hand flew up to her mouth.

"Get back." He pushed her away from the door. She resisted, but was no match for a Drakul's strength, he dragged her back to the safe spot against the hallway wall and propped her there. "Stay *here*, goddammit. Don't make me repeat myself." *There might be a trap in the room. Just waiting for a Drakul to come back and poke around.*

Besides, you don't need to see this. I don't want you to see this. Even if it isn't my Malik.

She was even paler, if that were possible, and she stared at him as if he were speaking a foreign language. Her pupils dilated.

God, help me. "Stay here," he repeated. "Here's the safest place for you."

Her lips moved, but even with his demon-acute hearing he couldn't tell what she was trying to say. He tore himself away and stepped back into the doorway, the knife laid flat against his right forearm, the plain wooden hilt protruding just a little from his fist. He picked his way into the room carefully, one step at a time, sparing himself nothing.

The female smelled ripe, with the bathroom odor of death-loosened sphincters. No taint of demon on her; but the recent smoky smell of sex hung in the air, fading fast. Whoever this man was, he wasn't Paul. His wallet lay open on at the end of the bed, the green edge of cash poking out— two twenties lay in a congealed pool of blood. *Last night, then, the blood smells fresh but not that fresh. If I'd have dragged her out of bed and ran over here, it still would have been too late.*

The small table by the chair was empty, Paul's coat was gone too. Ryan checked the corpse's pockets, feeling his gorge rise briefly. Pointlessly. There was nothing he could do, nothing he *could* have done, even if his stomach hadn't twisted into a knot over the woman who had disobeyed him once again and stood in the doorway, her fingers pressed against her mouth, her eyes huge and darkly dilated, the two violent spots of color in her cheeks standing out against pale skin.

I don't want you to see this, Chessie. The thought was tinted with sadness—and rage. Paul had broken cover to leave a message with the librarian's coworker; a demon had come up here and killed a man and a hooker who were, in all reality,

unconscious of the danger they were in. Where was his Malik?
Goddammit, Paul, I hope you're all right. I'm glad it's not you in here.

But the sick chewing of worry wouldn't go away. And that was something else to worry about; his worry wasn't for Paul or even for the two hapless victims. No, the only person he was worried about right now was *her.*

Ryan retreated to the door, pushed Chess aside. She didn't resist, but she did make a small, hurt noise. "Quiet," he warned her. If she started screaming now, she wasn't likely to stop. He swept the door closed, shut his eyes briefly. *Go to God, whoever you are.*

His next problem looked up at him with eyes that threatened to break his heart. "What is . . . Who did . . . *Why . . .*" She couldn't even formulate a question, and that disturbed him too. She wasn't taking this well.

What, she can handle demons but a dead body gives her trouble? He shook his head. It was an uncharitable thought. "Demon." He grabbed her arm and pushed her toward the stairs. "We've got to get out of here, we've already left more traces than we should have. Come on."

"But . . . *police* . . . the . . . the . . . " She struggled, but he used his strength ruthlessly, pushing her through onto the stairs.

"No police. Not now. I'll call in from your apartment and a cleanup crew will come out. They'll—"

"But—" She took a deep, gulping breath, and he didn't like the way her paleness was turning slightly green.

"Dammit, Chess, move. A demon was here. God alone knows what it left incubating in that corpse. We have *got to get out* of here." His fingers sank into her arm and she swallowed another soft sound, this one of pain. He knew he shouldn't hurt her but he had no *choice.* "Move."

She stumbled on the thin, cheap, carpet, and he held her up. *I won't let them take you, Chess. I won't.*

Outside, the sun was sinking below the horizon, a soon, short winter sunset. And now, he didn't have any *time.* Because as soon as dark hit the Inkani would be spreading through the city, and it didn't take much imagination to think that perhaps they'd show up here. Just as he thought that, he heard a low, chilling growl, and his eyes focused on the end of the hall.

Oh, great. Not an Inkani, but one of their spiders, already in the process of shedding its humanity. Its eyes glowed with sparks of red, its fingers crackling as they lengthened. It wouldn't be able to go out into full sunlight, but the room was windowless and the hall only lit by the dimmest of bulbs. And outside, it was cloudy . . . and the light was already fading.

"Stay still, Chess," he said, quietly. "This will only take a moment."

Eleven

Her knees turned to water. She slumped against the wall, staring at the young man who had just appeared. He was slim, Vietnamese, and no taller than her—but then he started to *grow*.

The horrible stench from the room full of dead people made her want to gag as she watched the human shape at the end of the hall stretch grotesquely, as if he was made out of rubber and was being pulled from both ends. Her jaw went slack, and she wondered when, exactly, her life had gone down the rabbit hole.

There're dead people in there. She'd only looked for a moment, but the sight was seared into the inside of her head. She suspected even a hot shower and scrubbing her eyes with bleach wouldn't make it go away. The horrible throat-cut grin under the slack face, blood spattered in a high arc and soaking into tattered wallpaper, the gassy, terrible smell—

The man at the end of the hall made a low, hoarse sound like a scream of pain. He wore a faded Jericho Warriors sweatshirt that kilted up at the bottom as his lanky frame stretched into something skeletal and hunched, bones cracking as his dark eyes lit with red sparks. His hair, in the layered razor-cut so popular with young men nowadays, fell in his eyes as his shoulders rotated inward, hunching. He looked like a cartoon, except for the claws that sprang loose from his lengthening fingers. The claws looked like bone, and his bony hand jerked out, claws slicing through the faded paint on the walls, dust puffing down.

Ryan moved forward, his shoulders almost seeming to fill up the hall. "Just a spider," he said, the razor edge of contempt slicing the air. "An Inkani spider. Used to hunt during the day. A filthy maggot with the worm inside him."

That doesn't make any sense. "Um," Chess managed through the pinhole her throat had become.

"Left here to provide a little surprise, eh? Only you wandered from your post, slave."

The boy snarled back at him, a thin thread of sound that ended on a yip. Chess wished she could stuff her fingers in her mouth to bite down and push back the scream trying to work its way free.

Then the bone-clawed boy yanked his fingers free of the wall and leapt forward, claws outstretched. He didn't aim for Ryan, who was definitely in his way, seeming to take up most of the space; instead, his red-flecked eyes fixed on Chess and his hands outstretched. He even foamed at the mouth, champing like a horse with the bit in his teeth.

Oh, Christ. Oh God. She stood frozen in place, staring as Ryan reached out with one hand and backhanded the boy.

"No!" Chess yelled.

The boy went flying, smashed into the wall. More dust flew. He shook his head and scrambled to his feet, but Ryan was on him, moving with a spooky blurring speed, inhumanly fluid and graceful. His fingers sank into the boy's throat as the thing writhed and cackled, its claws tearing and beating at the air. Ryan's free hand caught the boy's right wrist and *twisted*, the sickening crack of bone breaking echoed in the hallway.

"*NO!*" Chess screamed. Ryan didn't pause, his own fingers turning into hooks and sinking into the boy's throat. One quick twist, another horrible sickening crack, and the body slumped uselessly on the floor.

Oh, my God. He just killed him. All the air left her lungs in a walloping rush.

It was all very well to kill demons. But this was a *person*. Ryan had just committed murder.

What kind of person goes around with claws? the particularly jolly voice of horror caroled through Chess's head. She smelled it again, the ripe gassy scent rising thickly to clog her nostrils and choke her. She hated that smell, *hated* it; it reminded her of a crooked alley and seeing a little human shape lying broken under an octopus demon's maw, and the sound of wet crunching as the *skornac* fed.

Ryan stood with another fluid movement, brushing his hands together as if ridding them of dust or dirt. "God grant you peace," he said harshly. "Chess?"

She pressed her fist against her lips. *No. God, no.*

"You all right?" He glanced back over his shoulder, black eyes burning.

No, I don't think I'm ever going to be all right again. I think I'm going to throw up. Then scream. Then repeat as necessary. Then I'm going to go home, bury my face in a pillow, and forget all about demons. I don't want this. I never wanted this. She took a deep, endless breath, the scream rising in her throat.

Footsteps, coming from the stairs. Ryan tilted his head, his face suddenly easing. "Finally, some good luck. Come on."

Chess shook her head, beyond words. To go that way she would have to walk past the slumped, inhumanly-thin body on the floor; the hall was narrow and she might even have to *touch* it. Her gorge rose at the thought. *I'm rough, and I'm tough, and I can kill demons . . . but no way am I walking past that. No way. Uh-unh. No way.*

"Chess?" He was right next to her, his hand closing around her upper arm again. Chess flinched. She stared up at his now familiar face, his dark eyes horribly human. She'd just seen him kill someone with his bare hands, and he only looked faintly worried. "We've got to go, sweetheart."

"Ryan? *Orion?*" Someone shouting on the stairs. Ryan dragged Chess forward. She struggled, but he was too strong, it was no use. He *did* grab her waist and lift her over the tangled stick-thin legs braced across the hallway. Her stomach gave an amazing cramp. "Christ! *Orion!*"

"Make up your mind," Ryan answered, low and fierce, reaching the arch that gave way to the stairs. "Paul? Quiet down."

"Up," the other voice said, and Chess's heart gave a huge leap. It was the tweedy hunk who had asked her about Delmonico's book.

Then who was dead in the room there?

He arrived in the doorway, looking a little worse for wear—his sport jacket was torn and charred in places, his short sandy hair disarranged, and with a shiner puffing up around his left eye. He was also limping. His jeans were tattered too, and he had a red bandanna tied around his left calf—no, it had been white once, it was just soaked with blood. Chess's jaw dropped.

"Go *up*, there's Inkani dogs on the street in broad daylight. They're goddamn seri—" The man's eyes flicked past Ryan to her, and widened. He didn't look happy. "What the hell are you doing with *her?*"

Ryan let out a short, sharp curse. Then he moved forward, pushing Chess in front of him, shoving her up the first two stairs. "She's a Golden, Paul. Or at least a *potential.* You were too distracted by the fucking *sheela* to notice. Come on, if they're on the low road we'll take the high road. How fast can you move?"

Wait a second, I don't want to go anywhere with you, leave me alone, go away, what's going on? Her feet slipped on the cheap carpet, and she almost fell. Ryan set her on her feet again, absently. *Gee, thanks. Oh, my God.*

"Fast enough." Paul tipped her a mocking salute. His cheeks were rough with stubble, and she smelled a faint, horrible scent that wasn't like the gassy odor of death. *Demon,* she thought. *He's been close to demons.* "How are you, Ms. Barnes?"

She managed to find her voice as Ryan shoved her out onto the stairs and started pushing her up them. "No. Stop it. Let go of me. *Ouch!*"

"You've had your hands full," Paul said from behind them.

"You have no idea," Ryan replied dryly. He sounded amused. "Chess, you okay?"

Why do you keep asking me? No, I'm not okay. I'm not. "Who—the room, *who*—"

"They rented the room right out from under me, some businessman. I've been waiting for you to come back. She's the potential?" Paul spoke right over the top of her words as Ryan kept pushing. Chess stumbled, Ryan set her on her feet again as if she weighed less than nothing. Her arm hurt where he'd grabbed her, she could feel the bruise rising up underneath the skin. "Ah, shit."

"You're never going to live this down." Ryan sounded a lot happier. *Well, he's got his partner back. I suppose that would make him happy. Now all I have to do is go home and bury my head in my pillow. I'll call Charlie and have her bring over a chick flick or two. We'll eat popcorn and giggle. Yeah, that's it. That will be good.*

Her throat seemed to closed, her heart hammering, a funny roaring sound filling her ears. *I'm dealing really well with this. I just saw him kill someone and I'm not screaming. Right? I'm not screaming. Doing good.*

"Hey, I never mistrust what a woman tells me—at least not at first. Besides, the *sheela* is an Other; I've never seen a potential."

There was a low, harsh growl like broken glass scraping her ears, and Chess flinched. Wet meaty thuds began from below, and she wondered with a fainting sort of horror what was going to happen next. Ryan let go of her arm. "Take her.

Keep going up." He sounded deadly, and her heart began to pound. The stairs seemed to stretch up forever, like a rickety staircase in a Looney Tunes cartoon. *What's up, Doc? Nothin, just being chased by demons. Expanding demons. K-k-killing p-people . . .* "Don't let anything happen to her."

Wait a second—

"I'll look after her. Be careful." Somehow Paul was right next to her, Chess craned to look back over her shoulder as Ryan turned back. She heard the faint double click as he pulled the hammers back on two guns.

"Careful as I can be. Spiders out in broad daylight. What next?" Then he was gone, moving down the stairs so silently he seemed to vanish.

"Ryan—" she whispered. "*Ryan.*"

"He'll be okay." The Malik pushed her up the stairs. His hands weren't as brutally strong as Ryan's, but his thumb ground into a fresh bruise and she bit back a yelp. "He's done this before. One time we were trapped in an abandoned warehouse in London, that was worse than this."

Her brain began to work again. *Christ. Jesus Christ.* She reached down with her right hand, digging in her bag and trying to shake free of the grasp on her arm, scrambling up stairs that suddenly seemed far too narrow to hold breathable air. "What—those things, what *are* they?"

"Spiders," he replied shortly. "Take the next arch on the left. The Inkani put little soldier-demons inside their human servants, they can make drastic short-term changes in the physical structure of the host. Kind of like a disposable assassin; the body back there will rot inside of three hours as the stresses on cellular structure take effect." He pushed her into the next hall on the left, opening directly off the stairs. The hall receded back into darkness, the light bulbs in the fixtures either dim or burnt-out; Chess's fingers closed around the hilt of her knife. "Secondary exit. Always have a secondary exit." He didn't sound nearly as arrogant as he had before. "Christ, I hope he's careful. I'd hate to have to pick a new Drakul . . . here we are." He yanked her to a stop, then gathered himself and kicked at one of the flimsy doors. A long vertical crack opened alongside the doorknob, one more kick and the door busted open, revealing another dingy room, this one with a window spattered with rain and gray, fading storm light. The storm had broken, and the early winter twilight had begun.

She dragged the knife free as Paul's hand came up, full of a gun. There was a sudden, amazing wall of noise from below, the entire building seeming to groan under a shuddering impact. Squealing groans and a terrible, bloodcurdling screech followed the thump, and the sudden incredible sound of gunfire. *Ryan's down there! Oh my God!*

Paul swept the room, moving like a cop in a movie, making sure nothing was inside. There was a single bed and a small table with a broken porcelain lamp perched on it; the dun carpet was thin and raspy. He grabbed her arm again. Seemingly not noticing her knife, he dragged her to the window and wrenched it up, letting in a burst of chill, rain-laden air. Lo and behold, there was a fire escape here. The battered man glanced out, blinking painfully against the light, then motioned to her. "Looks clear. Let's go."

"I d-d-d—" Her voice refused to work properly. The knifehilt was solid in her sweating hand. *I don't want to go with you. I want to go home.*

For Christ's sake, Chess, you took on an octopus-demon in a sewer. Snap the hell out of it! The welcome sharp voice was her mother's, and it spurred Chess to action. She yanked the knife free of its sheath, seeing the hard blue glitter spring into life, jetting against the walls. He ducked out through the open window. He still had his backpack; it was as battered and singed as the rest of him. She glanced back over her shoulder, the awful smell belching and blooming, streaming out the window. Fresh chill air poured inside.

"Come *on!*" the Malik yelled. "Let's go, he'll catch up!"

Mechanically, Chess climbed out. The fire escape swayed dangerously, rusted and rocking under their weight. "Follow me." Paul moved cautiously but swiftly, paying attention to each footfall. She edged after him, heard another roaring crescendo of gunfire and a thin chilling deathsqueal. *Ryan,* she thought, pointlessly.

They made it down, Paul holding the ladder and catching her waist when Chess was three rungs from the ground. She squirmed away from him, landing hard on her feet. *You jerk. I can take care of myself.* The alley, sheltered from the wind, was still full of rain; the simmering smell of garbage made her stomach rise. *I'm spending a lot of time in trash-laden alleys lately. Must be my personality. Become a demon hunter, see the sights, smell all sorts of wonderful new things.* Her breath sobbed in her throat. The knife glittered, throwing out hard darts of blue light.

"Christ, what's that?"

She half-spun, but his eyes were on her right hand. He looked shocked, brown eyes wide and the rain starting to plaster his short hair to his skull. "It's my goddamn knife," she spat. "What do we do now?"

"That's a *Fang!*" He almost squeaked with surprise. Chess glanced around the alley nervously. The sudden rainy silence, wind moaning at the alley's mouth, made her nervous. "How the *hell* did you get that?"

"I bought the knife at the Army-Navy surplus store and consecrated it myself." She tried to look everywhere at once, unsuccessfully. "What do we do now?"

Paul had gone pale. He stared at Chess like she'd grown another appendage, and not a socially-acceptable one either. He simply stood there, eyeing her, and Chess began to get a very bad feeling about all this. Then, of all things, he started to grin, a wide satisfied smile.

The fire escape began to rattle above them. "*Move!*" Paul barked, as if he hadn't been the one just standing there gawking. "Move, goddammit!"

Where am I supposed to go? But he grabbed her arm and hauled her toward the mouth of the alley, weaving between piles of garbage. Her boots slipped in greasy scudge, and the urge to throw up crested. *Oh please don't let me blow chunks here, oh please God, please.*

They burst out onto the street, people scattering as gunfire rang out behind them. Screams, produce flying as he hauled her through a sidewalk fruit stand, footsteps thudding. "*Run!*" he yelled. "*Keep running!*"

Then his hand left her arm and he spun away from her.

Chess didn't stop to look back. She heard the hoarse cries and cracking that meant more of those stretching-things behind her, and flung herself forward, her boots pounding the pavement as something zinged past her. *Someone's shooting at me— maybe because I'm running down a city street carrying a knife?*

She tore around the corner at Harkness and Thirty-Eighth, stuffing the knife back in her bag. Rain splashed down, and she heard distant sirens. *Keep running. Sure. I can do that.* A stitch grabbed her side, her breathing echoed, and she realized what she was making for just in time: the Thirty-Eighth and Strange street subway station.

Chess put her head down and bolted, running for her life.

* * * *

Charlie's office was on the edge of downtown, in the plush Graber building. It was early on a Friday evening, and the secretary nodded as Chess walked in, damp and trying not to look like she'd just been chased through garbage-laden alleys and witnessed a young Vietnamese boy growing bone claws. "Hi, Lucy." She tried her brightest smile and wished she'd worn something other than a sweatshirt jacket and jeans. *I probably smell like garbage. God.* "Is Charlie in?"

Lucy nodded. "She just finished with her last client. Go on back. Heard you got food poisoning." Lucy's blond hair was a helmet of marcel waves, a close-fitting cap that added to her cherry-red lips and pale cheeks to make her seem like a 1920s flapper trapped in chic, tasteful business wear. She would look right at home on the running board of a Model T in a beaded dress and cloche hat, hanging onto a dapper swell's arm. Right now she was shuffling papers together into a file folder. Her purse was on her desk. It looked like quitting time.

"I'm still feeling urpy," Chess replied, which was the truth. The subway's rollicking motion hadn't helped, and she'd had to take three trains to get here since she'd flung herself into the Piers Express on the platform, not caring that it would take her out of her way, caring only that the train had been at the platform and she could get *away*. Her heart was still going a mile a minute and she was sure her hands, stuffed in her pockets, were shaking. She'd gotten a couple of strange looks on the subway.

At least nobody tried to mug me. "Thanks, Luce." She walked, deliberately slowly, past Lucy's desk, through the door, and into the expensive offices of Graber, Fawkes, Linton, and Barnes.

Charlie's office was a corner suite. Her secretary Phil— short for Philomela—wasn't at her desk so Chess just walked past. Phil had probably already gone home for the day. *Francesca, Charlotte, and Philomela*, she thought with a ghost of amusement, taking a deep breath. *No wonder we like our nicknames better. We sound like the Three Stooges. Only maybe not quite as funny.* A jagged laugh escaped her, and she knocked on Charlie's door and walked right in.

Sleek, tall, slim, and auburn-haired, her older sister looked up from behind the large cherry desk. She'd done her office in cream and blue, soothing colors; the view of the misty, rainy city below immediately cheered Chess up, as usual. Wooden barrister file cabinets in cherrywood, a fishtank on top of one with brightly-colored tropical fins waving gently, and a soft deep couch just right for corporate clients, as well as a tasteful glass coffee table and two more plush chairs set just subtly too far from Charlie's desk. The framed print on the wall was a Thompson, showing a ballet dancer *en pointe* on a lasso of stiff rope floating in empty space, watched by a tiger that might or might not be a sculpture. It was a beautiful print, even if slightly disturbing.

"Chess!" Charlie, in a couth gray suit, jacket and skirt and softly feminine blouse, almost leapt to her feet. "Mom said you were out with food poison . . . " Her hazel eyes—more green than Chess's, just like her hair had more red—widened, and she took in Chess from scalp to toes with a look that was *very* much like Mom's. She leaned over, scooped up the phone, and punched something in. "Lucy? Please call Zoftow, get his secretary to reschedule him for tomorrow. Thanks, sweetie. You're a doll." She dropped the phone and crossed the room, in long swinging strides, her tortoise heels sinking into the thick cream carpet. One quick flick of her fingers locked her office door. Then she turned around, her back to the door, and folded her arms. "Well? What's going on?"

A profound swell of relief swelled through Chess's chest. *God bless you, Charlie. I can always count on you.* "You're going to think I'm crazy," she rasped. She coughed, felt her stomach rise again, pushed it down. "You're going to think I'm fucking *crazy.*"

Outside the office, the last shreds of day faded and rain tapped and fingered at the window. Charlie shrugged. "I know what you make a year. You're already crazy." She lifted one manicured eyebrow. "And you dated Tommy Dalton. What kind of crazy are we talking?"

Oh, Lord. I can't believe I'm about to do this. "Charlie, do you believe in demons?" Chess's voice broke on the last word. *I can't believe I'm doing this.*

Her sister stared at her for twenty of the longest seconds of Chess's life. Then she unfolded her arms and stalked across the room to the antique teak sideboard that held a small tasteful collection of antique teacups. She opened the bottom right door and snagged a bottle of Scotch, two glasses, and poured them each a healthy dollop. She capped the Scotch deftly, set it back on the sideboard, then turned around with a drink in either hand. "You want one of these?" she asked. "Or do you want to go straight for the bottle? Sit down on the couch, and tell me *everything.*"

Twelve

Paul looked like hell and reeked of Inkani. He had a black eye, bruised ribs, a severely-bruised arm, and his leg wouldn't stop bleeding. He propped himself against the side of the phone booth and scanned the street. Ryan, his heartbeat finally beginning to come back to something like normal, glanced behind him. Rain came down thick and steady, cold and piercing; it had already started to slide down the back of his neck. *Clear of Inkani*, he thought, and a shiver touched his back. His shoulder hurt, he'd had to pop it back into the socket. The bullet wounds hurt too, and the claw-swipe along his ribs smarted as it began to heal. He was covered in blood. Again. He'd have to cover them both with a savagely-draining shell of illusion; they couldn't take a cab in this condition.

"She's a potential," Paul said grimly, into the phone. "My Drakul's been keeping watch. Send everyone you've got, for Christ's sake, the Inkani know she's Golden and they're on her trail. We're going to pick her back up and keep her in a safe locale until we get some goddamn reinforcements." A pause, while he listened. "I'm sure. She made a Fang, and Orion says she smells Other. She's a potential and damn close to a full Phoenicis. If they get their hands on her we're *doomed*. Just send everyone! And pour what you can into the account we're using for this run, we need emergency supplies." Another long pause. "Orion's got it under control. He made initial contact, she trusts him. He deserves a goddamn gold medal. He just fought both of us free of a whole net of soldier-demons. Give us some help out here, we're dying, all right?"

Another pause, and Paul muttered a goodbye and hung up. "Reinforcements on the way." He hunched his shoulders miserably. "I can't believe I fucking lost her on the subway platform. She was running like she wanted to take off into orbit."

Well, she never does anything halfway. "Thanks, Paul." And he meant it. The Malik was decent, at least. He hadn't mentioned what any fool could see: that Ryan was in a knot over this woman and had gotten a little too close for comfort. "Really."

"I can't believe I didn't see it. A *potential*." Paul winced as he eased himself out of the booth and into the stinging rain. The booth was in the corner of a grocery store parking lot, the main avenue one block away and buzzing with the sound of traffic. "I've been moving from bolthole to bolthole, one step ahead of Inkani with no time to call in. It's been pure fucking hell. Looks like you got yourself in trouble too."

You're lucky, if that's all you got from the Inkani. This is light damage, we both know it. Ryan grabbed the other man's shoulder. The faint tingle of healing sorcery spread over his palm, slid down into Paul's body; the Malik sighed and straightened when he was through. "Better? Can you breathe? That was a nasty shot to the ribs you took there."

Paul nodded. His pulse was a little too fast, and he was breathing in short shallow sips. He smelled of fear, too; that was normal. "I can breathe. I'm good. Where do you think she went?"

Who knows? The important thing is, she got away. You drew the Inkani fire to allow her to get away. I owe you my life. "Probably back home. I mean it, Paul. Thank you."

Amazingly, the Malik shrugged. His handsome face lit with a shadow of his old feckless grin, a shadow Ryan was suddenly glad to see. At least Paul understood Drakul and how to keep them in line. "You're a good Drakul, Ryan. The last thing you need is any static from me. So you like this girl? Is she nice?"

Nice? I can't figure out if I want to shake some sense into her or kiss her breathless. "I guess. Let's get you off the street, we'll catch a cab. Her apartment's warded, it shouldn't be too bad."

"Warded. You do that?" Paul hitched himself up straighter. He was indeed a sorry sight, from his torn clothing to his battered bag; he also looked, extremely happy to see Orion. Damn near bursting with glee, under the sour stink of fear. *Well, he should be. I'm the Drakul, I'm here to take care of anything too big for him. Living without me for a while might have taught him a little serious appreciation.*

But then he thought of the soldier-demons, each maggot one of them intent on getting past him, and the shudder almost managed to become visible. "No, she did it. It's what alerted me." *That and the Fang.*

She'd been terrified, of course. Her eyes had been huge, and she'd resisted him; the Inkani spider was something any skin would have trouble with. And the corpses inside the room had been hosting baby *brilnac;* he was damn lucky they hadn't hatched where Chess could see. He hoped he hadn't frightened her, hoped she would go straight home from the subway. At least she'd gotten away safely. He couldn't *do* anything right now except get his Malik to safety and hope.

Paul hunched his shoulders miserably against the rain. "Let's get out of here and hope she has the sense to go home."

"It's not sense. Home is the one place she shouldn't be going." *But I told her to. "If anything happens, come back here and wait for me." She's smart, she'll remember.* He checked the street absently, all clear. If Chess hadn't run for the subway he might have been able to track her, even with a wounded Malik in tow. But now her trail was broken in the subway and the thing for him to do was go back to her house and wait for her to come trundling home. Combing the city at this point would just confuse the issue—*especially* with a wounded Malik in tow. "But she doesn't know that. Let's move."

They moved off, Ryan checking the street frequently and keeping himself to Paul's slower pace. *She got away,* he thought, his heart suddenly pounding with relief and fresh frustration. If this kept up he might well have a cardiac arrest right out in the open and save the Inkani a load of trouble. *She got away. Paul held them long enough for her to get away. Thank you, God.*

However much of a skirt-chasing idiot Paul was, he'd saved Chess. And indirectly, he'd saved Ryan too.

After all, if a Drakulein's mate died . . .

Don't think about it, he told himself, hailing a cab with a swift motion and a thread of *glamour,* the thin illusion that made both him and Paul look like normal businessmen caught in the rain instead of battered, bloody Knights of the Order with demons to escape and a potential Golden to find. *Just come home, Chess. Come home like a good girl, and we'll get this all straightened out.*

* * * *

"Nice place." Paul snapped the towel, hung it up neatly. The bathroom door was mostly closed. They were both glad of a chance to clean up. "Interesting girl. Good books."

She dances while she cooks. Hope she doesn't mind us using her soap. And for God's sake, leave the toilet seat down. "She's a librarian."

"I've been thinking." Paul limped out into the main room. He'd had extra shirts in his backpack, both for Ryan and himself, he lowered himself down on the couch with a sigh.

God save us all. Ryan held up the small blue jar of ointment. "Thinking? You? Christ, more trouble. Here. Put this on your leg, and try it on those bruises too. She makes it, it's fantastic stuff."

The blind, turned-off television watched them both as rain smacked the windows. Ryan sat cross-legged on the floor, mending the NIN T-shirt; he'd been waiting for the chance to do that. It just didn't seem right to have destroyed the only thing she'd given him so far. A stack of DVDs sat by the television—Charlie Chaplin, Buster Keaton, the Marx Brothers—no Three Stooges, but there were several Bruce Lee and Jackie Chan films too. And a DVD of *Casablanca*, strangely enough. She was indeed an interesting girl.

The more he thought about it, the more uneasy he was. She might have been in shock, pale and stumbling, the chemical odor of her fear so thick it threatened even now to trigger the rage in him. He took a deep breath. *Come home, Chess. Come back. If anything happens to you . . .*

Paul grimaced. The smell of wormwood and mint filled the air, over the smell of Chess's skin and the deeper smell of Drakulein. Paul coughed. He still reeked of fear, but thankfully the smell of Inkani was less. "Christ, this is foul. Does it work?"

"Works well enough. What are you thinking?" The smell of her rooms soothed him on a basic level, made the demon retreat into watchful silence. Waiting. Waiting for her to come home.

"She's a librarian." Paul rolled the leg of his jeans up, smoothed some of the greasy goop on his calf. "Ouch . . . oh, *shit.* Damn. That stings."

Ryan kept his eyes on the black cotton he was mending. Thin threads of etheric force bled out through his fingers, fueled by the demon part of his inheritance, and the rips in the fabric blended together seamlessly. "I know she's a librarian. Does it work?"

"Damn. It stings, but that's better than it was." Paul sounded grudgingly admiring. "Smart girl."

Too smart for her own damn good. He thought of her eyes, flecked with gold and wide with fear, thought of how she'd shook his hand to make them partners. Thought of the soft smell of her hair, herbal shampoo and that fresh golden scent. *Come home, Chess. Or I just might do something stupid like going out to look for you, Inkani be damned.* "Very smart. Don't try any of your charming little tricks on her." He filled his lungs again with her scent, the smell they made together.

"You kidding? Not my type. Too bookish. The *sheela*, now . . . she was something else. Wish I had made that dinner. Anyway, I was thinking. She's a librarian in the building Halston worked from. I managed to do a little checking in the public records. Halston endowed the library with a trust." Paul rolled the leg of his pants gingerly back down. He was still shaking, from adrenaline overload and fear. Was he combat-sick? "What if the cache—Halston's books—are somehow in the library itself?"

Ryan's fingers stilled. "Huh." It made sense. It made too *much* sense. *Chess, you sneaky little girl.*

Paul spread a generous glop of the luminescent blue ointment along his bruised but no longer cracked ribs. He moved gingerly, blowing out short little chuffs of pain. "So check this out: librarian is a *potential*, she's poking around in her library and finds the cache. She starts playing around, ends up triggering her abilities. She starts changing, and somehow a *skornac* ends up getting killed here."

"She killed it." His heart gave a nasty leap again at the thought of her facing down the *skornac*.

The Malik let out an unsteady laugh. "You know, a few days ago that would have surprised me. So she killed a fucking *skornac*. Luck, or talent?"

"Both, I think. Mostly luck. After all, what demon expects to face an almost-Golden with a Fang anymore?" *Christ, you could have been killed, sweetheart. Come home so I can tell you never to do that again.*

Paul gave a slight groan, agreeing with him. "Anyway, we end up running across her before the Inkani have a chance to, just out of—again—sheer, dumb-fucking luck." Paul capped the small jar with a vicious twist of his wrist. He settled back on her blue couch, looking oddly out-of-place—a tall Malik sitting right where Chess liked to sit, her legs curled to the side, watching television. Ryan strangled the flare of territorial anger. The Malik's short sandy hair clung to his skull, and he had a large dark circle under his unwounded eye. He'd dabbed a little of the goop over his shiner, too, and that was starting to look better. "Just how involved with her are you, Orion?" Suspicion colored his voice.

Don't ask me that. He dropped his gaze again, looking down at the shirt. He was almost done mending it. The claw-swipe he'd taken to the ribs was almost healed. He was lucky.

Silence stretched between them, broken only by the persistent rain. He could imagine her curled up under her down comforter, reading and sipping hot chocolate. He could imagine her standing at the window watching the rain bead on the glass and slide down, the gray light touching her sleek dark hair. *Where are you, sweetheart? Come home. Get your ass back here so I can be sure you're all right.*

"Christ." Paul let out a long-suffering sigh. "Now you've gone and done it. She's a Golden, Ryan. And she's . . . God. You're a good Drakul, why'd you do this?"

Like I had any choice. "She went out to kill a *skornac* because it was taking schoolchildren." *And she sat right over there at that table and cried. She's treated me like a human being, like I'm untainted. She's . . . goddammit.*

The silence returned. Paul sighed again. "So the Inkani have been in town for a while. And she just went out to take care of it. A fucking skin went out to take care of it. A skin girl. A *librarian.*" It was hard to figure out what gave him the most trouble, Chess's job or her gender. "You've gone and gotten attached to her, haven't you."

Of course I have. Right now I'm trying like hell not to pace, or go out that goddamn window and start tearing this city apart brick by brick to find her. He stared at the T-shirt, the last rip melding itself together under his fingers. The burning threads of etheric force sank in, tied themselves off. He said nothing.

"Jesus. How am I going to get you out of this one?" Paul was making himself comfortable on the couch. The sounds of his movement were nothing like Chess's, but they were close enough that something hot burned behind his eyes. Dark would start falling soon, the rain was intensifying. Where was she? How long would he be able to hold out before the mounting frustration forced him into action? "Well, she's a Golden. I'll see what I can swing, all right?"

Don't do me any favors, Malik. It was altogether more reasonable than he'd thought a Malik was capable of being about this sort of thing. "Sure." He held up the T-shirt. It was good work, and he felt slightly mollified at having repaired it. Paul's breathing evened out, and he dropped into slumber with the ease of a man who had learned to sleep where he could. As soon as he was safely sleeping, Ryan stood, wincing a bit as his leg reminded him he'd almost been eaten alive by three Inkani spiders at once, more on the way, his entire world narrowing to holding the hall so she could flee. He couldn't ever remember fighting with such incandescent rage before. The thought of the dogs going after Chess had triggered a fey madness in him. He paced to the window, looking down at the alley. What a view, for her. Nothing but a blank wall, a slice of sky, and the Dumpsters down below. She deserved better.

Rain ran in rivulets down the window. The warding on it shimmered uneasily, brought to humming alertness by the presence of a demon, even a half-demon like him.

Half-demon. Drakul. Tainted. Impure.

He felt like an intruder here in her comfortable, cluttered apartment. And when she came back, Paul might . . . what? Send him back to the Order in disgrace?

I'm not going. I don't care what they do to me. I'm not leaving her. I can't.

He hoped like hell she came back soon. Even if she was furious at them for taking over her couch and using her soap. He should make something to eat, too. They would both need a protein load with all the energy they'd expended.

Come home, Chess. Please be safe, and come home.

Thirteen

It was past nine p.m. by the time they reached Chess's apartment building. She felt a little more sanguine, having napped on the couch in Charlie's office while her sister finished up some paperwork. All in all, she actually felt pretty good. Relieved.

Of course, the fact that she'd performed a spell or two to *prove* this was real and she was sane might have something to do with it. It felt good to show someone else, good not to look at her sister with the profoundly empty feeling of keeping a secret.

"Only you would live in an apartment building without an elevator," her sister complained, her heels clicking on the stairs. "Is it a secret demon-hunting lair?"

"Shut up." *I thought she'd have more of a problem with this. But I guess the fiat lux trick convinced her. Hard to argue with a woman who can throw light like a flashlight. And that trick with the glass of water—boiling, then ice, then boiling, then ice—helped too, although the cleanup's a bitch.* All in all it had been easier to convince Charlie than she'd hoped.

Then again, Charlie read science fiction when she wasn't reading law; it was a family quirk. She didn't have to be hit on the head to be convinced. Besides, she trusted Chess implicitly. *I've never been so glad to have an older sister.*

But Charlie hadn't seen a demon yet. That was kind of the point at which all this stuff became well-nigh unbearable. And Chess hadn't mentioned the murder on Harkness Street. There were some things even family couldn't handle.

How about that? I just saw Ryan kill a man with his bare hands, and I'm still protecting him. Keeping a secret. But to be fair, the man he killed was stretching out like that kid in Charlie and the Chocolate Factory. And growing big bony claws. Not to mention coming for me, and I don't think he was going to ask me to dance. She shivered, a shudder rilling up her back.

"I'm just *asking*." Her sister sounded delighted. "Ooh, is there a secret handshake? For demon hunting?"

"No. But I get tossed into Dumpsters. Oh, and held up

against walls and sniffed. Not to mention taken underground by trolls." *And kissed. Did we forget kissed?*

She hadn't forgotten the kiss. She was glad the stairwell was only dimly lit; the hot feeling in her cheeks had to be blushing. *Ryan. I hope he got away okay.*

"No wonder you haven't been answering your phone." Charlie apparently couldn't resist one little goose. But all in all, she was taking this calmly.

They reached Chess's floor, and she pushed the fire door open. A slice of yellow light pierced the gloom of the stairwell, and her own familiar hall stretched away toward the other door, the one she'd banged out to go down the utility stairwell and out into the alley. Her bag weighed against her shoulder, and she felt greasy and cruddy. "I'll pack, and then we can stop at that Thai place on the way to your house. I really appreciate this, Charlie Lou." She held the door for her sister, who still looked immaculate despite finishing a day of work and dealing with a crazy younger sister and the news that there were, after all, demons in the world.

"Don't call me that, Chessie Ray. I wish I could have seen this guy get rid of Robert. Didn't I tell you he was bad news?"

Chess winced. Trust Charlie to pick the most embarrassing instead of the craziest thing about this. "You were right."

"He really tried to barge into your apartment? Creepy." Charlie made her "men-are-idiots" noise, a slight, sharp puff of air past clenched teeth.

"Way." Chess glanced over the hall. Uneasiness crept under skin, and she reached into her bag, pushing the flap aside and curling her hand around the hilt of her knife.

Immediately, the prickling buzzing sensation washed up her arm. *Oh, no.* "Crap," she breathed, and pulled the knife free, leaving the sheath in the bag.

Blue light sprang loose as soon as the blade left the bag, and Charlie actually gasped. "What the . . . oh. Oh, man. Wow."

"Shhh!" Chess hissed fiercely. "Let's get you inside the apartment. If there's a demon I'll have to deal with it."

"Chess, what if the demon's *inside* your apartment?" It was a good question. Charlie's green eyes were wide, and the color had drained from her face. She stared at the knife as if it was a snake; the blue glow struck the walls and cast their shadows behind them.

"I warded my window, and if a demon came in through the

door it would be all smashed. They're not the type to pick locks." She transferred the knife to her left hand and dug for her keys, approached her door cautiously. "Watch that end of the hall. If the door opens, yell."

"I feel like I'm in a bad movie. This is exactly the point where I'd be screaming *'don't go in there!'* at the screen." Charlie lifted her chin, her eyes glittering.

They approached Chess's door. She stuck her key in the top deadbolt. It was undone, and she frowned. She *always* left both deadbolts locked.

Oh, shit. She tried to second deadbolt. Unlocked too. *Double shit.*

The doorknob was locked, though. Time seemed to slow down, and she motioned Charlie back. "If anything happens," she whispered, *"run."*

"Shit all *over* that," Charlie whispered back. "I'm not leaving you in the lurch."

"Don't argue with me." Chess pulled the key back out. Dropped her keys in her bag, transferred her knife to her right hand. *Here goes nothing.* She turned the knob slowly, slowly, the knife's prickling buzz in her hand reaching a crescendo. The door ghosted open, Chess hanging back and staring into darkness.

She lifted the knife, the blue glow penetrating the gloom. Saw nothing but her front hall, the back of her couch, the window beyond orange with citylight. *Come out come out wherever you are. Or did I leave the deadbolts unlocked? I was nervous, I might have . . . but I don't think I did. I don't leave my deadbolts unlocked. Ever. That's like begging to be robbed.*

"Chess?" Charlie whispered.

She motioned for quiet and took a step forward, pushing the door open wide. *Nothing hiding behind there. Probably in the kitchen, that's where I'd hide if I wanted to surprise someone—*

She barely had time to choke out a cry when the hand closed around her wrist and jerked her off her feet. The knife went flying, another hand clapped over her mouth, and Charlie zoomed around the corner, yelling Chess's name. Chaos descended, the door kicked shut and Chess suddenly struggled with frantic fear, *"Charlie! Charlie!"* Screaming through the hand on her mouth, striking out with fist and knee and fingernails. She finally regained enough presence of mind to sink her teeth into the hand and heard a faint hissing in-breath. He was strong, locking her wrist with his free hand and actually picking her up off her feet. He had to work to subdue her. She kept biting, kept kicking, and heard Charlie yell again, sounding more surprised than hurt.

"Calm *down!*" a familiar voice sliced through the hubbub. She heard a thump and a male cry of pain, sounded like Charlie had scored one. "Calm down, Chess, it's me! You're safe, it's okay, just *calm the fuck down!*"

Ryan? She went limp, breathing heavily, and he slid his hand away from her mouth. Chess found herself caught in a bear-hug. He squeezed just short of pain and buried his face in her hair again, her cheek was smashed against something that felt like his chest. He was warm, very warm, and it even *smelled* like Ryan, the peculiar scent of male and demon-tang that followed him around. *Oh, my God.* "Ryan?" *I sound dazed. I feel dazed. How did he get in?*

The hall light flipped on, and Chess heard a slight, definite click. "Let go of my sister, asshole." Charlie wasn't messing around. "Or I'll blow your fucking friend's head off."

Oh, boy.

A definite tremor went through Ryan's body. Chess wriggled free, his arms going loose and dropping down to his sides. He stared, not at Charlie but at Chess, his eyes unblinking and gone deep and dark. He had never looked more feral, his eyebrows faintly drawn together and his hands slowly curling into fists. She wondered if he was fighting those "instincts" again.

Charlie had her knee in the other man's back, and Chess saw, with no real surprise, it was the hunk in tweed, Paul. And her sister was holding a very nice baby Glock, the end of the barrel pressed to the back of Paul's skull. Charlie's hair was wildly mussed, her eyes all but snapped sparks, her linen jacket was torn and she'd lost a shoe.

She looked magnificent. Chess's heart hammered in her throat. The wild urge to laugh rose up inside her throat, died away. *Where did you get that gun from, Charlie?*

"Chess?" Her older sister was breathing rapidly, her ribs almost flickering. "These guys friends, or should I put a bullet in this asshole's head?"

Oh, Charlie, God bless you. "Charlie, this is Ryan. The

one on the floor is Paul. Guys, this is my sister, Charlie." *I saw you kill a man with your bare hands, Ryan. But wouldn't you know, I'm actually glad to see you.* "You can let him up off the floor and put the gun away. I don't think they're here to kill me."

"Are these the good guys?" Charlie didn't look convinced.

"Ryan is." She heard the conviction in her own voice and winced. "The guy you're holding down is an arrogant fuck, but he's basically all right."

"What are they doing hiding in here?" But Charlie eased up on the gun with an ease that spoke of long practice. "Did you give them a key?"

"No, I didn't." *But it's not the first time he's grabbed me just as I got through the door.*

Ryan was still staring at her. He was *shaking*, she realized, his fists visibly trembling. His jaw was set, his eyes glittering— he looked like a man on the edge of murder. "Ryan?" Her throat was suddenly dry. "You okay?"

"*Ow,*" Paul spoke up. "Get *off*, woman! God, I've been beaten to a pulp by goddamn Inkani today, I don't need any more." There was the sound of movement, then a long, low whistle. "Shit. Stay still. Listen, Ms. Barnes, you'd better touch him."

She stared, fascinated, as a muscle twitched in Ryan's cheek. He hadn't blinked once. He stared at her like he was trying to stare his way *through* her. "What the hell are you talking about?" She shifted her weight as if to step back, and Ryan twitched.

Chess froze.

"Look," Paul said quietly. "Just step up to him, nice and easy, and touch him. Skin on skin's best. He's worked himself into a state worrying about you, and right now he's fighting to stay calm. Just trust me on this one, okay?"

Trust you? Oh, sure. You're an arrogant fucking Malik who wants to steal my library . . . but you did help me get away from those things. All right. "Ryan?" *I sound like a little girl, all breathy.*

"I'm serious, woman. You want him to snap? Calm him *down*, or he's going to go ballistic."

Since when is that my problem? But she swallowed, and stepped forward slowly. Very slowly. He watched her, his eyes half-closed and volcanic tremors going through him in waves.

Christ, he looks ready to explode. "Ryan? Take a deep breath, calm down. Okay?"

Another step closer. He watched her; if his fists got any tighter his palms might start bleeding.

"What the hell's wrong with him?" Charlie whispered. Chess didn't blame her, the waves of rage coming off Ryan shimmered like heat over pavement.

"He's fighting his instincts," Paul whispered back. "Don't worry. She'll calm him down, he won't hurt her."

"How do *you* know?" Charlie didn't sound convinced.

Hear, hear, Chess seconded. Ryan stared at her, the glimmer of eyes under his lids oddly hot.

"She's about the only person safe from him right now. Stay still." Thank God Paul sounded calm.

You and I are going to have a long talk about this, Mr. Tweedy. A nice long coffee klatch. Chess reached out, her right hand meeting Ryan's. Her fingertips touched his fist, hard as rock and shaking a little. *What am I supposed to do? Last time he got this upset he wanted me to talk to him. I wonder if that would work now?* "Ryan." She heard herself using her firm-but-gentle voice, as if she was talking to a five-year-old at the library, or a feral cat. "Take a breath, calm down. It's all right. Everything's all right. I didn't know you'd come back here. I thought you were gone with your partner."

A shudder went through him. His fist unloosed, his palm turned out, and he grabbed her wrist. She almost flinched, expecting him to squeeze, but his fingers were gentle. Almost exquisitely gentle. He still stared at her, a muscle flicking irregularly in his cheek.

Keep talking, you idiot. Calm him down. Okay. "I hope you guys didn't clean out my fridge. I'm a little hungry. We were planning on going out for Thai. I'm going to spend the night at Charlie's, it seems safer than staying home alone. Now you've got your partner back everything's cool, right? I'm glad he's alive." *But who was in that room? And your fingerprints are probably in there. God. What are you going to do if the police come after you?* "I'd ask you what happens next, but you seem a little occupied right now. This is my sister, she's a lawyer but don't hold it against her. I had no idea she was carrying a gun."

The tension was slowly leaving Ryan's shoulders. A little sense began to come back into his eyes. Chess tried again.

"I'm glad to see you. I don't like you picking the lock on my front door, though. *Or* leaving it unlocked. Although who would come in and try to steal my TV with you in here, I don't know. Nobody's that stupid. I hope."

He took a deep breath, his eyes closing and his mouth relaxing. His face smoothed out. The rage simmering in the air drained away. Chess let out a long, soft breath, relieved. She pulled gently against his hand, trying to free her wrist, but he didn't let go.

"Chess." His voice was harsh, strained. "Are you all right?"

He sounded like he was being strangled. Chess swallowed, hard. "I'm fine," she soothed. "I think I pulled something running away from there, and I'm not at all happy about this turn of events, but . . . I'm fine. I'm glad you didn't disappear. I thought you were going back to the Order."

He shook his head. "They wouldn't have me," he whispered. The last of the tension left him, his shoulders sagged. "I told you, I'm on your side. I'm useless to them now."

"I wouldn't go that far," she pointed out. "You're the only one I trust." *Christ, did I just say that? I think I did. Lord help me, I've gone and got myself attracted to a guy who scares the hell out of me and kisses like a thunderbolt. Not to mention kills people with his bare hands. We're going to have to talk about that, Ryan.*

Amazingly, one corner of his mouth curled up in a smile. "Really?" He sounded delighted and hoarse all at the same time. "You mean it?"

"Of course I mean it," she soothed. "We're partners, remember? Now, how about you calm down and quit scaring all of us?"

Ryan nodded. There was a shadow of coal-black stubble on his cheeks, his shoulders slumped, and he suddenly looked tired. "Sorry." He *sounded* sorry, too. "I was worried about you."

Oh, Lord. I'm in too deep. Who would have guessed? "You were? Well, I'm okay. I'm here. Are you okay now?"

He nodded, once, sharply, then let go of her wrist. Chess almost flinched again, controlled the movement. His eyes opened back up, and he looked down at her. She caught a flash of something far back in his dark eyes—something like resignation, maybe—and her heart leapt into her throat. She was suddenly very conscious that her hair was sticking up all

over her head, she was wearing damp clothes that smelled like
an alleyway, her face felt sandy and her mouth foul from
sleeping on Charlie's office couch. Her heart was in her throat,
and the world seemed to have shifted off its axis by a couple
of crucial degrees.

"I'm sorry," he repeated, as if she hadn't heard him the
first time. "Really, I am."

"It's all right." She got the idea he was apologizing for
more than scaring her, and that she was agreeing to more than
she'd bargained for. "I'm glad you're okay."

"I'm very far from okay," he said calmly. "But you're alive.
I'll be fine. Now who the hell is this, and where the hell have
you *been*?"

* * * *

Charlie took a whiff of the luminescent blue goo in the
glass jar and wrinkled her nose. "What the hell is *in* this? It
smells like Wrigley's gone bad."

"Rotten Juicy Fruit? I never thought of that." Chess,
standing in the bathroom doorway, scrubbed at her hair with
the towel. She was beginning to feel a little more like herself
now that she had taken a short, hot shower. *God bless whoever
invented indoor plumbing.* "It's good for bruises and scrapes,
and I think it healed a concussion."

Paul was at the window, looking out into the alley. He was
extremely quiet, and Chess found out she liked him better that
way. He kept glancing back over his shoulder at Ryan, who
seemed much calmer now. But still, there was a gleam in Paul's
eyes she didn't think she liked.

"Concussion?" Charlie had brushed her hair and found her
shoe. She eyed Ryan uneasily as she capped the jar; he sat
across the table from her, loading a clip with bullets Paul had
produced. "Did *he* do that?"

Charlie was not convinced of the advisability of letting two
armed men stay in her little sister's apartment, but even she
had to admit that Ryan didn't seem like a threat. And that it
was, after all, Chess's house, and Chess got to say who stayed.
A full half-hour of discussion had brought them that far, at
least.

"Indirectly. He pushed me out of the way when a demon
came for me. I fetched up against a Dumpster pretty hard." In
fresh jeans and a T-shirt, with her bag on the table and her
knife safely sheathed—even if blue light did glitter out between

the hilt and the sheath—Chess thought she just might be able to handle this. "It wasn't his fault."

Ryan glanced at her. It was a short look, somehow managing to convey gratefulness. She found herself smiling back at him, an expression that felt natural. Even unshaven and obviously tired, he still looked extremely . . . attractive. In a stubbly, dangerous, dark-eyed sort of way.

Stop it, Chess. He killed someone. And you still haven't asked him about those bodies in the room. Who were they?

Charlie yawned. She had probably been at work since six and was a little punchy. "You still coming over to spend the night? I'm famished, Chess, in case you've forgotten. I need food."

Chess was dying to ask her where the gun had come from, decided it could wait. *I haven't forgotten. Christ, I only took a ten-minute shower.* "I'll go for Thai with you. I don't know if staying here is a good—"

"Staying here's safe," Ryan interrupted. "I'll stand watch." He finished loading the bullets into the clip and examined his work, satisfied. The bullets themselves looked odd, silvery and more slender than any other ammunition she'd seen, which granted wasn't a lot. Guns made her nervous.

"That's very nice of you," Charlie said, politically enough, "but you're not on the lease, and Chessie hasn't invited you. And I can't say I'm impressed with your behavior either." She sounded like Mom. "Chess, can I raid your closet? These shoes are killing me."

Chess waved a hand, picking up a comb and starting to fight with her hair. "Knock yourself out. But you leave that black cashmere sweater alone."

"You're no fun." Charlie hauled herself up from the table, gave Ryan one of their mother's patented I-Know-You're-Up-To-No-Good looks, and whisked away into Chess's bedroom, pointedly closing the door behind her.

Ryan met Chess's eyes. "Staying here's safe," he repeated. "I'm sorry."

Boy, this is turning into a situational comedy. All we need is the wacky gay friend and a laugh track. She sighed, dragging the comb through her hair and leaning against the door. *I feel like I could sleep for a week.* "I want to ask you something."

"What?" He didn't look toward the window, but she felt

his attention shift all the same. Paul had been extremely quiet. *Too* quiet, as a matter of fact. It didn't take a genius to figure out he wasn't happy with this chain of events, despite being rescued. Wonder of wonders, though, he hadn't made a snotty comment since she'd gotten home. Instead, he just kept glancing speculatively at Ryan.

"Those . . . in the room. Who were they?" *It bothers me, you see. It bothers me a LOT.* Chess yanked a tangle out of her hair, wincing.

Paul piped up. "Businessman." He sounded flat and bored, but something in his tone told her he wasn't as blasé as he wanted her to think. "They rented the room out from under me, and I had to stay away, the Inkani were everywhere. I guess they thought he was me. And the hooker—"

"Woman," Chess corrected. "Woman. Not *hooker.*" *You arrogant son of a bitch.*

Paul's shoulders stiffened. "Woman," he echoed, tonelessly. "Sorry. They might have thought she was you."

Not fucking likely. I'd never be alone in a room with you. Chess dragged the comb through her hair, dropped her eyes. "And the . . . the boy." *The boy. The one who grew like Michael Jordan on crack. The one who stretched out and produced big-ass claws that looked like his phalange bones were popping out through his fingertips. That one. What about him?* "He . . ."

"He bargained his life to the Inkani for something. In return, he got a soldier demon in him. He was an assassin, Chess. He was coming for you." Ryan slid the clip into a gun, chambered a round, started in filling another clip. His hands moved easily, habitually, as if he did this all the time.

Maybe he does. "I . . ." *You killed him. You killed him, Ryan, and acted like it was no big deal. I'm not sure how I feel about that. Killing demons I can handle, but people . . . no. No.* "So you've found your partner." She half-turned, tossed the comb so it landed on the counter, an accurate throw that didn't delight her as much as it should have. "So what now?"

"Paul's called in," Ryan said steadily, his eyes on his work. "In a couple days the city will be full of Malik. They'll get the Inkani under control and start apprenticing potentials to you, with your permission. The sooner we get more potentials awake and on the track to becoming Golden, the sooner they can start spreading out to other cities and taking them back. The Inkani will try to take you for their Rite of Opening, but they won't get close enough to touch you. If we can get through the next week, it'll be smooth sail—"

"Hold on. I told you, I don't want anything to do with your *Order.*" *They're after my library, dammit, and I won't let them have it.*

"They won't take your library," Ryan said softly. He still stared at the clip, loading it with quick fingers. "I won't let them. And you have to play ball with them one way or the other, Chess. It's a good way to protect yourself. You're not just a skin hunter, you're a Golden. They'll behave themselves. Besides, if you play ball with them they won't hunt me down like a rabid dog."

"Ryan—" Paul's shoulders hunched. He was looking more miserable by the second.

"No." Ryan's tone was soft but utterly inflexible. "Don't sugarcoat it, Paul. I just broke Rule Number Two for a Drakulein. They'll retire me, and I might as well be dead. I'll be shunned, and I'll die. Separated from the woman I've tied my instincts to, I'll die. I've seen it happen, two Drakul who got too close to Malik researchers. They faded." He finished loading the clip and examined it, racked it into another gun, chambered a round "Unless she makes a point of retaining me as her bodyguard, I'm doomed."

If my jaw drops any further, it's going to fall off. Doomed? Fade? Die? When was I asked about this? "You're kidding me," Chess began.

"*Stop* it," Paul interrupted. "Just stop. They're not going to retire you. Not if I have anything to say about it." He stared out the window, still running with stray rivulets of rain; it was one of the patented Jericho City slushers, the beginning of two days of steady, drenching, persistent rain. "You could give me a little credit, goddammit. I know I'm not the best Malik in the world, but you trained me and I'm not going to watch you fade."

He doesn't even sound like he's convinced himself. "Fade? What the hell are we talking about?" Chess's heart gave a strangled thump. "Ryan?"

"He's become attached to you," Paul snapped. "If they separate him from you, he'll start to fade. You need to learn how to deal with him, Ms. Barnes, or he's going to—"

"Leave her alone." Ryan's voice, still very soft, sliced through his; the air seemed to chill a whole five degrees. He slid the gun into a holster. "She doesn't understand. The important thing right now is getting her through the next week or so."

A very nasty thought began to worm its way up through Chess's head. "Protective instincts," she said flatly, raising one eyebrow and fixing Paul with a glare he could probably feel even with his back to her. *Shoving me up against the wall and kissing me is not protective behavior. I am sensing a very big problem rearing its ugly head right about now.*

"Possessive instincts," Paul supplied, turning away from the window. "Mating instincts. The Drakulein—"

"Whoa. Hold on. Wait a minute." Her cheeks certainly couldn't get any hotter. *I'm blushing like a teenager. Dammit.* "So you're saying . . . oh. Oh, wow." That put an *entirely* new shine on things. "Wow. That's . . . wow." *Oh, I'm an idiot. Can't I ever say anything right?* "Does . . . I mean, do you have any control over . . . this sort of thing, Ryan?"

"Enough control." Ryan's tone was still soft, but it was less scary than it had been. "I'm not *all* animal, Chess. Your sister's listening behind the door, by the way."

The bedroom door opened and Charlie appeared, wearing Chess's coveted Buddy Holly silkscreened T-shirt. She'd also resurrected a pair of her old jeans, kept at Chess's in case of emergency or sleepover, and had stuffed her feet into a pair of Chess's old Nikes. *Thank God we're the same size in shoes,* Chess thought. Then her brain ran up against the last few minutes again and stuck like an engine without oil.

"Thai," Charlie said grimly, with a fierce look that suggested she'd heard all of the last few minutes and had a few problems of her own. "You coming, Chess?"

She nodded, mute. Her cheeks were on fire, and the blush spread its way down her neck. *Wow. I'm going to have to think about this one.*

Ryan gained his feet in a single movement. "We'll go with you."

"No way," Charlie said firmly. "She's coming with me, and spending the night at my place. Pack your bag, Chess. We're leaving."

Ryan's eyes narrowed, his shoulders squaring. "You don't understand. The Inkani are *out there*, and they know she's a potential. Not only that, but they know she's being guarded by a Drakul. They will find her, and when they do you'd better hope I'm there to protect her, goddammit."

Charlie folded her arms, her chin coming up. Her hair was on fire under the lights, and Chess suddenly felt very glad her sister was here. "Listen, mister. I don't know who you *think* you are, but my sister doesn't need weirdos like you running her life. You haven't done anything but get her in over her head with this demon crap, and it stops *here*. By the time she comes back you'd better be out of her apartment and observing a respectable distance, or I'll get a restraining order against both you and your collection of playmates. Is that clear enough for you?"

I think that's the first time I've ever seen Ryan speechless. Chess took a deep breath. "Let's just calm down, all right? Charlie, I can't just throw them out, they don't have anywhere to go. I'll head out for a spot of Thai with you, and they can stay here and rest up. When I come back we'll hash everything out. Okay?"

Nobody looked mollified in the slightest. Paul, who had turned away from the window, exchanged a long meaningful look with Ryan, who simply started stuffing items into his bag as if they had personally offended them. The silence stretched, became brittle, and Chess sighed, stalking across the apartment to the table to open her demon-hunting bag, since it had her ID in it. She slipped her knife and her ID into her purse, wincing as she contemplated how cluttered her table was. "Good," she said. "I'm glad we have this all—"

Ryan's hand closed around her wrist. "Don't go alone. Not after dark, Chess. Please." He said the last word as if it choked him.

"Get your goddamn hand *off* her!" Charlie's voice hit a pitch close to Mom's during the great Soccer Leg Break of Chess's seventh-grade year. Ryan simply glanced at her, as if she was a persistent but not terribly noteworthy insect.

Chess studied his face. He dropped his chin, looking down at her, his eyebrows drawn together and his mouth a tight line. She could feel the tension return, thrumming through him like the sonic massage of the trolls in their stone underground. "You want me to trust you, right?" she reminded him softly. "I need to get away from this. I need to be normal for a little while."

His jaw turned to stone.

I wonder if he's going to grit his teeth down to nubs. Or shatter them. Christ, my imagination just works too damn well. Chess tried again. "I'll come back tomorrow night. We'll talk."

"They will find you, Chess. It's only a matter of time." His thumb brushed the underside of her wrist, a slow, even movement that made her breath catch. "I'm not going to let you do this. I *can't*."

She felt her eyebrows raise, couldn't stop herself. "*Let* me? I don't think so. You've been shoving me around ever since you showed up, and I've had enough of it." One step back, her wrist twisting and breaking free of his grip. "You want me to trust you? Back *off*. I know what I'm doing. I took out a *skornac* without your help, mister. And I've managed to stay alive so far. I'm going with my sister, and *you're* going to stay here and wait for me. I'll be back tomorrow night, and if you want anything to do with me at *all*, you'll sit your silly ass right here and *wait* for me. You got it?" She hitched her purse up on her shoulder. *Screw packing. I'm leaving. I can use Charlie's toothbrush.*

"Don't do this." Did he actually sound *pleading*? "Don't make me force you."

She turned on her heel, wondering if he'd explode into action. She'd seen just how *fast* he was, if he was going to try to stop her from leaving it would probably get nasty very quickly, and no amount of Al's kickboxing would stop him. "Charlie? We're leaving."

Charlie's eyes flicked over Chess's shoulder. She steeled herself, but nothing happened. Charlie edged for the door.

"When the Inkani come for you, they won't care who's with you," Paul said quietly. The words hung in the room. "You're putting your family at risk."

Why do you think I kept all this a secret? It doesn't take a genius to figure out that any demon with enough brains might try to take my family hostage. "If you guys don't shout it to the heavens that I'm your new best friend, I don't think it will be a problem," Chess lied, and pushed Charlie into the entry hall. "Let's go. I want a nice cold beer when we get to the restaurant."

"Good thing I'm driving." Her sister sounded strained. "I think I'll order curry tonight. You?"

"You know my heart belongs to phad Thai. Goodnight,

Ryan. See you tomorrow."

He didn't respond. She heaved a sigh of relief as her door closed behind her, and she locked it, including the two deadbolts.

"Are you sure it's safe to leave them in there?" Charlie whispered.

"If they wanted my TV they would have taken it before I got home tonight." Chess replied grimly. "Let's get out of here before anything *else* happens."

Fourteen

The sister lived in a tony high-rise on Vaskell Street, on the fringe of downtown, an apartment that probably cost more a month than Chess made in two. She was a real barracuda; she'd nailed Paul in the nuts and held a gun on him. For a Malik to be held down by a female skin was embarrassing, to say the least, even if Paul had been trying to be careful and not kill anyone. Even if Paul had been wounded and tired, too. Ryan was beginning to think that toughness ran in Chess's family.

The older sister drove her silver BMW like a bat out of hell, and they stopped at a hole-in-the-wall that apparently produced good Thai food, from the smell and the steady stream of customers. Emerging with takeout cartons, they had piled back into the BMW—and it had been a load of fun keeping up with them and dealing with a Malik's speed constraints at the same time. If he hadn't taken the precaution of checking Chess's address book, he might have had to track them on the ground, and that wouldn't have been pleasant. As it was, he'd barely managed to keep the silver car in sensing range as it sped through the streets and disappeared into the parking level of the Vaskell Arms.

Ryan hunched next to the HVAC unit, on the roof of a Chinese restaurant across the street from the sister's apartment building. All looked calm, except for the persistent rain—and Paul, huddled in the lee of the unit, with a turn-aside charm carefully applied to keep him dry. They were in their fourth hour of watching, and Paul was starting to get the fidgets. As usual.

Ryan's shoulders were wet, and rain dripped in his eyes. It took effort to keep his voice low. "I don't know. I don't think she understands. I tried."

"Christ. A potential, and she doesn't have the sense to stay where a Drakul can keep an eye on her." Paul was on his fifth repetition. "Women, eh? Nothin' like 'em. Little spitfire, isn't she? And her sister. Both pretty. What a pair."

I didn't notice her sister, Paul. I was too busy being glad she was alive and unharmed. Ryan ignored the persistent drip of rain down the back of his neck, soaking into his scalp.

There was only so much a turn-aside charm could do if you were right in the path of the wind. He'd given his Malik the sheltered place, as usual. *Just leave it alone, Paul. Let me brood in peace, dammit.*

He could see her even now, standing with her chin tilted just so and her hair lying wet against her shoulders, the vulnerable pulse beating in her throat. He should have argued harder, done something, distracted her . . . but he'd been fighting the damnable need to grab her shoulders and *shake* her, not to mention kiss her forehead and her cheeks and a few other places, just to prove how happy he was to see her.

I need to get away from this. I need to be normal for a little while. Her lower lip had trembled just a little, the circles under her beautiful eyes taunting him. She probably didn't know how her hands shook just a little, and how the persistent iron-copper smell of adrenaline and fear hung on her.

That was the exact point Ryan had realized he was in deeper trouble than he'd ever thought possible. Because he'd realized, as she twisted her wrist free of his hand, that he would rather stand guard on a rooftop or in a dingy alley than destroy her peace of mind any further. And if he couldn't do what was necessary to protect her, what use was he to *anyone?*

"Women." Paul shook his head, a slight movement Ryan could sense even in this darkness. It was the long, deep time of early-morning dark, when old people succumbed and the streets seemed bare and empty of all but the homeless and the criminal.

And, of course, the demonic.

"I thought she was an ice-queen." Paul's voice was a bare murmur. He still smelled of fear, but not so badly. Ryan didn't blame him, this was one fucked-up situation. "She played it really well, acted like she didn't even know who Delmonico was. Goddamn."

If he says that again, I am seriously contemplating throwing him off this roof. Ryan filled his lungs. Her scent still clung to him, a faint soothing reminder. She was beginning to smell like sunlight, and he was beginning to feel faintly nervous when she wasn't in sight. Faintly nervous? No, *really* nervous.

When I come back we'll hash everything out. As if she was really coming back. As if she thought he would let her spend the night unguarded anywhere.

Her sister apparently had no trouble believing that demons were after Chess. That was odd; most skins literally wouldn't believe the proof of their own eyes when it came to sorcery. He wondered what she'd done to convince such a hardheaded left-brain type of the existence of demons. Then again, the sister was by all appearances very close to her. The Barnes were probably a hell of a family.

I don't think she'd take me to meet her parents. He sounded bitter even to himself, but he wasn't the type of guy a girl brought home. Just a big, dumb, brainless Drakul, and he'd scared her just when he was doing so well. She trusted him, she wanted to be partners . . . and Paul had to open his big mouth. It was the wrong time to tell her.

Christ, you mean there could be a right time? The thought was amused and sour in equal proportion. He was in a hopeless situation, and the sooner he learned to live with it, the better. If the Malik didn't tear him away from Chess and sentence him to a slow, lingering fade, the Inkani would get him—and while he might die defending her, he might also die without being able to do even a quarter of what he wanted to do to her.

The demon part of him fixed its gaze unblinkingly on the building. *Go find her,* it whispered. *Find her. Touch her. Make her see.*

He wasn't an animal. He was *human,* as she had reminded him. What would a human man do?

I don't have a goddamn clue. And who am I going to ask, Paul? Yeah. Right. Like he can keep a woman around for more than a night.

The rain kept coming down, smacking and dripping, a hundred cold, wet kisses. He scanned the dark empty streets, listening with half an ear as Paul began again. "Can't ever predict what the female species will do. And a potential too. You certainly know how to pick 'em. Hey, Ryan?"

Oh, for Christ's sake. "What?" He pitched his voice loud enough for human hearing.

"Can I ask you something?" Paul shifted his weight, maybe glancing uneasily at the corner of the HVAC unit. He was thankfully out of the wind. If the Malik caught a cold, there would be no end of bitching.

"Ask away." *You will anyway. At least Chess knows when to shut up. Or maybe I just don't mind hearing her voice.*

"Was it my fault? I mean, I should have known she was a

potential, then I ran across the Inkani. I'm goddamn sorry, Ryan." And he did sound sorry, for once. The Malik might have been hidebound and anachronistic, but they were fighting the good fight. And while some Malik were actively sadistic to their Drakul, the majority of them were decent guys. And the nasty Malik were generally eased out into research instead of on the front lines—any Malik who lost a few Drakul due to stupidity was investigated. They weren't all bad. And the rules were there for a reason, they were good rules and had stood the Order in good stead.

"It wasn't you, Paul." Again, he pitched the words loud enough for the other man's hearing. *I saw her sitting at her kitchen table crying and that was it. I fell in love peering through her window. Like a goddamn voyeur.* "Really, it wasn't your fault."

"Then what was it? She's a *librarian*, for Chrissake. I mean, she stacks books for a living and probably hasn't had a date since the last presidential administration. She's a brainy type. I would have figured you for someone a little earthier, you know." Paul warmed to his theme. "She doesn't seem too well equipped to handle demons. Probably break a nail or something and start screaming. You know how women are."

I can't believe I'm standing here in the rain with my Malik giving me dating advice. The image of Chess mourning a broken nail made an unfamiliar smile pull on the corners of his mouth. *I can't wait to see Paul's face the first time he sees her on a heavy bag.* He scanned the street again. "I like her," he said, his eyes moving from streetlight to streetlight, each with a circle of wet orange light underneath. "She's got good taste in music."

"You fell in love with a librarian because of her taste in music?" There was a strangled sound, and Ryan realized his Malik was laughing. It did sound funny when he put it that way.

"She likes Buster Keaton, too." *This is no time for levity, dammit. Keep watch.*

"Ryan?"

"What?" *I feel like the parent of a five-year-old. But he's probably talking to keep himself awake.*

"Why'd you let her go? You could have kept her there. I could have brought her sister home." He sounded genuinely curious. "Or we could've kept them both there."

Because I can't stand the thought of her unhappiness, Paul. I'm an idiot. "Best to keep on a potential's good side, Paul. Besides, she needed a little rest." *I need to be normal for a little while,* Chess's voice floated through his head.

Normal. Yeah. He didn't have the heart to tell her it wasn't going to be "normal" for her ever again.

"Um, Ryan?"

He brought himself back to full awareness with a start. Cursed himself for letting his attention wander. "I see it." Down on the street, moving from patch to patch of darkness, a shape too quick and light to be human fluttered in and out of existence.

Ryan's skin went cold and prickled with gooseflesh. His pupils dilated, and the demon in him rose in a single snap of red flame. *Soldier demon, without a host. Looks like one, anyway; the rain's damping the smell. What's it doing out here?*

They came, a solid pack of twelve. Twelve black-smoke spider shapes flitting through the streetlamp-scarred dark, followed by a slightly slower, more solid-looking humanoid that moved from shadow to shadow. There was a flash of red eyes, and Ryan's hand curled around a knifehilt. *Karhanic and a group of twelve, a full hunting pack. Goddammit.*

They called *kaharnac* "squeezers," because of their preferred method of taking prey. They weren't as loathsome as the *skornac*, most squeezers looked like very tall, very pale humans with long, soft, grasping fingers and oddly smooth noseless faces. But they were very, very good hunters, and even with the rain blurring Chess's trail they still might catch onto her. She wasn't exactly inconspicuous.

He watched, barely breathing, his attention taut and focused, as the pack swirled down the street, taking no more notice of the high-rise than of any other building. Unfortunately, that meant nothing; they could be on an errand or simply out nosing around. On the other hand, the low, fluid, smoky shapes of the demon hounds weren't sparking or fizzing with excitement, and that was something.

The group vanished down the street, and Ryan strained his preternatural senses. They kept moving; he heard the faint chilling silver stroke of an ultrasonic hunting cry. Whatever prey they were after tonight, it wasn't his Golden.

The flare of possessiveness no longer surprised him. *My Golden. As if I have any right to think that.* Water fell from the skies, steady weeping that had probably saved them all by erasing the smell of a potential from the air.

"Squeezer. And a pack. Was it a full pack?" Paul sounded calm, but a stray breath of wind brought the smell of adrenaline through the rain. The sound of Paul's pulse thudding frantically reminded him of Chess. Ryan's nose wrinkled slightly.

"It was a full pack," he confirmed. *I hope you're sleeping, Chess. I hope you're oblivious to all this.*

"Christ." Paul shifted, the click of a hammer easing down audible under the sound of the wind. "Jesus Christ. We can't wait for reinforcements, we have to get her out of here."

"She won't leave."

"Goddammit, Drakul, don't be an idiot. If there are packs scouring the street and *skornac* taking humans, this is worse than we ever dreamed, and we have *got* to get her out of town. Two of us against all of them? She'll die. They'll take her, and use her for the Rite. You know they will."

The fact that he was right didn't help. But still, it would be easier to catch them in transit, Paul wasn't thinking clearly. "So we hit her over the head and carry her off? Great. That will really gain her trust."

"If they use her for the Rite, we'll lose this city and the two to the north, probably the ones to the east too. They'll be able to bring another mass of *them* through, the High Ones. We can't fight that. Jesus Christ, Ryan, use your head. We've got to get her out of here."

"You're right." *Shut up. That's rabbit-talk.*

"If you don't, I will."

Like hell you will. I'll find some way to make her listen. I have to. She's safer staying in a bolthole than trying to escape the city. They've probably got this place cordoned off tighter than a Grand Master's asshole. Ryan's hand tightened on the knifehilt. He said nothing, hunching his shoulders against the rain as the turn-aside charm thickened, trying to cope with all the water from the sky. He wondered if he'd ever dry out. *Sleep well, sweetheart. I'm standing watch.*

Paul didn't say anything else either. He didn't have to. Two more hunting groups, both with a higher-class demon to keep the hounds in check, swept the street before dawn.

Fifteen

She didn't go straight home like she promised Charlie she would. Instead, she took another long shower, ate two whole-wheat muffins, got back into her clothes from last night and brushed her teeth with Charlie's toothbrush. It was a Saturday morning and her sister was already at work, leaving a twenty for cab fare on the kitchen counter, as if Chess didn't have her own job, thank you very much.

Charlie's apartment was sleek chrome and clean glass, pale linen pillows and bookshelves full of frowning, fat leather-bound law books. Her stash of sci-fi and fantasy was in the bedroom, ranked neatly on stripped-pine shelves, Chess took a moment and went through the familiar titles, soothed by so many old friends. There was Tolkien and Peter Beagle, Tanith Lee and Robert Heinlein, Asimov and Gaiman . . . all the greats. Chess frowned, seeing a new Gabaldon paperback. *I didn't think Charlie went in for time-travel. Wait 'til I tease her about this. Scottish time travel, no less. Mom will have a fit. Still thinks anything romance is porn, but de Sade is okay 'cause he's dead. Got to love you, Mom.*

As usual, the books made her feel steadier, more alert. More like she actually had a clue about what was going on. She picked out the copy of Joan Vinge's *Psion* and opened it, her fingers finding the gap. There, between the pages, was the flat spare key.

Oh, baby. Come to Mama.

She tried not to feel guilty—after all, she'd paid for the bike too, and Charlie had it all the time because parking was hell around Chess's building. Chess even kicked in for the horrendous insurance, and *that* was a strain on a librarian's salary. But on the infrequent occasions when she needed transportation she couldn't get by cab, bus, or her own two feet, the bike was a welcome luxury. Even if it did rain more in Jericho than it should.

She shoved the key in her pocket and left a short note on the counter, sweetly informing her sister she'd taken the bike and borrowed the helmet. Ten minutes later she was in the underground parking level, fluorescent lights buzzing and reflecting off the smooth concrete. She penetrated to a far, dark corner, little-used and stocked with a Viper and a few slim leaning shapes under tarps. One tarp she twitched aside.

The sleek, gleaming Ducati 999 leaned slightly on its spring-loaded kickstand. Chess's heart began to pound. The bike was beautiful, a little prissy in its lines, but capable of amazing things once you got it out on the open road. It wasn't really a town bike. For one thing, it pulled too hard and you really didn't get the full effect until you were well above a normal speed limit.

But *damn*, it was beautiful. And the library had a few standing subscriptions to some of the better cycle mags. The only thing better than looking at pictures of the bike was riding it.

It's going to be cold. But I'll get there quick. She was able to fiddle with her purse strap to lengthen it so she could settle the strap across her body under her coat. *I'm going to get drenched. At least if anything demon shows up I'll be able to outrun it. God, Charlie's just going to die. Well, too bad, it's my bike too, dammit.*

She straddled the bike, popped the stand, and eased the helmet over her hair. The world immediately took on a distant wavering sound. The sudden claustrophobia of the helmet was soothed when she clicked the key over and pressed the button, hearing the engine rouse itself. It wasn't a Harley's growl, but then again, nothing was.

I haven't been riding in months. She grimaced at the odometer; Charlie had been taking the baby out on walks again. Sneaky older sister, always lecturing Chess on being cautious and law-abiding. *Come on, baby bike. Be nice to Mama. Let's go to the library, shall we?*

It wasn't as wet as she feared, since the storm was taking a brief break. But it *was* cold, and she was shivering by the time she'd gone half a mile. Traffic was the lightest it ever got on the fringes of downtown. Chess penetrated the tangle of one-way streets, taking a looping circuitous route that nevertheless got her near the library in a shorter amount of time than if she'd gone the direct way. There was even— hallelujah—a parking spot in the far corner of the pay-for lot on Vox Street, under the drooping, dripping branches of a cedar tree whose roots were beginning to crack the pavement on the other side of the chain-link fence. It was a miracle the tree had survived, but the lot was dotted with small islands of greenery, and the owners made more in parking fees than they could leasing the plot for development. Unfortunately, they didn't believe in giving the library employees a break, a fact bemoaned regularly at staff meetings.

She paid the pimpled, greasy attendant, who barely looked up from his skin mag. The windows of his little hut were clouded with condensation, and Chess grimaced as she walked away, swinging her helmet. If she went in through the side door nobody would see her. Everyone would be too busy dealing with the regular Saturday circus. Tomorrow would have been better; the library was closed on Sundays and she could have walked right in the front door singing a few Gilbert & Sullivans at the top of her lungs and nobody would have been the wiser.

Needs must when the devil drives, she thought, fishing her keys out of her pocket. Rain began to flirt down, kissing already wet pavement. Chess glanced nervously over her shoulder, seeing only the blank back wall of the bank and an alley holding Dumpsters. She normally didn't work Saturdays, taking a few hours on Sunday to come in and deal with the ever-increasing reams of paperwork her job required. Still, she felt guilty, and the back of her neck crawled as if she were being watched.

Ridiculous. You sound like a Looney Tunes cartoon. Any moment now Bugs is going to pop out and say "Eh, what's up, Doc?" And you'll scream like a girl. Where's the tough Francesca Barnes, demon hunter extraordinaire?

Unfortunately, the tough Chessie had taken a powder. Maybe it was the sound of bones creaking and crackling that had pervaded her uneasy dreams and made her thrash Charlie's spare futon out of all recognition. Or the horrible, chilling sounds of gunfire as Ryan was left to deal with more of those things alone.

Or maybe it was the vision of the dead man's eyes, staring into Chess's own with wide, horrible calm. Of the woman's slumped, half-naked body, her hair clotted with drying blood.

Stop it, Chess. You knew what you were doing when you went out to hunt the skornac. Deal with it, dammit. Just deal with it.

The trouble was, she didn't want to deal with dead people. Dead demons, certainly; sometimes she could even pretend she was a character in a movie, watching particularly gruesome special effects. But a dead body she just couldn't pretend her way around. She stepped gratefully through the door and pulled it shut. It locked automatically as she slid her keys back in her pocket.

A short, dim hall turned into stairs at the end, the broom closet was to her left and the stairs going up to a back hall on the main floor slanted up on her right. She heard the drone of a weekend at the library, the indistinct noise of people speaking softly and pages turning, not to mention computers humming, and relief wrapped her in a warm blanket even as she sniffed back a sneeze. She was so cold she'd stopped shivering, and damn near soaked through. It was a blessing to be out of the wind.

She edged down the hall, grabbed the banister, and descended into the cavern of the basement. Shelves full of boxed files and other supplies jumbled together, the old boiler crouching far back and seeming to glower even though it was dead and dusty, turned off. Chess moved to her right, penetrating the tangle of odds and ends, sloping metal bookcases and boxes of decorations.

Along the far back wall, two bookcases leaned crazily next to a blank space of wall. The first time she'd found the library, she'd been feeling around in total darkness, muttering imprecations against anyone who had voted down the last bond issue and their families unto the seventh generation, when her hand had closed around a chill, carved iron doorknob.

Now she simply strode for the blank piece of wall. It looked just like a bit of wasted space, the bookcases on either side arching over to slump against each other higher up, both twice as tall as Chess, the top shelves reachable only with the help of an ancient stepstool. Her wet sneakers squeaked and probably left prints on the dusty floor, but it was such a jumble down here nobody would notice. She sniffed, getting a good lungful of dust and the unpleasant smell of a cellar, before reaching out toward the blank wall and confidently closing her fingers.

The knob was there, cool and hard and solid even if she couldn't see it. Chess twisted it and stepped through the door, keeping her eyes closed against the sudden vertigo that would happen when her eyes tried to convince her brain this was a *solid wall, and dammit, you can't walk through it!*

Just as she swept the door closed from the other side she thought she heard something, a soft footstep or a sigh. But she sneezed immediately, destroying all hope for getting through the beginning of winter without a cold. *Dammit. I knew I should have taken some zinc.*

She snapped her fingers twice. *"Fiat lux."* Her voice fell flat and chill, as if she had suddenly closed herself in a windowless space. Well, she had. "Light."

And the silver trickle of light bloomed. Chess heaved a relieved sigh. Nobody knew about this place, which made it the safest damn place for her in the whole damn city.

Time to do some research, she thought, and sneezed again, miserably. *How about we make a hot cuppa tea and dry off a bit first, though? Don't want to drip on the books.*

* * * *

The room was long and rectangular, with a vaulted ceiling that was much higher than it should have been. It appeared to be walled in solid stone, with flagstones that seemed oddly like the ones in the troll tunnels under Jericho, fitted together with such precision the floor was a little slippery if you weren't careful. Long butcher-block tables almost black with glossy varnish marched down the middle, and along all three walls were high bookshelves full of leather spines. Dust never seemed to settle here, and the light came from silvery crystal globes hanging from the ceiling, brightening in response to need—soft and luminous when she was mixing up the salve or experimenting with the jars of herbs and other substances from the cabinet in the far left corner, bright and clear when she needed to read. She'd given up wondering how the lights seemed to know what she was doing.

The only thing wrong with this library was that it had no electric plug-ins. The bathroom was a small closet off to the side, with a sink and an antique commode, but no mirror. And forget *hot* water. She suspected the plumbing in here used a well or something, since the water had a flat mineral taste different than city water. Just to be safe, she'd brought down water-purification pills and a rack of bottled water.

On the furthest table were beakers and pristine antique spirit lamps, racks for holding glass jars, candles, and other assorted objects. It had looked, when she'd first stumbled into the room, as if the owner had just stepped away for a moment, a book open on the table to the recipe for the salve, and a capped jar of the stuff next to it, amid a jumble of assorted minutiae. She'd cleaned everything up, over the six months of study, and wondered about the anonymous owner who wrote his small crab-cramped words in the diaries.

Now she knew.

A stack of towels and a spare pair of jeans, not to mention a dry shirt, worked wonders; keeping a spare set of clothes at work was second-nature to her. After boiling some water for tea with the same trick she'd used to convince Charlie, she went straight for the back wall, where on the third bookcase bottom shelf was a long row of antique composition books, each written in with a firm, clear hand. She'd only worked her way through three of them, they were closely written and hard to decipher as well as rambling, a nameless narrator that she now suspected was Melwyn Halston giving advice on the books in the library, shortcuts for killing or repelling demons, recipes, and other useful information.

She took the last book on the far right, gently, and carried it back to one of the tables. Hopped up on the varnished wood surface, sitting cross-legged and setting her tea mug aside. She sneezed, twice, lightly, and touched her hair, wrapped up in a towel. *Yet more laundry. Nobody told me the cleanup is worse than the demon hunting itself.*

She opened up the diary, flipping through it until she came to the blank pages at the back and then backing up a few more pages. *Bingo. And I thought I was just being systematic when I started from the earliest ones. I should have started with the latest.*

For there on the page, written in the spidery, clear, small hand of whoever had built this room, was the word *Drakulein*, repeated several times through the text. She paged back even further, found that the whole book had references to them salted through. The Inkani were also mentioned, and once or twice she saw the word *Malik*.

Perfect. She opened to the first page, settled down, and began to skim, paying special attention whenever the Drakul were mentioned. *The Golden usually have one or two Drakul bodyguards. It's not as bad as it seems. I'll be careful, I just need you to understand a few things.* Ryan's voice floated through her head.

I wonder if he's still back in my apartment. If he knows what's good for him, he is. She scanned a few more pages, came across a drawing of a human hand, beautifully executed, a man's hand with a heavy, square antique ring. The caption read, *Samuel's hand.*

She began to get the idea that Melwyn had been a little

closer to Samuel than she'd suspected. A few passages were almost blushworthy in a repressed, Victorian fashion. And the drawings were something else. *Looks like ol' Mel had his artistic side freed. I've heard May-December relationships can do that.* Her own sniggering giggle made her feel a little dirty.

Ryan had told her the truth. He just hadn't told her *how* serious the situation was. Once a Drakul got "attached" they didn't live without the object of their "affections." Mel mentioned that same-sex pairings were rare; and he didn't have the angst she would have associated with a nineteenth-century homosexual relationship. Then again, if Mel was as old as Ryan said, he might have a whole different view of that sort of thing.

She also began to suspect that Ryan had deliberately not shown her just how strong and quick he *really* was. Some of the terms Melwyn used were thought-provoking, to say the least.

It was a constant battle for Mel to keep his "territory" clean of Inkani and other demons, and she had a hazy sense that he was talking about a much larger piece of land than just Jericho City. Then again, this was in the age of carriages and bad roads, distances might have seemed larger then. There were other Drakul, mostly identified with a first initial; Samuel was the only one who rated a whole name. And Melwyn constantly bemoaned the lack of "potentials" to help him out. Sam suspected that the Inkani had found some way of killing them before they "awakened," but Mel pooh-poohed that idea, saying that people simply weren't as smart or as good as they used to be.

Melwyn, you sound like a cynic. And a grumpy old man.

By far the most interesting were the references scattered through the text to books she hadn't gotten around to yet. She found herself making a mental list and wishing she'd started with this particular diary first. That was the trouble with finding a library of antique sorcerous books, one never knew the right place to start.

She finished the tea and ended up lying on the table, wincing as she shifted and her body reminded her she'd put it through hell lately. *I should go home. But this is so interesting. I suppose I could fit it in my purse, but I don't want to damage it and I don't want anyone knowing for sure where these books are.* She yawned, stretching, her ribs protesting at the hard table. *Need to find a way to smuggle a pillow in here. This is getting ridiculous.*

Chess rolled over on her back, looking up at the vaulted ceiling. Her sock feet were a little chilled, but she'd long since grown used to the even sixty-five degrees down here. It was probably thanks to the stone walls that the temperature never wavered. Her hair was almost dry now, and she'd only sneezed twice. She reached up, touched her lips with her fingertips, felt Ryan's mouth on hers again. *I'm not* all *animal,* he'd said, with that bitter twist to his mouth. The unspoken attitude—that the Drakul were somehow second-class because they were part demon—got to her. Even Paul, who might have turned out to be decent, had acted like he had the right to boss Ryan around.

About the only person in this whole goddamn thing who understands anything is Ryan, she realized. He'd believed her when she'd denied knowing anything about Paul's disappearance, he'd fought a demon away from her window, been waiting in her apartment for her, worried sick. As men went, he wasn't half bad. And he was easy on the eyes, definitely. Nice shoulders. A good mouth, when it wasn't pulled tight with bitterness. Those black eyes.

From now on, it's your side I'm on. Trust me.

He'd been telling the truth all along, even if he hadn't told her *everything.* Of course, she wasn't guaranteed to react calmly to any of this.

Chess sighed and stretched, almost knocking over her empty tea mug. It took ten minutes to clean everything up, leaving the diary on the table nearest the door with all the other books she wanted to take a look at as soon as she had time. The lights dimmed as she made one more circuit of the room, checking for anything left out, a habit learned after years of working in a library. Everyone should be home by now, she felt as if she'd been down here for hours. ·

He's probably worried. No wonder he didn't want me to go to Charlie's last night. Maybe I should have stayed home. She shrugged back into her damp jacket, pulling it down over her purse. Carried the helmet to the door, stopped to glance one last time over her shoulder. *Maybe I'll bring Ryan down here. He'll probably have a better idea of what to do with all these than I will. And he can probably tell me a better way of going about doing my research.*

The thought made her heart feel a little lighter.

It was well past sunset, and misty rain hung in the uneasy, windy air. Ryan was probably climbing the walls by now. The streetlamps were all out. Darkness slid oily up against the side of the library as Chess tucked her keys in her pocket. *That's odd.* She set off along the side of the building, her head down against the wet wind; the library was dark too. Of course, a Saturday evening, who would want to spend it here?

Nobody except me, I guess. Nobody except a boring old demon-hunting librarian.

Vox Street was uncharacteristically dark as well. Her sneakers made soft wet sounds against the pavement as she walked, the wind now cutting across her path only when she crossed the street. Dampness began to soak back through her jacket. *I'm wet, I'm cold, and I'm hungry. I can't wait to get home and fix myself some chicken-noodle soup. And have a big jigger of Scotch. It might be time to open that bottle.*

The sound was soft and distinct, a soft dragging. Like a wet footstep. She didn't speed up or slow down, but she did pull up her jacket, her right hand rooting around for the flap of her bag. Her heart started to hammer. *I don't like the sound of that.* Her nape suddenly began to crawl, her damp hair chill and cold against her skull. *What is it? Is something following me? Oh, goddammit. Now's a fine time to wish Ryan was around.*

Her hand closed around the hilt just as she heard something else.

A low, chilling growl that made her skin feel tight and stretched thin, as if electric needles had suddenly been pressed against her and switched on. She tore her hand free of the bag, the knife's hilt slipping a little in her suddenly sweaty palm. Her sneakers scraped as she whirled, blue light suddenly darting harshly from the blade; she'd yanked it free of the sheath. *Thank God for small favors*—But her mouth was suddenly cotton-dry, heartbeat thudding in her ears and throat. *Oh, God. God . . .*

"Grady?" she whispered. *OhmiGod. He's one of them.*

Bones cracked and crackled as the library aide, his shoulders hunching, seemed to grow a full foot in under twenty seconds. His horn-rimmed glasses fell, one lens cracking as they hit the pavement and spun away. Grady's shirt hung on him as if he was a scarecrow in last year's model. His jacket fell too, his face becoming skeletal as it thinned, his jaw suddenly swelling. His teeth seemed to shift shape, one of them popping out of his mouth and curving to a wicked point.

Was he waiting for me? I thought I heard something as I went through the door. Oh, God.

Her hand, holding the glittering-blue knife, lowered slightly. Her helmet hit the pavement with a sharp cracking sound. *Fucking hell. I can't kill him. He's a volunteer.*

"Grady—" Her voice wouldn't work properly. She sounded as if the air had been punched out of her.

What do you know, that's how I feel. Grady? One of them? What did he sell his soul for?

Grady made a chilling little squeal that sounded like he was trying to laugh. Then he leapt.

Sixteen

"Get *down!*"

The scream came from his right, but he was too goddamn busy to worry about it. Paul moved with the speed trained into Malik by constant practice, smashing her out of the way, and Ryan hit the Inkani dog *hard,* felt bones snap under the force of his blow. The knife tore up, the curse glowing along its blade, ripping through skin gone hard and leathery with armor-plating. He only had a few critical seconds while the dogsbody finished changing to get in the final blow. If he let it go much further he'd have to spend some serious effort kicking its ass.

Etheric force crackled, a Drakul's fighting-aura, almost visible in the wet air. Paul yelled, a shapeless sound. The dog's neck cracked as Ryan backhanded it with just the right amount of force, the sound like a dry branch snapped in half. The body crumpled, he shook foul black blood off his knife and half-turned on his heel, scanning for more of them.

Christ.

The street was dark, all the lamps either busted or refusing to work. Chess lay on her side, her hair ripped free of its usual sleek braid and her eyes wide, dark, and uncomprehending just before they closed. His chest hurt, a swift slicing pain—*she's alive, thank you God, alive, I owe you one*—and Paul was on one knee, crouched in front of her, his left hand reaching down, fingers tented, to touch the wet pavement. His right hand was up, the gun trained on the *irikornac*, which hunkered down growling, its red eyes infernos and its forked tail lashing. *Just greaAt. A leaper.*

The *irikornic* looked like a humanoid flea with red eyes and high pointed ears, its skin smooth and gray. It crouched, tail lashing, muscles bunching in its massive legs. You didn't often see leapers. They were unable to camouflage their essential weirdness and, as such, were often kept as bodyguards or personal pets by the High Ones, much as human druglords kept pit bulls and mastiffs.

Don't tell me there's a High One in this city. Please God, don't let there be one here so soon.

"Ryan?" Paul didn't sound panicked, but the leaping iron taste of adrenaline filled the air. Chess groaned, a shapeless sound.

"Got it." Ryan reached for another knife, spinning the hilt of the one in his right hand until the blade lay flat against his forearm. "Be mellow, Grasshopper. I'm on it." *Irikornic* tracked with their aural receptors. Ryan deliberately scuffed his feet, attracting its attention. "Come on over here, you stupid little bitch. Come on."

It leapt, blurring with demonic speed. Ryan dropped, a sullen-red flash sparking as he shoved etheric force into his knife and smashed upward, ripping. The thing screeched, an unholy sound, and he heard the sound that was every Drakul's nightmare: the thin, high, silver chill of an ultrasonic hunting-cry, far too close for comfort. His head met concrete with stunning force. He shook off the blow and ended up flat on his back.

Steaming meat collapsed, rancid black blood boiling on his skin and scalp, slicking his hair to his head. He'd hit the soft spot just under its ribs and nicked a blood-channel. Lucky shot, luckier than he deserved. His foot socked into its solar plexus and he shifted, ready to push it off to the side.

"Ryan? *Orion!*"

He shoved the limp, rotting body away, made it to his feet. "*What*?"

Chess's knife spun between Paul's fingers, its light scoring into Ryan's eyes. Paul lowered the knife. "They're close. *Really* close."

"Where's the key?" He made it to them in record time, almost skidding to a stop and going down on one knee. "Is she—"

"Just stunned, I think. Her pulse is good, respiration sound." Paul held up the broad, flat motorcycle key. "I'll get her bike. Can you handle her?"

We shouldn't split up, but on that motorcycle you can outrun anything short of a High One. "I can handle her. She's lighter than you."

"A little bitty thing."

"But sharp." But his eyes were on Chess even as Paul fished in her purse, yanking her coat up. For a moment, the idea of another man touching her—even a Malik—made red rage rise under his breastbone. She lay on her side, her eyelids fluttering and her skin waxen-pale. He reached down to take her shoulders and gather her up. *How hard did he hit her?*

It's a damn good thing he got her out of the way, the spider was almost on her. He touched her cheek, a rill of pleasure spreading down his arm. She looked just like she was sleeping, instead of knocked unconscious by a Malik pounding her with both physical and sorcerous force to get her *out* of the way. But she wasn't bleeding.

Paul got the knife back in its sheath, shoved her purse back where it belonged, and yanked her jacket down with one quick, efficient jerk, the Fang safely stowed. "Come on."

It took a moment, but he had Chess over his shoulder and carried her to the empty parking lot, where the motorcycle crouched sleek and gleaming under a cedar tree. *I'm not even going to ask you where you found that thing, sweetheart.* The attendant was gone, his cubicle dark and forlorn, and that didn't seem quite right. He discarded the thought as immaterial. They wouldn't be here long. He could hear her heartbeat; it was, as Paul had said, reassuringly strong. She was breathing too, beginning to stir.

The motorcycle roused itself, its kickstand popped up and its seat swiped free of water. Paul grinned. "She's got great taste."

She obviously loves it. The way Chess had touched the motorcycle before leaving it here this morning had told him *that* much. Even if he had almost missed her speeding out of the parking garage on it. "Take care of that thing, or I'll sic her sister on you. Godspeed."

"You too. See you soon." And Paul eased it out of the parking spot and turned right on Vox Street. Then he gunned it, and Ryan sighed.

Another high, crystalline hunting-cry shook the air. Ryan didn't hesitate, cutting diagonally across the lot and gaining the safety of a dark alley. He muscled up a metal ladder bolted to the side of a brick building, handling her slight weight carefully. He reached the roof just as she stirred again and made a low moaning noise.

Hang in there, sweetheart. He reached the roof just as the heavens opened. Cold rain began slashing down, the storm front he'd been smelling for hours while watching the library dumping yet another load of water on the weary earth below—and not so incidentally, blurring his trail.

The hunting-cry came again, like a crystal glass stroked just right, chilling his skin and calling up a tide of instinct from the darkest basement of his mind. *Hunting. And she's the prey.* More speed, breath tearing in his lungs. She was awake and starting to struggle.

He found a handy, defensible corner behind a billboard tacked to the top of a three-story concrete building that, from the smell, housed a dry cleaners, and eased her off his shoulder. The billboard cut the force of the wind, and he found himself holding Chess's slim shoulders and restraining the urge to shake her. "Calm down, sweetheart. It's only me." *I hope you're glad to see me.*

"Ryan?" She sounded dazed. Her eyes were dark, her hair sticking in damp tendrils to her forehead. But her pupils were even, her breathing slightly fast but nothing to be worried about, and she wasn't bleeding. "What the . . . *Ryan?*"

Sorry, sweetheart. He leaned down, kissed her forehead, slid his fingers under her hair and checked her skull. She hadn't hit her head. He checked her ribs, too, sensitive fingertips trying to sense even hairline fractures. "Christ," he whispered against her forehead. *I never want to do that again. Trying to track you across a city while keeping a Malik with me is not a good time. And if there's a High One in town . . .*

"Ryan?" She tried to twist away from him, and his fingers clamped down on her nape, stilling her.

"Just *stay still*. What the hell were you thinking, woman?" He scanned the rooftop, heard the hunt-cry rise again. Was it farther away? Chess shuddered, and the small movement brought her closer to him. He filled his lungs with her smell, under the thin copper of adrenaline: warm gold, female, the summa of every good thing in the world now. "Christ. Thank God you're safe."

"What are you doing here?" It was a fierce, shrill whisper, but at least she held still. "Did you *follow* me?"

He was about to answer, but glancing out over the rooftop again made him uneasy. The instinct was unerring, born of wars in dark places, protecting a Malik and keeping back the tide of demons so normal people could go about their oblivious lives. He clapped his free hand over her mouth, gently, the touch of her lips sending another hot flare of sensation through him. "Be quiet. Can you be quiet?"

Her eyes were huge. It wasn't his imagination, the gold in them was much more pronounced. *I think that was the worst fucking moment of my life, wondering if I was going to get there in time. Thank God for Paul.*

She nodded deliberately. Swallowed, the movement visible even in the darkness. The wind shifted, rain smacking the other side of the billboard, and he heard the slight shifting sound that meant something had arrived on the rooftop. Chess's eyes flicked past him. Whatever color she had left in her face drained away and her right hand patted her side, desperately searching for her knife, safe in her purse.

"Don't worry." She probably couldn't hear him over the rain and the sudden inaudible sound of bloodlust curling over the roof, but he told her anyway. "Everything's all right." Here, with possible avenues of escape and only Chess to worry about protecting instead of both her *and* the Malik, things were much more palatable.

He let go of her and half-turned, his eyes moving over the rooftop. *Not bad*, he thought. Three leapers and a spider. *That tears it. Of course a High One's in town. The question is, where is he? Not like a pretty piece of high demonflesh to come out in the rain. So this is a tracking party, probably under the control of the spider there or another spider on the ground.* The knife appeared in his hand, and the rain began to steam before it hit his skin. He was radiating again. Of course. Here with her to protect, he wasn't disposed to play very nicely with his new friends.

Ryan moved out from the shelter of the billboard just as the first *irikornic* sprang. He heard Chess's short terrified inhale and felt a nasty flare of happiness that she was, at least, worried about him before the red rage of combat took over.

* * * *

"Hold still." She bit her lip fetchingly, and dabbed at the scrape with the cotton ball. Her hair, tangled and dark, fell in her eyes. She found her apartment comforting, her pulse rate dropped as soon as she was inside. Paul hissed out between his teeth, Ryan's eyes were locked to Chess's profile. She was pale, extraordinarily pale. Her sodden sweatshirt jacket was tossed in the laundry hamper and her jeans were damp to the knee. But her hands were steady, and she cleaned the long, vicious claw-swipe on Paul's forehead before dipping her finger in the mint and wormwood ointment and applying a thick streak of it. "There. Does it sting?"

"Yes."

"Good. How long have you two been following me?" She

slanted a dark glance at Ryan, who stood by her window, occasionally looking out and down into the alley. His T-shirt was in rags, his coat wasn't much better, and his jeans were just starting to dry. For all that, he felt the slight trembling in his bones, weariness over a deep well of fury. He was wound far too tightly, accepted it, and kept breathing, not seeking to calm himself down.

He'd fought them free of the leapers, and she'd put up with being carried by a running Drakul. *Manhandled* was the word she'd used, and she wasn't too happy about being followed. It was probably the damn library, it would take a fool not to figure out what she'd been doing inside that building with its soaring, beautiful lines. Paul had canvassed the place from top to bottom during the day and hadn't found her, but Ryan's instincts had shouted with crystal clarity that she *was* in there, and hours after she'd gone in, she'd walked right out again. So either there was a library inside the library, or it was a way to shake pursuit . . . but that was ridiculous. With the amount of demonic activity on the streets, she'd have been picked up if she surfaced anywhere else. She'd spent the whole time inside the library, in some corner that for some reason a Malik couldn't find.

"You didn't seriously think we'd let you wander out on the streets alone?" Paul didn't sound conciliatory in the least. "We saw hunting teams last night, out looking for you. You're in danger, girl."

She shook her head, as if he was too dense for words. Dug in her purse for her knife, jammed it back into her demon-hunting bag. Ryan hoped she wasn't planning on going out again tonight. Spending the night on a rooftop with a complaining Malik was never fun. He had no desire to crouch outside in the rain again, even if it was to protect his Golden.

"You *followed* me. For how long? To Charlie's? All *night*?" Chess's tone could have broken glass.

"We spent all night on a goddamn roof, and we've spent all day in alleys, freezing our asses off and waiting for you. And when you come out, you prance right up to an Inkani dog—"

"That's enough, Paul." The flat tone of finality in his own voice startled Ryan. It startled Chess, too. She gave him another, longer glance before capping the ointment jar and setting it with a precise click back on the table. Was that gratefulness in her eyes? If it was, he'd bottle Paul's mouth physically, if he had to. "Leave her alone."

"I told you guys to wait here," she muttered darkly, swiping her tangled hair back out of her eyes. "I *distinctly* remember telling you to wait here!"

"Would you have preferred to face the Inkani on your own?" He had the small nasty satisfaction of seeing her shudder, her cheeks white as paper. "The nice thing to do would be to thank me." *I am, after all, fucking covered in blood. Not to mention with half my clothes shredded. But that's okay. I don't mind fighting, if you're safe.*

Her hands curled into fists. "You know, I was actually feeling *charitable* toward you when I left the library."

Well, that's something. "Thank you." *If I sounded any more sarcastic I'd probably choke on my own words.*

She stared at him as if she couldn't decide whether to scream or throw something, and finally settled for stalking toward her bedroom. "Get cleaned up, get bandaged up. Then we're going to have a little talk about what *stay here* means."

His mouth threatened to curl into a smile. "I sit and heel like a good boy. But I don't play dead very well." *Oh, Christ. Did I just say that?*

Chess stopped so quickly she almost overbalanced, staring at her bedroom door. Her tangled dark hair fell down on either side of her face. Her eyes glittered, and her hands were clenched so tightly he was almost afraid she would hurt herself.

She was so goddamn beautiful his heart threatened to stop.

"I don't want to do this anymore."

He doubted Paul heard her. She merely whispered, as if she thought she was speaking but couldn't get together the air to do so. Ryan's mouth had gone dry. She smelled of paper and dust, and the night outside drenched with rain. She smelled of the adrenaline of recent danger and of the clean gold that was *her*, the same woman who sat at her kitchen table and sobbed into her hands, quiet and alone.

The woman he had fallen in love with.

And over that smell, the sharp spike of fear and anger, taunting his control. He was vulnerable to her fear. *Be gentle, Drakul. Be as gentle as you can, she's not used to this. She should never have had to see any of this.*

"Don't want to do what anymore? Hunt demons?" His voice sounded strange even to himself. Paul glanced up from the table and just as quickly looked down, his cheeks flaming with embarrassment Ryan could smell, as well as the persistent tang of fear. *I could have lost you.* "That's a profound relief to me, really. Because you're going to get yourself killed, Chess."

She all but vibrated with tension, and it teased at his control. The demon in his head stirred, tested the air, and subsided, secure in its strength. Soothed by her presence, even though she was strung tighter than a tripwire. But if she became much more upset, the demon would wake. This time, he wouldn't be able to put it to sleep without her body, without the oldest tranquilizer known to man.

If she pushed him too far over the edge he wouldn't be able to stop when she said *no.* And there was only one word for that, not a pretty word either.

"I don't mind the demons." She swallowed, her throat moving. Stared at her bedroom door. "It's the dead bodies I can't handle. You *killed* people, Ryan. People are *dead.* I *don't want to do this anymore.*"

Paul spoke up. "Then come with us. We've got to get you out of town. It's too dangerous. In a week or so, when the Malik have arrived in force, we can—"

"No." She shook her head.

Goddammit, Paul, rabbit-talking again. We're staying here where it's safe. "Chess—"

"No."

Ryan was fast losing the battle with himself. "Goddammit, Chess—"

"*No!*" She all but screamed, rounding on him, her eyes burning with gold and a faint golden glimmer crackling in the air around her. Ryan's jaw threatened to drop. *A mantle. She's producing a mantle.*

Holy Christ. He'd been told about mantles, the etheric force of the Golden taking on the shape of a full Phoenicis, golden wings and golden proportions, the beauty of a bird made of sunfire. But he had never dreamed he'd ever *see* it. The wings trembled, furled close to her body, not yet ready to spread. Few demons could stand even a weak mantle. And not even a High One could stand a full-grown Phoenicis with a full mantle. That's why they killed potentials. If he could just keep her alive long enough to train her, she still would be be fragile—but not nearly as easy to kill. She would have a *chance.*

For a few moments it glimmered, and a hot wind seemed to slide through the room, touching every surface with a golden flush. The smell was unutterably sweet, as if Chess had been distilled down to her bare essence and tinted with amber. He took a deep breath, even as the golden light threatened to spear through his eyes and strike pain into the cold darkness of his demon-bred bones.

He took another deep breath. Held her eyes, squinting to see through the shield of golden light that drained away, swirling as it dissipated. *We'll be lucky if nobody notices that, she's pulling on all the etheric strings around here, making a big disturbance. Christ.* "Chess." His voice was flat, level. "I'm on your side, remember? Nobody's side but yours. You're upset. You've had to deal with something no rational person should have been forced into dealing with. Just relax a little."

"Relax? *Relax?* People are *dead.* Grady's *dead.* They're *dead!*"

Who the hell is Grady? "If you're talking about the Inkani spiders, they were dead the second they signed their souls over to the demons. If you're talking about the civilians . . . yeah, they're dead." *No reason to sugarcoat the truth.* "My job is to make sure you don't join them. And, if I can, to keep any more people from dying. I didn't kill them. The Inkani did." *Come on, sweetheart. See reason. Help me out here. Use that fantastic wonderful brain of yours and figure this out.*

Her fingers loosened, her shoulders slumped under the now-dry T-shirt. Had he gotten through to her?

"Get cleaned up." Her voice was toneless. "Then get out of my goddamn house."

I don't think so, sweetheart. Nobody in this apartment is going anywhere until I decide it's safe. "I am not going to let the Inkani kill you." Just as toneless. "You're not getting rid of me. That's final."

"It's *my* house."

That doesn't mean shit to a demon, sweetheart. "And I'm *your* Drakul. Have the sense to listen to me. Go change. Paul will cook you dinner."

"I could call the cops. I could call *Charlie.* I can have you evicted. You can't—"

He met her glare with one of his own, peeling his shoulders away from the wall and drawing himself up to his full height.

"Try me." He heard the growl rattling in his chest. "Just try me, sweetheart. Give me an excuse." *If you don't stop this I'm going to drag you into your bedroom and undress you. After we get a few things straight about who's in charge when there's a city full of Inkani and no goddamn help in sight.*

She whirled away, stamped toward her bedroom, and slammed the door. The bathroom light came on, and the shower started. It was no use. He could still hear the sound of her sobbing.

"Good one," Paul muttered.

"Shut up." Ryan unfolded his arms. *If you weren't a Malik I'd kick your ass for pissing her off.* "Don't you start too. I'm going to go up to the roof, take a look around. If she leaves this apartment I'm going to be very upset."

"Hurry up, then." Paul's tawny head bent over the tabletop, but his shoulders were shaking. Whether it was from tension or repressed mirth, Ryan didn't want to know.

Seventeen

Chess didn't bother to leave her bedroom, simply took a long, hot shower and collapsed in bed, unwilling to let the day get any more complicated. If the world wanted to go on, that was fine—but it would have to go on without her. Besides, she was bone-deep exhausted. Pulling a pillow over her head to shut out her problems sounded like a *damn* good idea, better even than eating.

She woke out of a sound sleep when Ryan's hand closed over her mouth; his other hand touched her shoulder, shook her. Gently, but she wasn't fooled. He could dislocate her arm in a hot second if he felt like it. He smelled like a winter night, cold and full of rain, with smoky anger boiling off him in waves. Chess instinctively tried to squirm away, her pulse skyrocketing; he didn't let her move. "Quiet." A mere breath of sound, somehow menacing anyway. "Or I'll tie you up."

He sounded serious, and Chess's eyes suddenly seemed far too big for their sockets. She yanked the blanket and tried to wriggle away again. He didn't even seem to notice. "Don't be ridiculous, I wouldn't," he whispered. "Just making sure you're awake, you slept all day. Get up, get dressed."

His hand left her mouth slowly, his fingertips brushing her cheek. "What's going on?" *I slept all day?* The room suddenly didn't seem to have any air left.

"Get dressed, Chess. There's something going on, and I'm nervous." His eyes glittered in the near-dark, dusky light fading in her window. She *had* slept all day. "Want to be ready to move." He loomed over the bed, and Chess suddenly felt like an idiot. Now that she'd had a chance to catch up on sleep in her own bed, she felt a lot less unsteady—but *hungry*. She wanted an omelet, dripping with melted cheese. Bacon. Pancakes with maple syrup. It was nighttime again, and all she was craving was breakfast food. Her body clock was *all* screwed up. It didn't look like she'd be able to sleep in Monday morning either.

He let go of her arm, too, and straightened. Buster Keaton looked mournfully over his shoulder, his eyes infinitely sad.

"What's happening?" *Don't let it be any more dead bodies. Please, God, don't let it be any more dead bodies.*

"It's too quiet out there. I've got a bad feeling about this. Come on, get dressed."

"I suppose you're going to watch." *Why am I whispering?* "A little bit of privacy would be nice."

"Maybe I like watching you." She saw the gleam of teeth in a smile, before he ghosted across to her window, peered out. "I promise I won't look. Unless you want me to."

She stretched, yawning. It was cold, so cold she wondered if the heaters had stopped working. Slid her feet out of bed, shivering. "I can't figure out whether I like you or want to heave you out the window."

"You don't have to like me. I'm just here to keep you alive." The way he said it almost hurt.

"I spent the day reading Melwyn Halston's last diary. Did you know he was involved with a Drakul? Guy was named Samuel. They were apparently really tight—"

"Chess, get dressed." His shoulders were rigid. "Please."

"I *am* getting dressed." She was already in a T-shirt and boxers, and she grabbed jeans, underwear, and socks, retreating to the bathroom. The light stung her eyes, and she shivered as she used the toilet and dressed quickly, tying her hair back in a sloppy ponytail. *You idiot, I'm trying to be nice to you.* Her teeth almost chattered as she opened the door and stepped out, was temporarily blinded when Ryan reached around the corner and flipped off the bathroom light.

"There's a scout in the alley." His tone was so calm, he sounded like he was ordering a pizza. "You'll need a coat."

A demon? Outside? "Did you turn the heat off?" She edged for her closet, found a sweater by touch, and pulled it over her head.

"No. Are you cold?"

She nodded, forgetting it was dark. "My coat's in the hall clos—"

He seemed to blur through space, ending up with his arm around her, spinning as the window shattered and the warding laid across it fluoresced into the visible spectrum, popping and hissing as threads of energy snapped. Chess let out a short, sharp yell, found herself shoved toward the door as Ryan cursed, a sharp vehement sound. Her fingers closed around the doorknob as something snarling and smelling horribly fetid landed with a thump inside her bedroom window. Chess yanked on the door and found she was breathless. The high, thin screaming sound was *her,* and she tore the bedroom door open and spilled out into her living room.

Growls and thumps shook the building. She heard Ryan's voice, cursing again, and the shivering sound of breaking glass. *That was probably my Keaton print! Goddammit!*

Her demon-hunting bag was on the kitchen table. Chess bolted for it, running behind the couch and hooking around the wall into the dining room. There was another confused flurry of motion, more glass breaking, and Paul appeared out of the darkness near her living-room window, a gun roaring. She actually *saw* the muzzle flash and ran into her table, almost tripping over a teetering stack of physics and English textbooks. Her bag was over her head in a trice, thank God she'd put her knife back in it.

All right. I think I can handle this. She plunged her right hand in her bag, whirling back toward the window, her hip banging the table a good one. Her fingers closed around the hilt and she yanked the knife out just as her bedroom door shattered, something dark and human-sized flung through it with incredible force, demolishing the flimsy wood.

I am never going to get my damage deposit back. She took a deep breath, and blue light burst out as she dragged the knife free of her bag. "*In nominae Eumenidae, coniurat vax!*"

It was bastardized Latin, meant to show any demon hidden in the vicinity, but it worked. She heard a chilling scream of demonic pain as Ryan hauled himself up from the floor. He'd just been tossed through her bedroom door.

"*Ryan!*" Paul backed up, two guns in his hands, both leveled at a patch of snarling, rabid darkness cringing in the corner near the entertainment center. The TV screen glowed with blue phosphorescence, the smell of ozone crackling through her apartment. Her teeth chattered. She expected to see her breath plume on the air. *Why is it so cold?*

"I'm on it." Ryan sounded calm. "Chess?"

"What the fuck is it?" *Well, for once I sound capable of kicking ass.*

"Get her out of here, Paul. There's a High One close."

"Holy shit." Paul kept backing up, skirting her couch gracefully without looking. His guns were steady, but his hair stuck up anyhow. He looked as if he'd been awakened a little less gently than she had. Chess stared at the cringing thing. *High One? What does he mean, High One? I don't like the sound of that.*

"What do you mean, High—" The smell of burning charcoal and dried blood tainted the cool night wind pouring in through the broken window. Chess ducked reflexively, Paul let out a shapeless yell, and Ryan was suddenly *there*, colliding with the thing a scant two feet from Chess, driving it down next to her kitchen table with a cracking sound. He'd broken the floor, he'd hit it so hard.

Even the skornac wasn't that fast. It's a kibbik. Oh my God, a kibbik in my living room! She finally placed the smell, charcoal and copper, according to the books it was all teeth and hair and appetite.

And they usually roamed in packs.

It squealed in a falsetto that sawed right through Chess's head. She might have stabbed herself with her own knife while trying to clap her hands over her ears to shut it out, if the cry hadn't been cut short with a gurgle.

Ryan rose, spinning his knife around his fingers, black demon blood exploding free of the shining metal. "Put that thing away, Chess!" he barked. "Paul, get the fuck back here!"

"No need to shout." Paul had Chess's arm, hauled her up. He tried to wrestle the glowing-blue knife free of her numb fingers. Chess ripped away from him. "Let's go. Put the Fang away, girl, it might cripple him!"

What the— Understanding flashed. The knife affected anything demonic, it glowed whenever Ryan was around. It was either put the knife away and trust the Drakul, or keep the knife out and risk affecting him, maybe to the point he couldn't fight. "My knife," she said, numbly. "It's *my knife*, I'm not going to—"

"Please, Chess." Ryan had her arm. He squinted, his black eyes suddenly alive and alight with a feral intensity that made his face not only sharp but handsome. He dragged her into the kitchen, Paul moving behind them with his guns trained on the windows. "Just stick the knife in your bag or something. It *hurts.*"

Nope, definitely not going to get the damage deposit back, she thought inanely as she heard more scrabbling little sounds from her bedroom. *God, if you're listening, I'd really like to take all this back. Okay?*

"Christ, there's a whole tribe of them." Paul's voice was a little higher than usual. Ryan paused at Chess's front door just long enough to flip the locks. "The trouble with fucking Tribbles."

"Steady, Malik." Ryan pulled the door open. Chess flinched as yellow light from the hall fixtures flooded in. "They're planning on driving us out through the front door. Sloppy."

"Are you sure it's the front door they're planning on?" Paul dragged the door closed behind them and ran to keep up, Ryan's long strides eating the distance. "Chess, goddammit, put the knife away."

"That's my *house*," she heard herself protest. "They're in my *house!*"

"Everything in there can be replaced, one way or another. You can't." Ryan reached over, grabbed her wrist, and shoved her hand back into her bag. "That's better. Remember the rules, Chess? Move with me, stay behind me, don't grab my arm. And run when I tell you to." He was going the wrong way down the hall, toward the utility door instead of toward the door that led to the main stairs.

"Kibbik." Her voice was high and thin. "Roams in packs, smells of copper and the burning of charcoal. According to Morelly, vulnerable to garlic crushed into a paste; Delmonico scoffs at the idea—"

"We know what it is," Paul hissed. "Shut up."

"Leave her alone." Ryan's hand was bruising-hard on her arm, he all but dragged her. "It's her way of coping." He actually kicked the fire door off its hinges, the heavy door crumpled as if made of paper. "It's okay, Chess. Just keep close."

"Scavengers," she whispered. The knifehilt was slick against her palm, her hand trapped in her bag. Her teeth chattered as Ryan pulled her down the stairs, she honestly couldn't tell if her feet were even *touching* the steps.

"There's a High One out there." He sounded grim. "You've read about them if you've read Delmonico, the *siafeaine*. The Unnamed."

"The *Unnamed?*" Her voice bounced off the stairwell walls, it was oddly silent otherwise. Ryan made no more sound than a hunting cat, and Paul moved very quietly. "There's one of *those* out there?"

"There is. It's why you're so cold. Now be *quiet*, for God's sake, sweetheart."

Quit calling me that. The flood of irritation swept through her, slapped her into thinking again. *The Unnamed. Big, tough, unstoppable, another one of those "if you meet these, run and kiss your ass goodbye. Or in O'Mailey's words, "Make thy peace with God, hunter, for thou wilt face Judgment soon." Wonderful.* "How do you kill one of them?"

Ryan dragged her around a corner, his feet barely brushing the steps. "You don't. You get the hell out of here with Paul and leave it to me."

"Ryan—" Paul sounded as breathless as she felt. "You can't—"

"If I'm going to die, I'm going to die protecting her," he replied shortly. They reached the last flight of stairs, he slowed and glanced down at Chess. "You *go with Paul* if I tell you to. Clear?"

I am not leaving you to face an Unnamed alone. The words rose up, and she wondered why exactly she'd think something like that at a time like this. But she felt a burst of panic just under her breastbone when she thought of him facing down the worst type of demon—a demon that looked like a tall, thin humanoid with pale skin and incandescent eyes. Most demons were ugly, but the books couldn't agree if the Unnamed were ugly in a particularly beautiful way, a way that induced nausea—or if they *were* beautiful. Beautiful enough to warrant the worship some of them had received from human cults of spilled blood and flayed flesh.

The idea of a pretty demon made a hysterical laugh rise under her breastbone as Ryan stopped between one step and the next right inside the utility door. "I mean it, Chess." He looked like he did, too; his eyes flashed and his mouth drew into a thin line when he wasn't speaking. "*No* heroics. You get on your bike with Paul, and you get the hell out of town."

She shook her head, mute. *Not going to,* she thought. Her fingers tightened inside her bag, the hilt of her knife slipping in sweat.

Ryan didn't argue, he simply let go of her arm and ghosted to the utility door. He cocked his head, listening, and Chess clenched her jaw to keep her teeth from chattering. Her demon-hunting bag lay heavily against her hip; her fingers still curled around the hilt of her knife. The blurring, buzzing, prickling sensation of the knife reacting to demons jolted up her arm, now that she had time to pay attention to it. Her heart pounded thinly, and her mouth was dry. Creeping cold spilled through her arms and legs, she swayed.

Paul caught her arm, kept her upright. He said nothing,

watching Ryan. There was no trace of superciliousness or arrogance. Instead, he looked like a professional waiting for the right moment, having done everything he could and commended his soul to God.

She winced inwardly. *Why do you think of things like that at a time like this, Chess? Jeez.*

Then she began to hear little soft sliding sounds.

Gooseflesh prickled up her back. The sounds were too quick and light to be human. She'd never before imagined that the *sound* of footsteps could be terrifying in its inhumanity. Her eyes locked on Ryan's shoulders, his quarter-profile as he listened intently causing a funny flutter just under her ribs. *It's going to be okay. He's here.*

Ryan held up his hand. "Alley's clear," he mouthed. "They expected us out through the front, didn't know about this door. Cover Chess."

"Locked and loaded, baby." Paul sounded serious. There was a double click—hammers, on guns, drawn back. "No fucking Inkani's going to get his mitts on your girl, Drakul."

Up the stairs, there were little tapping sounds. Creaking. A snarl.

Ryan tore the door open and moved out. Paul pushed Chess in front of him. Darkness folded around them, the darkness of an alley where night came early, the last light fading from the cloudy sky. Cold caressed Chess's entire body, cold and the spilling terrible weakness she'd felt before. The alley slipped by in a blur, Ryan stopping to herd them through a door in the apartment building opposite, a door he simply wrenched open as if it wasn't locked. Metal pinged and hit the alley floor; it *had* been locked. The deadbolt glinted in the dim light as Paul dragged her past. "Ryan, she's passing out or something."

"Might be the High One." Ryan sounded thoughtful. They were in a long, dimly lit hall, doors opening off on either side. "This should bring us out on the street, and we'll have a fighting chance to get out."

"We like getting out. Getting out's good."

"Getting out safe's better."

"Well, nobody's disputing that."

They sound like they're at a party. God, get me out of this. I promise. No more fried food. No more extramarital sex. At least, not without love. Her brain kept veering like a frightened rabbit. A utility corridor, she realized. This was storage space or a utility corridor, just above the basement in the building next to hers.

The relief that came from solving that one simple puzzle was short-lived. The cold robbed her arms and legs of strength. She could barely keep up even with Paul dragging her. The prickling up her arm from the knife was the only thing keeping her on her feet; a warm wire of strength flooding up her arm and into her chest. She took a deep breath. Darkness swallowed them, she stumbled, and Paul's hand curled around her shoulder, held her upright.

"Um, Ryan? We can't see."

"It's all right. It gets better in a little bit. Just keep moving."

"Just keep moving, the man says." Paul spoke under his breath, and Chess began to get the idea that the banter was for *her* benefit. If there was a chance they would be overheard, Ryan would have insisted on silence. Instead, they were lightening the situation. Making jokes. Gallows humor.

Her teeth chattered until she clenched her jaw. It was *cold*, the type of cold that stole into her marrow like frozen lead, making her arms and legs heavy. There was something else, too; something that teased at the edges of her mind, something she should remember, some important thing she wasn't thinking of.

"It's getting colder," she whispered. "We're getting nearer to it. It was c-cold in the t-tavern t-too."

"It was? Don't worry, Chess. Everything's well in hand."

Don't worry, he says. I'm thinking I should be worrying right about now.

"Ryan—" This from Paul, whose hand suddenly bit into Chess's shoulder.

"Hang on a second." There was a sound, soft and scraping, then a jingle. Chess stopped short, her breath coming in shallow sips. "Everyone involved in this is forgetting one damn thing."

"What?" *I sound breathless.* The cold bit into her bones, her knees turned to water, and Paul held her up with an arm around her shoulders. *It's so cold. So cold.*

"I'm part demon," Ryan said, calmly enough. "And I'm not stupid. Something's wrong."

A faint edge of light appeared, a slice of dimness widening as he swept the door open. "Besides, there's something else. Something doesn't smell right here."

"What the hell do you—" Paul sounded like he'd been

punched.

And that was when all hell broke loose.

Chess screamed as *something* boiled through the door, a wave of coldness so intense it burned. Then Paul shoved her aside, into the doorjamb, and there was the roar of gunfire. But it sounded *wrong* somehow. She couldn't quite think of why. A long, howling scream, Ryan yelling her name, and a warm hand closed around Chess's left wrist, giving a terrific yank that almost dislocated her shoulder. Her knife suddenly blazed with hurtful blue radiance, there was a confused flurry of motion as whatever had her arm let go. Chess's knees hit the floor with a grating shock.

A terrific impact smashed against her right hand, knocking the knife away; it skittered uselessly on concrete and Chess looked up, dazed, into Paul's dark horrified eyes. *What did he . . . Why?* He'd kicked her, *kicked* the knife right out of her suddenly numb right hand.

She heard her own horrified gasp and a low sound of pain that sounded like Ryan's. Another sound, awfully familiar, as if a fist made of concrete had just hit a heavy bag. But the other low sound of pain she heard told her it wasn't a heavy bag, it was *Ryan*, someone had smacked him a good one.

Paul held the gun, and it was pointed at her. "Don't move, Chess." His lips were pulled back in a rictus of a smile, white sharp teeth gleaming in the sudden flare of crimson torchlight. "They want you alive. It'll all be over soon."

Eighteen

Darkness.

It was not the mothering darkness of night, the dark that called a hurtful flower of strength out from his demon half. No, this darkness was different. It closed around him like the steel jaws of a trap. He simply *existed* for a while, floating in the blackness, struggling to remember something very important. Something he had to do. The word came slowly, rising from the depths.

Chess.

Where was she? He had to find her.

Then the pain came, rolling in a great wave over him, and he returned to consciousness with a jolt. Red agony around his wrists, weight against his shoulders, he could barely breathe. His ribs felt like they'd been smashed in, and anklets of fiery pain closed around his ankles. He was *hanging*, and that told him what he needed to know even as the demon half of him felt others of its kind drawing close.

He forced his eyes open, a millimeter at a time. The light stung him, ruddy torchlight, fire straining and smoking against the choking breathless smell that was a High One. Salt stinging his eyes, too, sweat and warm blood, he felt the hot trickles from gaping holes in his chest. Four of them, nicely grouped.

Chess. Where is she? And the second thought: *Who? What happened? They shot me, shot in the back, I remember that. But there was nobody behind us, I was certain of that Nobody except—*

"I think he's coming around." A familiar voice.

What the fucking hell?

Metal clashed as he stirred, unable to stop himself. He lifted his head, one slow screaming inch at a time. Stinging in his eyes, a rivulet of something warm running down his throat from his ear, his shoulders shrieking with rusty iron and broken glass.

He hung, his ankles loaded with weighted chains that crackled with etheric force. The black lightning of demon sorcery crawled over the cuffs at his wrists, too, shackling even a Drakul's strength.

Then another voice, a voice that slid along his skin like tiny, frozen, razor mouths, their bite so cold it didn't hurt for the first few seconds. A sibilant, soft, *evil* voice. "He iss traitor to hiss kind." It was a High One. An unspeakable demon, a foulness on the face of Creation, one of the lords of hell.

And it was speaking to Paul.

The light ran through him. Paul and an Inkani.

What have you done? Jesus Christ, Paul, what have you done? It was impossible. *Im*-fucking-*possible.*

His mind began to work again through the screaming raw agony of pain from his wrists and shoulders. He was trained to function even through this blinding misery.

Paul had been gone from the rendezvous for days. The room had been rented out, a trap left for Ryan. Once the Inkani realized there was a potential in town, the High Ones would have come. They had been hunting down potentials for centuries and were damn good at it. They'd probably been alerted by the killing of the *skornac* and the golden scent that even then was following Chess around.

She was valuable, a potential so close to becoming a full Golden. The closer she was, the more powerful their Rite of Opening would be, and the more High Ones they could bring through to lord it over the skins.

But Paul didn't know she was a Golden!

No, he hadn't . . . but the books. The books would be valuable to the Inkani, to be used against the Malik. The *sheela* and the head librarian both stank of sorcery, and one of the library volunteers had been an Inkani dog. The demons had been trying to find the library for a long time, and Paul had taken himself off to strike a deal, certain the two women he suspected of knowing the cache's location would stay right where he wanted them, guarded by the dumb, faithful Drakul.

But first Paul had to find a demon who would listen, and then he had to bait and set the trap for Ryan. Once he found out Chess was the potential the Inkani were searching for, Paul had struck an even better deal. It all made sense now. And Paul had plenty of time to call in Chess's location while she was in the shower and Ryan was on the roof, checking the neighborhood.

Not only that, but the Malik flooding in to protect Chess would be walking blind into a trap full of the worst demons around. There would be horrible casualties.

"I know you can hear me." Paul's voice, soft and bored.

"Come on, Ryan. Wake up."

"Usselesss."

"You don't know him."

At least he still respects my abilities. His mouth was desert-dry. He opened his eyes further, straining.

The torchlight ran wet over stonekin-carved, fluid stone. It was a high arched chamber, proportioned subtly wrong. The chains hung from a hook at the very apex of the ceiling, and he knew without looking that the weights dangled into a circular shaft cut in the middle of the floor. The floor itself was sloped toward that maw, which would be floored with sharp iron spikes.

Sloped down, so that the blood would flow into the hole itself. It was a *drakarnus*, a torture chamber, built for one thing. Killing a Malik—or a Drakul—slowly.

One sharp, panicked burst of thought—*Chess, where is she, are they doing this to her?*—and then control clamped down, the often-tested control of a Drakulein in who the dark inheritance of demons ran stronger than most. He raised his head still more, and saw Paul. The man's sandy hair glowed in the crimson light, and he looked very pleased with himself, wearing the smile he usually wore after a long night spent with someone female. He was even wearing fresh clothing—that is, if you could call the long, dark robe *clothing*; it was an Inkani outfit. His dark eyes gleamed.

He looked, of all things, satisfied.

Think, Ryan. Quit flailing and think. They won't hurt her, she has to be whole for the Rite. They need her whole and perfect for their dirty work. Think, goddamn you!

Next to Paul was a thin, attenuated shape, and the growl rose in Ryan's chest. He couldn't help himself.

The High One blinked its fathomless blue eyes. It looked like a human; that was the worst part about them. Wide blue eyes, a sweetly-curved mouth, and a shock of dark hair matted into dreadlocks, each fat strand bound with writhing, silvery etheric force. The bladed cheekbones were subtly wrong, as was the shape of the nose, and the creature was corpse-pallid. Its six-fingered, wax-pale hands hung loosely by its sides, and it wore plain, dark, unornamented breeches and a simple shirt. The clothes did nothing to hide the essential *alienness* of the being, the way its joints moved with horrid oily grace, and how the air itself seemed to cringe away from it.

A killing smile hovered on the demon's lips. "Ah, the pup

growlss. Mayhap it hath teeth."

Warm salt dripped into Ryan's eyes. The burning in his chest was slender, silver-coated ammunition, deadly to demonkind. *Malik* ammunition. He would heal from it, his human half doing what his demon half could not—but slowly. Too slowly. "Paul." The word was a stone in his throat. "Where . . . is . . . she?"

"Safe. For now." Paul was literally beaming. "All the women you want, Orion. Think of it. Money. Slaves. We can have it *all*. We're on the winning side now, Drakul. Maybe after they're done with the Rite you can have what's left of her. You'd like that, wouldn't you?"

Oh, you son of a bitch. There won't be anything left of her once they finish. You know that. His eyes threatened to close, he forced them open. His fingers were insensate wood, swollen and useless, the weights strapped to his ankles robbed him of leverage. And he heard the soft drip, drip, drip of his own blood, coating the iron spikes below. "Malik." It was as close to accusation as he could come, with his cracked lips and swollen tongue. The pain drove red-hot pokers into his side, but he'd had worse. Much worse. *Chess. Where are you, sweetheart? Christ. A traitor Malik . . . why?*

"I'm tired of being a loser," Paul said. "Tired of rooftops in the rain, of cheapass hookers and ice-cold Malik bitches. Sick of doing what I'm told. You are too. I know you are, I see it in you. You're stronger and faster than any Malik, and they treat you like *crap*." He leaned forward, his tone dropping, becoming confidential. "Come on over to the winning side, Ryan. It's better that way. They'll even give you the librarian, after they're finished with her."

For a moment, Ryan thought rage might blind him. The fury rose, shoving aside the agony for one glorious red second— then retreated before the onslaught of pain as his battered body hung stretched between roof and chasm. Metal clashed and ground together, Inkani sorcery spitting and crackling as he swayed like a plucked string. His head flopped down, his neck no longer having the strength to hold it up.

"Sso." The High One gave a chilling little laugh that sliced through the torchlight, making the oily, crimson glow gutter. "Usselesss he iss. Let uss leave him to reconssider."

A touch against Ryan's shoulder. The scream died in his throat, half-strangled. He would not give them the satisfaction of hearing him yell. The High One's breath washed over his face, loaded with its alien scent, and if he'd had a stomach left, that would have turned it. "We alwayss win, coussin," the Inkani hissed, softly. "*Alwayss.*"

Their footsteps retreated. "Think about it," Paul said, before the sound of their feet—the High One's almost weightless, brushing the drum-head of stone that shrank back from its passing; Paul's stumbling human tread—retreated. There was nothing wrong with Ryan's ears. He focused through the sheet of blinding agony from his chest and shoulders and maltreated wrists. Underground. They had him underground, in tunnels they had built with stonekin slaves; they went up through a tunnel. No door—and no guard. They were going to leave him down here to rot.

Rage returned again, fruitless rage. Paul. Whoever would have thought the feckless Malik had it in him?

Why am I still alive?

The answer was simple. They thought Chess had told him where the books were, or how to get at them—because Paul couldn't find them, even after searching the library. They would come back as many times as they had to, to get that information out of him. But that wasn't his problem.

How far away is darkmoon? The Rite is at its most powerful at darkmoon. Three days, five at the most, depending on how long I've been out.

He coughed, his body curving into a taut shallow arc as red-hot pokers drilled through his chest. The chains clashed, spat, jangled.

Chess. Francesca. He hung still, then, swallowing the tickle at the back of his bloody throat. Copper tainted the inside of his mouth. Christ, he was in bad shape.

Not as bad as those bastards are going to be when I get my hands on them. Chess. Think, you big, dumb Drakul! Think!

She *had* to still be alive. If they had performed the Rite, they would know how to get to the books, there was no way she could stand up to that kind of torture. She wasn't made for it. Stubborn, yes; brave, yes; determined to fight, yes. But they would rip her soul out of her body and use her to power a portal between here and the foul place the High Ones escaped from, and she would be left a battered, bleeding wreck. She would tell them anything they wanted to know, and they would kill her anyway.

Stillness, then. The chains stopped their clashing as he hung motionless, barely even breathing. Sweat and blood ran down his skin. He could barely feel any clothing. Had they stripped him? He wouldn't put it past them.

It all made sense now. Paul showing up battered . . . but not as battered as he should have been if he'd *really* run across Inkani. Showing up just after the first Inkani spider had triggered its change, suggesting Ryan keep both Chess and her sister in the apartment, talking all night to gauge whether or not Ryan was alert, suggesting they try to get Chess out of town, possibly to lure Ryan into a prepared Inkani trap, unaccountably nervous and fearful not because of combat sickness, but because he was playing both sides of the field. It *all* made sense. *How did they get to him? How? And for how long?*

Who cared? Forget Paul. He was only an obstacle now, and a fragile one at best. He was, after all, only Malik.

Only human, when all was said and done.

Slowly, infinitely slowly, Ryan tensed the fingers of his right hand. Blood slid warm down his arm. The metal crackled uneasily—but he was demon, too. More strongly demon than most Drakul.

His eyes closed, Ryan *concentrated*.

So much time spent keeping the demon down, keeping it chained, exerting control. Control. He'd tried so hard to be gentle with Chess, and ended up dragging her into a trap. What would have happened if he'd sent her out with Paul alone? *Christ.*

Think of her, then. Think of her dark hair, the way her eyes are growing golden. Think of the way she smells. She smells good, and she bites her lower lip a little when she's concentrating. Think of her sitting there at her kitchen table, with her face in her hands. Think about that, Ryan.

A thin wire of warmth slid down his lip. His teeth were buried in his own flesh, one more note in the symphony of pain.

Chess, then. Her braid bobbing back and forth as she punched the heavy bag, her hand in his. *You're a human being. You're the only one I trust. We're partners.*

The only one I trust. Her face, open and peaceful, as she slept in her bed.

The demon in him stirred.

It wasn't so hard after all. So much iron control, so much

denying himself, when all he had to do was relax for just a moment and let that other three-quarters of himself out. The black, roaring thing he kept chained and crouching stretched, finding itself trapped in a body hanging weighted from chains that crackled with power akin to it.

Chess, he whispered without speaking, the entire world narrowing to a pinprick of bloody crimson. Every muscle tensed against itself, his teeth driven into his lip, his eyes rolling back into his head as bones creaked under the strain and the chains stilled, even their static-laden murmur hushed.

Mine, the demon whispered, filling his veins with hot, bloody wine. *Mine.*

"Mine," Ryan whispered back, agreeing. He loosed the last shackle of his control, and let the demon take him.

Nineteen

She put her back to the stone wall, sitting cross-legged on the bed. It was a narrow single bed, covered in white silk; the little stone cell had a bathroom but no mirror, and no window. There wasn't anything in the whole damn room that could be used as a weapon, she'd already yanked up the silk and tried tugging at the bedposts, but they were somehow fixed to the floor.

So Chess sat, chewing meditatively on a fingernail, staring at the thick, heavy door, without even a doorknob or keyhole on the inside. The only light came from a single candle set in a shallow dish somehow curving out of the stone wall itself, the candles themselves smelled foul and were too thin to be of any real use as a weapon.

They'd taken her knife. They'd taken everything. And Paul had helped them.

Come on, Chess. Buck up. Think your way out of this one.

They'd beaten Ryan to a bloody pulp, the blue-eyed things, and she'd been so sick she'd lost everything she'd ever *thought* of eating while Paul held the gun on her and laughed. It wasn't so much their six-fingered, soft, long maggot hands or their sheerly pretty faces with their alien bones—it was the *cold* that emanated from them, and their hiss-clicking voices. And the genuine enjoyment they had seemed to take in beating Ryan up while they dragged Chess away. Five of them, and he'd still fought them; but . . .

They've killed him. You know they've killed him. There's no way someone could survive what they did to him.

She moved restlessly, eyeing the candle again. They came every little while to bring her food—human food, from God-knew-where. Each time it was either a colorless human slave with vacant eyes, shadowed by one of the Unspeakable—or it was Paul, with a demon leering over his shoulder. And that was somehow worse, because he grinned and joked about what they were going to do to her.

Now I know how it feels to be on Death Row.

"There is nothing bad or good but thinking makes it so," she whispered, her voice mouthing the cold stone walls. The bed was soft and deep, but she didn't feel like lying down. She didn't feel like eating, either; the latest tray with its cargo of chicken and saffron rice lay on the floor, congealing. The dishes were plastic and the tray itself was too flimsy to stand up to any kind of abuse. She knew, she'd broken three of the trays trying to make a weapon. *Any* weapon.

As if she wasn't so sick and cold when one of those things came in she could barely stand up.

The candle flame flickered. If she attacked Paul with the candle, they might take it away. And as much as Chess wanted to scratch the bastard's eyes out, she couldn't stand the thought of being locked up down here in the dark.

She shivered. Closed her eyes. Sought refuge, once again, in literature. "It was the best of times, it was the worst of times." She recited the long string of paradoxes from memory, then switched to poetry. "We were very tired, we were very merry . . . " Her voice cracked, sobs rising in her throat.

Come on, Chess. What have you got to lose?

She was hungry, drained, and exhausted. Her skin crawled and her mouth tasted foul. The food was starting to smell heavenly, even ice-cold as it was likely to be. But what if it was drugged?

"Whether tis nobler to endure . . . oh, wait a minute. Or by opposing, end them. Yeah. Sure. Who am I kidding?"

The candle flame flickered, guttered.

Oh, God, don't let me be down here in the dark. But the flame straightened again, strengthened.

She slumped against the wall, feeling its chill burn through her T-shirt. Ryan was dead, her apartment was probably ruined, and nobody knew where she was. She was kidnapped by demons who were going to sacrifice her in some funky ritual.

I keep thinking this can't get any worse. Then it goes and gets worse.

Her ears were sensitized by the absolute silence, it was so quiet she could actually *hear* the candle burning, a faint soft sound. She closed her eyes, leaned her head back against the wall. *This is bad. This is really bad. I wish I could think of something, anything . . . I'm so hungry. God, I'm so hungry. If I get out of this I'm going to get a big bacon cheeseburger and eat the whole damn thing. And French fries. With mayonnaise. Oh, and a bottle of white wine, so cold it hurts my teeth. Then I'm going to get a big chocolate-covered sundae and pour whipped cream on it, and load it up with nuts.*

She shifted restlessly. *Ryan. God, I'm so sorry. I should have done something. What could I do? I never even got to kiss him back.*

That was a good memory, even though she was terrified. Somehow thinking of Ryan made her feel better. He'd done the best he could.

What would he do? He wouldn't be sitting here moping. He'd be figuring out some way of getting out of here. Christ, I'm woefully short on practical experience. The researcher's doom, actual field conditions.

Think, then. She had to *think*, before she got any hungrier, any weaker.

She imagined the library, then. Not the secret hidden room of sorcerous books, but the plain, everyday, falling-apart library, with its faded carpet and heavy lamps, with the sound of computers softly humming and pages turning. The checkout counter, Chess's own cluttered tiny office. *God, I'd even welcome Pem the Indignant right about now. I'll bet she'd make short work of those demons. Probably beat them over the head with her little tartan purse.*

The laugh was forlorn and thin, but it made her feel better as well. Chess rubbed her fingers together. Her hair was mercilessly tangled and she would start to smell unwashed pretty soon. Mom was probably climbing the walls, and God knew what Charlie was thinking. They had probably found her apartment trashed by now. Charlie would come over to collect the bike and find Chess's door blown off its hinges and the window broken, her bedroom door hacked apart and—

A soft, sliding sound outside the door. Chess froze, nailed in place before she realized the creeping cold wasn't spreading up her fingers. More stealthy sounds, someone scraping at her door. A slight squeal, as if a key was turning.

Holy fuck. She was off the bed, as quickly and quietly as she could. Crossed to the shallow stone dish carved out of the wall and reached out, snapping the thin wax taper. Her sneakers made slight squeaking sounds as she turned carefully, shielding the flame with her cupped hand.

It was as close to a weapon as she could think of. And if there wasn't one of the Unspeakable outside her door, she might just have a chance. She ghosted across the stone floor, wondering if there were any trolls around here, and put her back to the wall beside the door, cupping the frail flame with her shaking hand.

More scraping.

Who's on first, she thought, shoving down the urge to giggle. *What's on second. And I Don't Know's on third. I come not to praise Caesar, but to bury him.*

The door squeaked as it swung inward. "Hey, baby," a familiar voice crept into the dark. "Let's teach you some manners—what the fuck?"

He probably sensed something wrong, because he shoved the door open, banging it against the wall with more force than was necessary, probably to make sure she wasn't hiding behind it. Chess leapt, her back leg providing leverage as she button-hooked around the corner, jabbing with the candle's sullen gleam and hot wax. *Ohgodpleasepleaseplease—*

She got lucky. Paul let out a short blurt of surprise, dropping into a defensive crouch that brought his face right to the level of the candle. The thin taper flew forward, and smacked him right in the eye with hot wax.

"*Agh!* You *bitch!*"

Chess almost froze. But months of practicing and training with Al rose under her skin, and she moved instinctively, snapping a low kick to his knee, a yell bursting from her own throat. She was weak, shaky, and starving, but she had surprise on her side; Paul went down hard. Chess lost her own balance, not expecting him to fold so quickly. The candle skittered out of her hand as the torch Paul carried flew down the darkened hall. Another miracle intervened—her knee landed on something suspiciously soft near his groin, and his yell abruptly became more of a strangled squeak.

Her fist flew, a rabbit-punch not to the face—her hands were too small—but to the throat, the best place to land a punch. She could still hear Al yelling, *if'n they can't breathe, they can't fight! Go for the throat shot! Neck, neck, neck, and I ain't talkin about kissin!*

There was a sickening crunch, and he started to thrash. Something clipped her hard on the side of the head. Chess fell, sprawling, barking her elbow on stone and letting out a hoarse, pained cry. *Ouch. Not another shiner, please, I don't want another black eye.* She scrambled blindly to get *up*, to run away, to use the advantage she'd been given for all it was worth.

She managed to make it up to her knees, tasting copper, and looked down at Paul. He'd stopped moving and lay on his back, a shallow whistling sound coming from parted lips. His eyes had rolled back into his head, and he looked very, very unhappy.

A useless sob hitched in her throat, her head throbbed with pain. Adrenaline made her stomach sour and her hands shaky. *Now what do I do? Think, Chessie! Think!*

Logic dictated that he had to have some weapon on him. Logic further dictated that he wasn't supposed to be here without one of the Unspeakable with him. Then again, he outweighed her. Maybe they'd thought she wasn't a match for him. Or maybe he thought he was more than a match for her, and was up to no good.

Yet another fool underestimating a librarian, she thought, rancid giggles rising in her chest. *Get up, Chess. God only knows how much time you have. Get up and drag him into that room, take whatever he's got, keys, weapons, anything you can use. Then get the hell out of here.*

Where exactly would she go? These were *tunnels,* for God's sake, and she had no idea where she was. And fumbling around in the dark . . .

Better to fumble around in the dark than wait for them to come back and kill me. The thought forced her to get moving, mechanically, her fingers numb and her legs unsteady.

Paul was a heavy deadweight as she dragged him into the room, she'd knocked him out. A quick digging in his pockets by the pale golden light of the candle, relit from the smoking torch, turned up a heavy metal key. He also had her knife in a sheath clipped to his belt. *You bastard. Why did you have my knife?* She took both, the knife buzzing in her hand, and yanked the door closed. On the hallway side of it there was a single keyhole. She stuck the key in and tugged at it, thinking she could break it in the lock . . . but then she thought about being locked in that room with no light, and rested her head against the cold heaviness. The door seemed made out of something alien, too cold to be wood and too light to be iron. It sounded like glass when she tapped it from the outside.

She yanked the key out of the lock and stuck it in her pocket, clipped her knife to the waistband of her jeans, and took a deep breath, holding the rescued torch high and hearing the sputtering hiss of the flame at its far end. Her other hand held the candle, saved against the torch's demise. *Which way do I go? Right or left?*

It was a fine time to wish she'd heard from which end the demons came from. *Come on, Chess. Right or left? Either way, I'm probably equally fucked.*

She finally turned left, for no reason other than she'd once read that people lost in the woods usually ended up making turns in the direction of their dominant hand. It was as good a decision as any, at this point. Her knife buzzed against her hip, sending prickles up her spine.

Two thoughts took on uncomfortable dimensions as she started tentatively down the corridor. The first was predictable enough: *I wish Ryan was here. I'd feel a whole lot better about this.*

The second thought was chilling: *"Teach me some manners?" What was Paul going to do to me? And how long do I have before they discover I'm gone?*

* * * *

The torch died a short while afterward, she managed to light the thin tapering candle from its last sputters and finally tossed the charred hunk of wood aside into one of the weird rooms that opened off on either side of the hall at regular intervals. Some of the rooms had chains hanging from the ceiling over round holes in the floor, and some had other chains attached to stone walls by rusting staples. Other rooms had items she couldn't even begin to imagine the use of, except that they looked painful.

It was starting to look as if she'd had it easy in her room, being fed and watered. *Just like the fatted calf,* she thought with a shiver.

Her knife kept buzzing. Demons everywhere. It was probably only a matter of time before they caught her.

Will you stop it, Chess? Things are actually looking pretty good, they're looking okay, why don't you just relax?

The candle had burned down almost to her fingers when she found something that could either be very good or very bad: a dead-end intersection with another tunnel, this one lit with ruddy torchlight. Torches meant someone used this corridor, which meant she had a higher chance of being discovered.

For a few moments she simply stood in the archway, her

eyes becoming adjusted to the relatively greater light. She blinked, then blew out her candle. *Save it for later. If there is a later.*

She had to decide which way to go. She peered around the corner, looked each way. The featureless hall stretched in either direction, starred with the fuming torches, and she wondered if she was going to succumb to carbon monoxide poisoning from the flames. *How do they ventilate this shit?* The laughter returned, crawling up her throat and filling her mouth with bitterness. *Who's on first, What's on second, I Don't Know's on third, and Chessie's underground. Get it? Get it, Chess?*

"Shut up," she whispered, and shivered. The shivers spilled up her back, cresting and flying down her arms, and her hands began to feel numb. The knife vibrated hotly on her hip. She wrapped her fingers around the hilt. A thin wire of strength slid up her arm. *Caught. Like a rat in a trap.*

It brought up an interesting question: Did she draw the knife now despite its glow—or did she back up into the dark, mathematically-straight corridor behind her and hope to be overlooked?

Unless, of course, the demon was coming up behind her. If she froze like a rabbit in a trap . . .

I have nothing to lose. She stepped forward, turned to her left, and started to run as fast as her weary body would allow. And she saw, at the end of the impossibly long hall, like a gift, the last thing she ever expected to see.

Stairs. Going *up.*

Twenty

Crimson, shot through with blackness. Moving on instinct, tucking his chin so the spider couldn't get purchase to rip out his throat. The demon's back broke with a sound like iron-laced glass shattering. He did not even recognize the sound he was making. A low, thrumming growl, the entire tunnel resonating to subsonic frequencies. *Making a lot of noise. Lot of noise. Can't be helped.*

The thing scrabbled weakly in his hands, already dying. It was a soldier demon. He'd already met one of the High Ones and was consequently bleeding again.

It didn't matter. He'd killed it, though it had damn near tried to take his spleen out the hard way. And once he'd killed it, he had to deal with the spiders. He had been down here a long time, an eternity, fighting, working toward the direction instinct told him would lead him to an exit. He needed to get out of here, go to ground somewhere. Lick his wounds.

Traitor. Traitor. Someone had betrayed him, and he was going to make them pay eventually. But to do that, he had to keep moving. Keep fighting.

His legs worked when he pushed himself forward, leaving the small hairless little demon writhing on the stone floor. It was the same type of thing they put in the human slaves, but past its pupae stage, with long sleek legs, compound eyes, and a caved-in nose. But still, it died.

The other one clamped its teeth in his calf, but he was ready for that and stamped down sharply, heel becoming a battering ram, then reached down and snapped its neck. The bodies slumped around him, each one terribly battered; the spiders roamed in packs when they didn't ride a human carrier. His breathing came hot and harsh, ribs flickering as he pulled in air tainted with death and demon.

Who am I?

He no longer knew. Or cared.

It took him a few moments to wipe the blood out of his eyes. He leaned against the cold wall, his heart pounding and his body shrieking as etheric energy crackled, his fighting aura patching together the rips in his wounded body, forcing his skin to close and muscles to reknit themselves.

Traitor. Kill the traitor. He stalked down the corridor, some part of him aware that he was seeing in complete darkness, heat and etheric force bouncing off the walls, acting as a kind of sonar to inform him of speed, direction, drift. There were torches lining the walls, but he was past using his eyes to see; they were merely blobs of heat, bouncing off the stone and showing him the way.

A breath of scent drifted across his senses.

Gold. Female. Young.

Familiar.

The bleak darkness in him stopped, a ceaseless spinning shifting its axis. *Mine.* He raised his weary head, taking a deep breath.

She had come this way. Just who *she* was he wasn't sure, but the deep well of instinct flooded over with possessive fury. Whoever that scent belonged to, he recognized it, and that made him temporarily able to think a little bit clearer.

Just a very little bit. The thirst for revenge faded under this new priority.

He smelled smoke, torches, the peculiar nose-stinging odor of others of his kind, ones that made a shiver of distaste fly up his spine. *Them,* the ones that smelled like danger; if he faced them in this condition he would die. Instinct told him this, clearly, unavoidably.

She's here. She was alive, not too long ago, passed this way, touched the wall here. Smell of burning fat . . . candle. Why a candle? Who knows?

He was used to tracking, so a few breaths told him everything he needed to know. The scent of another demon lay over hers, one that chilled his breath and sank into his skin. Following her, something with blue eyes and long maggot-waxen fingers.

He sensed them massing behind him. *Why am I underground? Who am I?*

The name would not come, no matter how he shook his head, so he discarded it and moved on, ignoring the soft slipping sounds as his blood hit the floor. He would stop bleeding soon enough, but for right now he had to follow this trail as quickly as he could. He'd figure something out on the way.

Mine, the blackness in him whispered. *Mine.*

Mine, he agreed, and began to run.

* * * *

The stairs stretched, and the trail was fresher. He pushed himself up, *up*, each step a song of agony from the time his heel touched down to the time his leg tensed to carry him upward. He wondered how far below the ground he still was. His fingers trailed along glass-smooth stone, reading from each slight vibration how far back the pursuers were—and how far ahead his prey was. He was slowing, slowing, each step an agony, his feet bare and oddly damp against the stone. He was leaving bloody footprints.

My name. Can't even remember my name.

It should have troubled him, but he was too busy forcing himself up to care. The golden scent in the air, beginning to falter, to be overlaid with the copper smell of devouring fear— *that* troubled him. The blackness inside him pulled swiftly on all the strings of etheric force it could reach, feeding strength into his weary muscles, but he was still only partly demon, and tired. Exhausted.

Blackness lay like a wet blanket against his eyes, even though he could smell the torches left at the stairs' bottom. He was operating on blind instinct, it could be deadly unless he could force himself to *think*.

Mine, the blackness whispered, subsiding slightly.

He blinked, his body moving smoothly, passed beyond misery into dumb endurance. *Keep going. She needs you. Needs you.*

Or it was a trap. The thought rose foggily, but he felt something else: wind. Cool wind on his cheeks, touching his blood-crusted hair. The wind was freighted with scent. Trees, mud, the outside world. And water. And the faint, straining smell of gold, under a heavy screen of demon.

Inkani, he realized, the word rising through deep, black water to whisper in his ear. *Inkani A High One. Following her.*

His feet tangled together and he fell, heavily, barking his forehead on a sharp edge—a stair. Other sharp edges dug into his hip and heels, he lay stretched out on the stone stairs and blinked.

All right, that's enough.

"I swear fealty to the Order." The voice was ragged, hoarse. Cracked, bouncing off the stone.

Who the hell's that?

"*O, quam misericors Deus est; Justus, Justus . . .*"

Coughing. He retched, tasted blood. Light began, piercing through his eyes again. Like a needle to the brain.

Christ. It's me. I'm talking to myself. Get up.

"*Misericors...*" A long, hollow moan.

You're the only one I trust. This voice spread soothing heat over his skin, like soft clean fingers touching his face. *We're partners, remember?*

It came back in a blinding flash, striking right through his eyes and into his brain like sunlight, that hated light that stole his strength. He *remembered.*

Chess. Goddammit, Chess. An Inkani following her. Get... UP!

Somehow it worked. He found his palms on stone, his tattered body mending itself as quickly as it could while he curved over, retching, shaking his head to clear it. "Ch-Chess..." He coughed, tasted more blood, and bile. *Goddammit. First make sure she's safe. Then kill him. Kill the traitor.*

But first, make sure she's safe.

He found the strength to stand, and found that the stairs had ended. A low, glassine door stood here, he would have to duck to go through it. It might have been locked at one time, but right now it was shattered off its hinges. Something had hit it in a hell of a hurry.

He also smelled sorcery. The familiar scent of *her* threaded through with smoky sorcery and water, wet earth, and crushed green things. Rain dripped off leaves, and there was a faint track that his dark-adapted eyes picked out with little difficulty. He smelled dawn coming, and the reek of blood.

Late. I'm too late. He pushed himself forward, following the great gouges torn in the earth; the High One had its claws out and was running. She couldn't match that kind of speed, she wasn't a Drakul. She wasn't even a full Phoenicis yet.

Chess, Chess, just hang in there, sweetheart. I'm on my way.

Roots reached up to trip him, but the old, tired flood of adrenaline gave him temporary speed. Still, when he burst out into the clearing he wasn't prepared for what he saw. Two slim shapes, one much taller and one so familiar he knew it even in the stew of agony and instinct. Dark hair, tangled back, a pair of jeans, her pale hands both clasped around the hilt of a knife whose blade glittered a hard, hurtful, deadly blue.

Her back was to a tree, and blood slid down the left side of
her face. And in the air around her, stirring like golden feathers
made of light, the beginnings of a mantle shone.

He didn't pause, his stride lengthening. He flung himself
on the Inkani's back just as he heard her scream his name.

So that's who I am, he thought, wonderingly—and then
the demon turned, swift and fresh, and tossed out one six-
fingered hand.

The stunning impact smashed against him, hurled him back.
He met something hard and felt a brief starry jolt of surprise
before losing consciousness for a few precious seconds.

When he struggled up out of it, he knew he was in trouble.
The thing was too fucking close, too *close*, and it was reaching
down, a smile tilting up its thin lips. Blue eyes glinted with
unholy light. "The pup doess have teeth," it chortled, and its
claws swept down. Flesh parted like water, and he heard his
own scream, like a wolf on the hunter's spear.

"Hey! Hey, *you*! Yeah, you! Blue-eyes! You sack of shit,
I'm *talking* to you!"

It was Chess's voice, but subtly different. How? He
couldn't think of how. *Christ, don't attract its attention,
sweetheart, just give me a second to get up and we'll fix
this.* But his body wouldn't obey him.

The High One, wonder of wonder, paused. It straightened,
and he wondered why he felt so cold. *Pushed myself too far.
Chess, get out of here while it's busy with me, go. Please.*
His arms were turning to lead, so were his legs.

"You are usseful, *imrahir*," the High One hissed, its voice
like the slow scald of boiling oil passed over shrinking skin an
inch at a time. "But we can find otherss."

"Hey, pal." She *did* sound different. Her voice was deeper,
richer, and it *hurt*, scraping along his skin in a different way
than the Inkani's. A purely inimical way, with the dragging pain
that told him sunlight was on him.

Brightness against his eyelids. *But it's raining,* he thought.
And it's not dawn yet.

"You're in my fucking city, Blue Eyes." Chess's voice
deepened, but retained all its low sweetness. "And you have
pissed off the *wrong fucking librarian!*"

It rose to a screech then, the unearthly hunting-cry of a
Phoenicis, hot wind flooding the clearing and screaming through
the leaves. The Inkani screeched too, but the force of its cry

was blasted away by a massive noise, as if every church bell, pipe organ, siren and foghorn in the world had rung at once into every microphone. His eyes flushed red as the light pressed against his face, light so intense he could see the faint traceries of capillaries in his squeezed-shut eyelids. The smell of burning amber and golden musk drenched the air, blotting out everything else in the world, and he heard a solid *chuk* sound, as if a blade had been driven into a side of meat.

Bit by bit the light lessened. He heard harsh breathing, and a string of obscenities that made him want to smile. *Damn, can that woman curse.* But he was cold. Very cold. Oddly cold.

"Ryan?" Her voice again, tired, without that deep edge of danger. The light was draining away, but he couldn't open his eyes just yet. "Oh, God, no. Talk to me. Ryan? *Ryan?*"

"The wrong fucking librarian," he heard himself say, in an odd, dreamy voice. "That's fucking beautiful, Chess."

She made a low, hurt sound, very much like a sob. *Don't cry, sweetheart. It's all okay.*

"Come on, get up," she said. "There might be more of them. Come *on*, we have to get up. Of all the *goddamn* places to come up out of those blasted tunnels, they have to pick the middle of a *park*. Come on. Please, Ryan. Please." She sounded very close to a nervous breakdown, and the demon in him raised its weary head, suddenly very close to relaxing. "*Please*, Ryan."

I can't. Christ, I'm dead. I can't.

I have to.

The world tilted and swayed drunkenly as he struggled to obey her. "I'm glowing like a Christmas tree on crack," she muttered. "Wonderful. Perfect."

"It's y-your m-mantle." *Why am I stuttering?* His tongue wouldn't obey him. "P-p-protects y-you."

And then, he passed out.

Twenty-One

Her left hand was bleeding too badly from the demon's claws to be of any real use and she had, par for the course, developed a black eye. At least she'd stopped glowing, mostly. Instead of sending streams of light in every direction she seemed to glimmer, a pale-gold foxfire glow hovering a few millimeters above her exposed skin. But she was exhausted, and the feeling of vital force bleeding out and away from her had been *awful*. She never wanted to do that again. *Ever*.

Doesn't matter. If they try to hurt him again, I'll do what I have to do. Whatever that was, I'll find a way to do it again. Whatever I did.

Rage. The feeling had been rage; she'd found something inside herself cracking as the demon had bent over Ryan, intent on killing him. And then the light had come, and a hot fury drove her forward to spit the blue-eyed demon on her knife as it writhed.

Chess shivered. Ryan was little help, he simply slumped against her, all of his weary attention taken up with staying vertical, and his dark eyes had a vacancy to them she didn't like. He looked like hell, he was *covered* in blood and guck, and his feet were bare. The only clothing he had left was rags, and vivid pink, swiftly healing weals showed against his pale skin—at least, the parts of him that weren't covered in dried blood. His wrists looked terribly swollen, and he moved jerkily, without his usual fluid, eerie grace.

And to add insult to injury, her eyes seemed to have gone a little haywire. She *saw* things, like pale lines of force swirling through the air, the trees as columns of liquid light, each living thing seemed to have its own aura. If she didn't concentrate on seeing the real world, everything started to look all wonky and glowy, connected with lines of blue or white humming energy. Ryan himself was a furnace of light, strangely geometrical and oddly alien. Maybe she had a concussion. It wasn't out of the question.

Quit it, Chess. You're out of ideas, and there's going to be more demons here soon. She struggled forward another step, her foot sliding in mud, the rain was pelting down now. The sky was gray in the east, but not enough to lighten any of the shadows under the trees. *A park, for God's sake. We can't come up anywhere where I can possibly hail a cab— though who'd stop for us looking like this? And my purse is at home. And to top it all off, I've got a glowing-blue knife.*

She'd buried the knife in the Inkani's chest, and the foul-smelling thing had damn near imploded, rotting right in front of her eyes. It was a good thing her stomach was already empty. Right now the knife buzzed in its sheath at her hip, and she was cold. Thankfully, it wasn't the ice-in-the-marrow cold of an Unspeakable too close . . . but it was still chilly. And *awful*.

Water slid down the back of her neck, she slipped again, and blinked back blood and water. Her head was bleeding again, she struggled to focus. Ryan ṣwayed. He somehow managed to pull her back up to her feet. "Now would be a good time for a miracle," she said, wishing she could look back over her shoulder. Her ass hurt, and the muscles in her thighs quivered with exhaustion from the stairs. The light in the sky was strengthening, but far too slowly.

"Call . . . in." Ryan's voice was husky. His breath made a faint white cloud in the cold air.

"What?"

"Find . . . a phone." His eyes were still blearily vacant, and his tone was slow and slurred, as if he was talking in his sleep. "Malik."

"We're in a *park*. I don't even know *which* park. And why the hell do we need more trouble? A Malik got us *into* this mess!" *I wonder if he's still locked in that room?* She felt a sharp pinch of weary guilt, shook it aside. Looked up, rain stinging her cheeks and forehead.

Holy God. There were streetlamps, shining orange, on the hill above them. Streetlamps meant a street, which was better than slogging through this mud and underbrush. And what was even better, they looked normal, there wasn't a hint of that funny glow on them. *Thank you, God. Thank you.*

"Call . . . in," he insisted. "Chess."

"All right, let me find a phone. We've got to get up that hill. If it's a jogging path it means Simons Park, and they have phones on the main jogging loop. Can you make it up the hill?"

"Will," he mumbled, and his head dropped forward. He kept moving, though, as she scrabbled up the slope, fighting through branches and greenery. Blackberry vines tore at her jeans, swiped a line of fire across the back of her right hand, plucked at her hip. The rain kept coming, kissing her face with cold, sharp needles. Ryan's arm was heavy and limp across her shoulder. Her left hand cramped, her fingers curled under the waistband of his shredded jeans, she could feel hot blood soaking through the tough denim. Each time she yanked on him, trying to help him stay upright, a fresh jolt of ripping pain tore up her arm.

It seemed to take forever to reach the top of the hill, and when they broke through the last screen of clutching branches and vines Chess let out a sobbing breath of grateful wonder, her vision returning to normal with a subliminal *snap*. It *was* Simons Park, and they were on the main jogging loop. And there, in its yellow box, was an emergency phone for joggers and bicyclists. *Oh, thank you. Thank you, God.* "I don't have any quarters," she managed, pulling Ryan out of the underbrush and onto the paved trail. "You think they'll take a collect call?"

Ryan lifted his head. She glanced up, and her heart began to pound. His eyes were rolled back into his head, and he looked asleep on his feet. *He's not okay. Neither of us are okay. God, help us out here, please? Just a little more help, and then you can retire.*

"Number," Ryan mumbled. "Number . . . "

They made it, haltingly, to the yellow box. She propped him against it and reached out, trying to look everywhere at once while she picked up the receiver. Wonder of wonders, a dial tone sounded in her ear. "Number? What number?" *If he can't think of it I'm going to have to call Charlie. But she can't come down here when there's demons around. Oh God, they could be in the trees even now.* She checked the sky. Getting lighter by the minute. She had *never* been so happy to see dawn.

Ryan recited a long string of numbers, she faithfully punched them in and was rewarded with a click. *Please don't tell me I have to deposit a dollar in quarters—*

"Code in, please." The voice crackled in her ear.

Chess gasped. "Code?"

Ryan recited another number. "314428-Henry-Zulu," she repeated. *Please, help me out here.*

"Holy shit!" The voice was young, male, and almost squeaking with surprise. "Where's Ryan?"

"Right here next to me," she managed, sagging with relief.

"This is Francesca Barnes, I've got an almost-dead Drakul here and a bunch of blue-eyed demons looking to eat me for lunch. I'm in Simons Park, on the jogging loop, and I could really use a little help. Oh, and Paul? That motherfucker turned us in to the Inkani. I left him locked underground, and I'm bleeding and I'm glowing like a Christmas tree on crack, and you had *better* be able to help us, or so help me God I don't know what I'm going to do, but I know it's going to be drastic." She had to stop to take a breath. Rain needled the sides of the phone booth, drumming its tiny fingers incessantly. Ryan closed his eyes, slumping against the side of the box, his shoulders loose and his hands dangling. He looked even more tired than she felt, and she wished he could talk to her.

There was a click, and a new voice came on. This one was older, male, and very calm. "Miss Barnes? This is Abraham Shelton, Deputy Master of the Order of the Dragon, West Coast Division. We have a lock on your position and are sending transport and cleanup. The first team is in your area and should reach you in ten minutes. How badly are you hurt? And what's this about Paul and the Inkani?"

* * * *

"We're calling it a home invasion." Abraham Shelton was a thin man with café-au-lait skin and curly black hair cut severely short. His face was a statue's, perfection burnished to a fine sheen, and his eyes were wells of calm, brown darkness. "The police report will state that you escaped your home and wandered around in shock. The library's put you on two weeks paid leave."

Well, that's mighty nice of them. Christ, you people are really serious about this sort of thing, aren't you. Chess's bandaged hand itched. She took another gulp of the scorching coffee, wishing she could wake up a little more. She'd slept for eighteen hours straight, according to the clock on the nightstand. She wished she could sleep for another twenty-four. Her knife dug into the side of her belly, they'd given her a new sheath for it.

The room was nice, if a little soulless: heavy four-poster bed with a red comforter and designer-matched sheets and pillows, a nightstand with an artful arrangement of white carnations, a gas fireplace and a window seat. Rain beaded down the window, an autumn storm she was *very* glad not to be out in the middle of.

The Malik "team"—four Malik and six Drakul, the Drakul glowing the same way Ryan did—had melted out of the shadows of the park, nearly scaring the life out of her and prompting Ryan to try to peel himself away from the phone to face them. It had taken some doing to calm him down, but he listened to her voice, and they had been bundled into a not-very-legal SUV that had suddenly appeared on the jogging path, in blithe disregard of its own weirdness.

To wake up here, in this nice little room, had been equally relieving and terrifying. Relief because there weren't any funky demons around, and they had even brought her fresh clothes and let her take a shower; relief because a tall, blonde medic had come to bandage her and check her for broken bones or concussion. And terror because Ryan was nowhere in sight, and nobody would tell her where he was; terror because the weird double-vision, normal world and glowing lines of force, hadn't gone away at all.

"That's really nice," she said finally. *That's uber-swell. Considering that it was one of your goddamn Malik that turned me over to the goddamn demons in the first place.*

No, she was not feeling charitable at all. "Where's Ryan?" she asked for the fifth time. "Is he okay?"

Shelton sighed. He had pulled a straight-backed, red-velvet chair up to the bedside. Chess perched on the rumpled covers with her coffee cup. She wondered idly if they would bring more food, she'd tucked away six pancakes and a pile of scrambled eggs and was having longing thoughts of nice crispy bacon to top it all off.

"The Drakul's recovering, he's in the dormitory with the others. This is a . . . a delicate situation." His tone plainly said he didn't think much of the situation itself. "On the one hand, you're the first potential we've been able to lock onto and bring in, for a very long time. And if what you're telling us is true, it was the Drakul who resisted corruption and the Malik who turned traitor. Which has never happened before."

"Not to your knowledge," she returned, her eyebrow raising. "*If* what I'm telling you is true? Are you calling me a liar?"

He held his hands up, placating, the loose sleeves of his red sweater falling back from his muscle-corded wrists. "No, not at all. Not at all. But this is very . . . irregular. There are certain . . . rules."

Is he talking about what I think he's talking about? "In other words, you want to punish Ryan." *You son of a bitch,* she added silently.

His calm brown eyes met hers. He studied her for a long time, the brushing of rain against the window oddly soothing.

A welcome flare of irritation sprang to life right in the center of her chest. "Look, Mr. Shelton, I'm going to put this into terms you can understand. Ryan's the only one of you inept jerkwads I trust. You want me to help you out, you want me to do something because I'm one of these Golden thingies? Fine. But *only* if you leave Ryan alone. He's my Drakul, and he stays, or no dice."

Shelton shrugged, crossing his long legs. "If we withdraw our protection, you might have to face the High Ones again." But his mouth twisted down bitterly. "We're not willing to compromise your safety, even though the Drakul has broken . . . certain rules. It was a very irregular situation."

Damn right it was. Feeling slightly more justified, she settled back into the bed. "So what are we talking about here? When do I get to see him?"

"You may not be able to do him much good." Was there a slightly cruel smile touching his lips, or was that her imagination? "He's already fading."

She barely realized she'd bolted to her feet, the coffee cup hitting the wine-red carpet and letting loose a flood of scalding liquid. Shelton stood, too, his eyes widening in a way that told her whatever reaction he'd expected, it wasn't this one.

Chess drew herself up to her full height, her right hand dropping to the hilt of her knife and her face freezing, the little tic in her cheek starting. It was, again, Mom's patented You-*Are*-Aware-I-Am-Potentially-Deadly? expression, and she saw with satisfaction that even though this man had a head and a half height on her, he still was no match for one of her mom's Looks. "Where. Is. He?"

And damned if that faint golden glow didn't start again, swirling in the air around her like colored oil on water. *Great. Am I going to turn into a light bulb every time I get pissed off?*

There were, she supposed, worse things. Like running in the dark and feeling a blue-eyed demon behind her. Goosebumps spread over her skin.

"There's no need for—" the man began hastily, his eyes

turning round as quarters.

"You listen, and you listen *good.* You're going to take me to Ryan right now, posthaste, young man." *I sound like Charlie.* "And you'd better pray he gets better. Because if you let him die, I am going to be all over you like white on rice. And believe me, after the week I've had, I am one librarian you do *not* want to mess with."

That sounds good, Chess, but how are you really going to force him to do anything? Her practical side spoke up about ten seconds too late, for once.

Doesn't matter, she told herself. *I'll do what I have to, even if I have to search this whole goddamn place. He'd find me—he did find me, no matter what they did to him. And I'm bloody well going to find him.*

Shelton shook his head. "Fine. You win. But you don't understand. They're animals, Miss Barnes, and you're not equipped to control him should some of his more aggressive tendencies—"

"Listen to yourself." She didn't bother to disguise the disgust in her voice. "He's not an animal, you son of a bitch. He's a *person.* Now get your ass in gear. *Where is he?"*

"You're determined to—"

She glared at him, the golden light still swirling in the air. "You better believe it, mister. You don't want to see how determined I can get."

He visibly gave up. "Then you'd better come with me."

Twenty-Two

Drifting.

It was gray, the place where he drifted. Infinitely gray, the world turned to comforting cotton-wool static. Nothing left to fight. Nothing left to *do* but lie still, staring blindly into the grayness, and feel the welcome numbness as it slid up his arms and legs, increment by increment, searching for his heart. When it reached his heart the gray would turn to black, and he would be released.

It didn't matter. He had done . . . what? Something. He had kept someone safe, and that was all that mattered. Now there was nothing left to do. Nothing but lie here and wait.

Sometimes people spoke softly, his brothers keeping watch as a vigil for the dead, some leaving, some arriving; their silence was laced with the subliminal hiss of demons watching what could well be their own fate someday. Despair turned to numbness, grief turned to apathy, the will to live sapped, gone, forgotten. The body healed itself, in fits and starts, but that was of no use.

Not now.

"Oh, Jesus." This voice cut through the gray, flushing it with gold for a bare moment.

The thought was slow. *What?* Stretched out like taffy, the single word hung in the gray mist.

"Jesus Christ. What have they done to you?"

Stinging, a faraway pain. He turned his attention away, fretfully, seeing the gray mist again. *Let me go. Just let me go.*

"Ryan? *Orion!*" She sounded close to weeping, and something jabbed him in the side. "Goddammit, wake up!"

Another voice intruding, this one smooth and male. Malik. One of the commanders. "You can't bring him back. He's too far gone."

"You stay out of this, you son of a bitch." Coldly furious. The woman's voice was familiar, so familiar it almost roused his interest. The demon stirred under the floor of his mind, a hurtful flower blooming.

No. Go back to sleep. Just let it go. Nothing more to do here, nothing more to see. Just go. Just let go.

More prickling pain, in faroff territory he recognized as his fingers and toes. Tiny needles jabbing, jabbing; each one a thin diamond star of pain. Like a frostbitten limb slowly waking up, like the painful scrape of sunlight . . .

"Wake up, goddamit! I'm not finished with you! Wake the *hell* up, Ryan! I'm *talking* to you, you big dumb jerk! Get up! I *need* you!"

That sent another uncomfortable spike of interest through him. *Need me? Nobody needs me. I did what I had to do. Now let me die.*

BLAM!

The impact jolted him; the sound of open palm hitting flesh. He heard a sharp collective intake of breath. Something against his side, two dimples of pressure on either side of his hips. The blow smashed through the shell of gray haze, white light bursting against his eyes, something pressing against his chest.

BLAM!

Again. The light burst through him, the demon rising snarling through layers of apathy, chemical adrenaline flooding his bloodstream, the listlessness shaking itself away. His hand shot up, closed around something soft and fragile. But gently. Exquisitely gently.

Ryan blinked. A low rumbling growl died in his chest; his pupils shrank, trying to deal with the sudden influx of light. "Quit it." He tried to make the words forbidding, could only manage a whisper. Why was his body so heavy?

Shock. Bodily systems shutting down. Jesus. What the hell—

He peered through the glare of light, slowly making out a familiar face, framed by the low ceiling of a Drakul dormitory. He could barely remember being dragged in here while they were setting the dorm up. The Order had probably moved in here in a hell of a hurry.

Chess's eyes were now mostly dark-gold, the hazel that remained merely flecks. She had braced her knees on either side of his hips, and her hair was loose, falling forward over her shoulders. She wore a blue V-neck sweater that made her skin look even more flawless, and she had the fading remains of a terrific black eye. The gash in her forehead had healed nicely. She smelled of Malik healing-sorcery, and of gold, and of female, the familiar scent he filled his lungs with, staring up at her, her wrist trapped in his fingers.

And she was *crying*. Tears spilled down her cheeks and

high color flushed along her cheekbones, she looked frantic.

She was so goddamn beautiful it robbed him of breath.

Life returned in a rush of color and sound. He was vaguely aware of the presence of other Drakulein, watching with bright eyes and reined interest. The Deputy Master also stood by the bed, his arms folded and his dark eyes narrowed. *You sadistic bastard . . .* He buried the thought. They'd made Shelton a commander because he had a habit of losing Drakul. What was he doing here? And with Chess?

He blinked again. *What the hell's going on? Chess? In a Drakul dorm?*

We made it. She's safe. Relief burst inside his chest, exquisite relief. What the hell was going on?

She let out a sound that was half a sob, half a sigh. Her left hand, wrapped in a white gauze bandage, was knotted in his shirt. At least the other Drakul had cleaned him up and dressed him before putting him in a bed to die.

"You *idiotic, infuriating, brainless*—" She seemed, for once, to run out of words, and tipped her head back, her jaw working. Ryan observed this curiously.

Finally, her chin came back down, and she fixed him with a glare he was exceedingly happy to be alive to see. "Don't you dare die on me!" she finally settled for saying, with barely-controlled violence. "We're partners, remember? Don't you *dare* die!"

He searched for something to say. His mouth opened. "Your bedside manner could use a little work, sweetheart."

For a moment he thought she was going to try to tear her hand free and slap him again, and he decided he'd let her, if only because the thought of her skin touching his made a bolt of fire go through him. Instead, her arm relaxed. She let out a long, sobbing breath, her shoulders dropping. He was suddenly, acutely aware of her weight against him.

"Don't call me that." She swallowed. "Are you . . . they said you were . . . "

He was acutely aware of other eyes watching. "I'll be all right. Are you okay?" *That* was the important thing. She didn't smell hurt; but the sudden stinging scent of her fear lashed him into full alertness, smashing at the remaining gray, cottony numbness. The demon stretched inside him, strangely satisfied—of course, he'd let it out. And it had feasted on blood and violence.

She nodded, biting at her lower lip. "Let go, I need to sit down. I spilled my coffee."

What? "What happened?" *Clue me in, sweetheart. The last thing I remember is you telling me to stand up since you'd . . . what? Killed a High One?* His skin chilled again, at the thought of her facing that alone.

She let out an unsteady, barking little laugh that it hurt him to hear. "What happened? I had to drag you through blackberry bushes and put up with *that* SOB—" She tilted her head toward the Deputy Master. "—trying to tell me to just let you die. You can't die, Ryan. Not after I dragged your ass up that goddamn hill."

I never thought I'd live to hear Shelton referred to as a SOB. Ryan made his fingers loosen. His entire body ached, yanked back from shock. He would need a little bit of bedrest and a few protein loads before he was near fighting capacity again. He'd pushed the limits of even a Drakul's strength. He vaguely remembered taking on a High One, blind with the rage of his demon half. "Yes ma'am," he mumbled, and she clambered off the bed, giving him a venomous look that cheered him up immensely. "No dying allowed." He sounded hoarse but much more alert now.

"You better believe it." Someone moved aside for her, and she dropped into a chair by the bedside, then reached over and grabbed his hand, lying discarded on the plain dun blanket. Against the bare white walls and low ceiling of the dormitory, she seemed almost to glow. She darted another glance at the Deputy Master, whose face had settled into an interested, bland expression. "This is *my* Drakul," she informed him, tartly. Ryan felt, even if he couldn't see, the sudden attention of the other Drakulein, each of whom held completely still, waiting. Her fingers laced through his. "I'm told the Golden have Drakul bodyguards. So this one's mine. If you want anything out of me, anything at *all*, you'd better be nice to him."

The Deputy Master paled under the rich tone of his skin. "You're the boss." He managed to make the words sound sarcastic, at least, even under the pressure of Chess's withering look. "Just be careful. They're not human, no matter how much they like to pretend."

"More human than the Malik who turned us over to the Unspeakable." She looked back down at Ryan, who almost wished he could be a fly on the wall at the next Council meeting.

Her fingers were warm in his, and she squeezed his hand, the feel of her skin electric against his. "More human than supercilious fatheads who treat other men like animals. If you guys want to hang out in my city, there's a few things that are going to change around here. Now get out, before I decide I dislike your face more than I already do."

Ryan winced, but the Deputy Master turned on his heel and stalked away. He waited until the door had closed at the far end of the dormitory's hall to clear his throat. *I could get up if I had to. I could. Yeah, sure I could.* "That wasn't wise, Chess."

"Wise, schmise." She shook her head, dark hair falling in her eyes. She blew a strand of it back irritably, and his heart leapt inside his chest. "Well, what are the rest of you staring at? Huh?"

Wisely, perhaps, nobody answered her. Instead, the feeling of *presence* leached away as the Drakulein slowly, silently, went back to their everyday lives, some leaving through the doors at either end of the hall, others moving to the tables at the far end of the room to clean their weapons and talk in hushed tones.

"Are you really all right?" she asked finally, reaching over with her bandaged left hand to touch his forehead anxiously, as if checking him for fever. The gauze scratched his skin, but her fingertips were warm.

No, I'm not. I feel like hell, and you just opened up a giant can of worms. The Deputy Master's not going to take this well, and he's an enemy I don't want to make. "Better." He squeezed her hand, too. But gently. Very gently. "You dragged me up a hill? Through blackberries?"

Her chin set, and she scowled stubbornly at him. "I wasn't going to leave you behind."

Oh, Christ. "Chess—"

"Don't." The color had drained from her cheeks, and she looked close to tears again. "We're going to have to talk about your habit of manhandling me. And that 'sweetheart' thing has really got to go. And maybe I should find another apartment, now that the Inkani know where I live. But . . . I mean, are you really . . . do you think you could stand to stick around me? For a while?"

Oh, my God. Is she saying what I think she's saying? "Stick around?" *I sound like I have a rock caught in my craw. Good one, Ryan.*

The blush came back. She dropped her eyes, staring at the comforter and shifting uneasily on the chair. "Well, I suppose this qualifies as dating, doesn't it? In a totally weird, twisted sort of way."

She is. She is saying what I think she's saying. Oh my God. "Um." He couldn't find the words he wanted, settled for whatever came to mind. "Jesus Christ, Chess. You're beautiful. I adore you. I've adored you since the first time I . . . God. Yes. Goddammit, *yes*."

Was that relief that passed over her face? She let out a heavy sigh, and he saw the dark circles under her eyes, the pallor of exhaustion on her. She'd need a little bit of a break. Of course, getting her to slow down would be like trying to stop the Titanic from sinking, probably.

"I really like you, too. Go figure, I finally find some decent boyfriend material and he's half demon."

It stung, but only briefly. He was part-demon, and he was grateful for it. If he hadn't been, he'd have died, and she might even now be chained to an obsidian altar while the High Ones tore the soul from her beautiful, fragile body. "You have great taste in music."

"Really?" She actually smiled, a tremulous, trying-to-be-cheerful smile. "Well, that's something. Do you think this is going to . . . work?"

Christ, sweetheart, I don't care if it works or not. All I want is to keep you alive; that's enough for me. "I think it will." He heard something approaching certainty in his voice, almost flinched away from it. His body sank into the bed, the demon satisfied, lying quiescent under the surface of his mind. "But we're going to have to work on our communication, sweetheart."

"What did I tell you about that sweetheart shit?" But her smile widened, and lying there heavy and fatigued on the narrow cot, in the middle of a Drakul dormitory, he suddenly felt . . . light. And happy, for once.

"Yes ma'am," he muttered, and closed his eyes, willing himself to heal.

Epilogue

"*Will* you hold still?" She bit her lower lip, her quick fingers moving, and he tried his best to stay absolutely still. The late-afternoon sun coming in through the window picked out highlights in her beautiful dark hair, sleekly pulled back into a French twist. She wore a blue silk T-shirt and a pencil skirt that were entirely too form-fitting for his comfort. Just *looking* at her was an . . . well, an *uplifting* experience, to say the least.

"Why do I have to do this?" It was only a half-serious complaint, but it earned him a single golden glance that could have broken a window.

"Dad likes boyfriends who wear ties. Don't worry, it'll be over soon. You're almost home free. After we go to dinner with them you can stop wearing a tie. It's the rules."

"How did you talk me into this?" He glanced around the apartment—stacks of boxes, the bookcases empty and forlorn, her couch and entertainment center already in the new apartment. Tomorrow the real moving would begin, several Drakul showing up to help. But for tonight, they were knocking off the packing early. The apartment smelled of disturbed dust, the golden scent of Chess's skin, and Drakul; it was a heady mixture. Heady, and soothing at the same time. The windows and doors had been repaired and the loose ends tied off. The Order had done all the damage control necessary.

"Sweetie, there's only so long I can keep a boyfriend away from my mother. She and Dad have heard a lot about you from Charlie, they want to meet you. We'll be in a public place, so you'll be safe. And tomorrow Dad will be amazed at how polite you are and how well you and all your nice, young, musclebound friends help carry boxes." She finished the half-Windsor, stepped back, and ran a critical eye down him. "Hmm, you look really nice in a suit. Who knew?" Her earrings, silver hoops, glittered as they swayed.

"Bite your tongue, missy." He shifted his shoulders uncomfortably. "There's no place to hide a gun in this getup."

She grimaced. "You'd look like a Mafia hitman. Take your bag, you can hide all sorts of stuff in there."

He caught her wrist before she could turn away. "Tell me

again why I'm doing this." But his mouth curled up into a half-smile, one she answered with a grin of her own.

"Because you adore me, and want to make me happy. And I will be *very* happy seeing you wriggle under Mom's eagle eye and Dad's pointed questions." Damn the woman, she sounded much too pleased with the thought.

He checked the fall of sunlight again. "We'd better get going." His thumb drifted across the underside of her wrist gently, and he was rewarded with her smile turning sleepy and her eyelids dropping a fraction. *Goddamn. If she licks her lips and gives me that come-hither look, I don't think we're going to get out of here on time, parents or no parents.*

The city still wasn't completely safe, but the High Ones had vanished. Chess refused to have any Malik standing watch. Instead, she took a page from Evrard Halston's book, and told the Order the Drakul were welcome to come patrol and stand guard, and that female Malik researchers were welcome to make appointments to study the books Halston had left behind. But no Halston book ever left the library building, and some of the Malik researchers had begun to show signs of *potential.* And with all the Drakulein around . . .

Chess met regularly with the Drakul who had requested permission to come and be part of the first Phoenicis Guard since Halston's time. All twenty of them, and more transfer requests were pending.

I don't care who you sleep with, she'd told them, folding her arms. *What I care about is you doing your job and taking care of this city. The safer this city is, the safer whoever you're sleeping with is. You're all old enough to understand that, am I right?*

It was a hell of an experiment, and one the Malik weren't happy about. But for right now, Chess was the Phoenicis of Jericho City, and that was the way it was, period. And her sister was beginning to show signs of interest in sorcery too.

Now that would be interesting. Between the two of them, it's going to be one hell of a time around here.

The stonekin had sent a delegation to her, and Ryan sometimes caught glimpses of them, especially at night while he and Chess patrolled the city for signs of demon activity. They were watching over her too, and that was comforting. The more help, the better. The remaining species of Others were observing a low profile, obviously waiting to see how this was going to shake out.

"Ryan?" Chess's voice pulled him back from contemplating the fall of sunlight against her hair. "You okay?"

"Just thinking, sweetheart. You ready?" He managed to let go of her wrist, one finger at a time.

"Just have to step into my shoes and get my bag. You look really nice." She reached up, fiddled with his collar, her knuckle brushing his jaw. "I never thought you'd be the young-professional type."

"Can't hunt demons in a suit." He let his eyes move over her face again, from her pretty cheekbones to her liquid eyes, dropping to take in the curve of her mouth.

"Mmh." Her hand slid around his nape, and she pulled his head down.

She was a little breathless by the time she let him go, and he kissed the corner of her mouth, her cheek. "We could always reschedule dinner," he murmured into her ear. That earned him a laugh. She still had nightmares, of course, but that was to be expected. He was just grateful to be there when she woke up. *And I used to think librarians were boring.*

"No way. Mom would *kill* me." She stepped back, he let her go.

"Not while I'm around, sweetheart." He meant to say it lightly, failed miserably. But she only smiled again.

"Pfft. Demons you might be able to handle, but Mom's entirely different. Come on, get your bag. Let's go."

"Yes ma'am." *You're the boss, Chess. At least for this run.*

"Hey, Ryan?" She stepped into a pair of black square-heeled shoes, and he tore his eyes away from the smooth muscles working in her calf.

"Hmm?" He found her purse and his bag on the cluttered kitchen table, made sure the Fang was safely stowed in her purse. *Always prepared, isn't she.* He took great care not to actually touch the knife.

"How do you feel about marriage?" Her tone was excessively neutral, as if she wasn't sure how he'd react.

Jesus Christ. His heart began to pound. "Sounds good." *Holy hell. I sound like I just swallowed a skornac egg. Jesus Christ on a crutch.* "But let's get dinner with the fam out of the way first."

"Tease."

He half-turned, settling the bag strap on his shoulder and holding her purse. *I think I'm having a heart attack.* "I can think of several ways to disprove that accusation, sweetheart."

The sun slipped behind a low cloud, and shadow drifted through the room. But Chess grinned, and the squeezing inside Ryan's chest wasn't unpleasant at all. The demon stirred uneasily inside his head. *Mine,* it whispered, and settled back, watchful.

"Okay, big guy. I'll take you up on that. Come on, let's go, we're going to be late." She held out her hand for her purse, and he had to step over a box full of books before he could approach her.

"Lead the way, Chess. I'm right behind you."

Don't Miss Lilith Saintcrow's
Watcher Series

Dark Watcher

Storm Watcher

Fire Watcher

Mindhealer

Available from ImaJinn Books
www.imajinnbooks.com

LaVergne, TN USA
15 December 2009
167080LV00002B/16/P